THE DO-RIGHT

THE DO-RIGHT

LISA SANDLIN

Cinco Puntos Press
EL PASO, TEXAS

Printed in the U.S.

First Edition
10 9 8 7 6 5 4 3 2 1

Library of Congress Cataloging-in-Publication Data

Sandlin, Lisa.
   The do-right / by Lisa Sandlin. — First edition.
     pages ; cm
   ISBN 978-1-941026-19-9 (pbk. : alk. paper)
   I. Title.
   PS3569.A5168D6 2015
   813'.54—dc23
                    2015024949

The cover photo is called "Blessing," and was taken by the amazing photographer Keith Carter in 1985 and used with his permission. Like Lisa Sandlin, Keith is a native of Beaumont, Texas. And Delpha Wade's room in the New Rosemont Hotel, like the room in Keith's photo, was likewise a blessing, rich and deep.

Book and cover design by Anne M. Giangiulio

I remember telling myself not to carry the hatred around,
although I know where it is. I have it in a trunk in storage.
SALMAN RUSHDIE

I

SHE ASKED ABOUT the job in the ad.

The middle-aged cabinetmaker in the sawdusty apron who'd wiped off his hands to shake hers, who'd said, "I'm sorry, Miss," while making eye contact—he was all right, he was more than tolerable. Truth was, he was about the best Delpha could imagine.

The pinch-mouth office manager that shook her head once, the young one that stammered, the C.P.A. that batted away her Gatesville business-course certificate, saying, "Not for us," the shoe store owner that chuckled nervously, helplessly throughout his refusal—she'd expected those turndowns, but that didn't mean she didn't feel them. She felt them.

The bone-weary, though, was brought on by today's prospect. White shirt, neck-roll over the starched collar. Called her *honey* when she walked in the door. That hinky light crawled into his eyes after he read her Gatesville certificate, flicked it back at her. "Aren't you the cool customer?" this one said. "Sitting there on my respectable chair. Lay your ass over my desk, I might could slip you a five." He leaned forward. "Honey, my business wouldn't touch you with a ten-foot pole."

Her P.O., Joe Ford, a six-foot five-inch talking handbook for the Texas Board of Pardons and Paroles, had advised her how to act in such a situation. Joe Ford had advised her how to act in *every* situation.

The parolee must maintain acceptable, non-threatening behavior at all times.

The parolee must follow their agent's instructions.

The parolee must obey ALL laws.

Must submit to search of person, residence, motor vehicle at any time.

No weapons.

No guns.

No bullets or anything that resembles a gun or bullets.

The parolee must not own any knife with a blade longer than two inches, except for a kitchen knife, and only if their parole agent says so.

Failure of any of these conditions will result in a return to prison.

"Tell you straight, Delpha, I hate pulling paper, but I do not hesitate. Don't wanna go back, do you?"

"Not ever, Mr. Ford."

"OK then, here's my Double-A life advice, Delpha. Number 1: Act."

"Act like what?"

"People come out, they run back to old friends and bad old ways to get comfortable. Don't go doing that. Act quiet and easy and eventually you'll feel quiet and easy. Till you get the hang of it, if you have to put on an act, do it, put one on." Joe Ford paused. "Now, second part: Ask."

"Ask," Depha repeated. Not something she had any practice doing. She shifted in the wood chair.

"Ask for a place to live, so you can leave that half-way house. Ask for a job. For what you need. Out here they won't knock you down for asking. You don't help yourself, nobody's gonna help you. Now, they show you the door, you still be polite. You don't burn any bridges because who knows if you might run into these people again. They say no, you just say, 'I appreciate your time. Have a nice day.' Then you smile and leave."

As Mr. Ford had advised her, Delpha didn't burn down this fat-neck man's bridge. Neither did she say, "I appreciate your time. Have a nice day," like she'd said a bunch of times already. She took the elevator down, parsing out her breath till she could get some clear air.

She walked a block, swerved into an alley to breathe, about tripped over a weather-beaten white person with wispy gray hair squatting by a grocery cart, a spray of azalea in one fist and a twig of dogwood in the other. Delpha startled, then became rigid, chin lowered, arms down, hands visible, including the one with her purse.

The person studied her sideways and thoroughly and then went back to contemplating the two flowers. "Which one you think?"

Manner, voice, puff-sleeve blouse were womanish, but the gray chin whiskers, the pleated-style trousers and stained suit vest were male wear. Tennies could go either way. Delpha knew close enough which it was though.

She pointed to the azalea. *Wouldn't it be fine Lord to step into a sunset-pink flower fluted like a party dress and pull it up fluttering round her shoulders? Wouldn't it be fine to be wrapped in that good-smelling, lighted skin?*

The old woman nodded, tucked the azalea into the vest's breast pocket, and looked up again, thready eyebrows raised, inviting comment.

"Fetchin'."

"Thank ye. I'm Miss Doris." She handed up the dogwood. "For you. Welcome back."

Delpha traced the powdery, tender, white, white petals.

"You can tell...I look that raw? Got it all over me, don't I?"

"Not like you think." Miss Doris jutted her chin whiskers toward Delpha's right hand. "You toting one of them handiworks."

Delpha looked down at her leather purse, cut, sewed, simply tooled in a basketweave pattern, adorned with neither rose nor lily. You could order either pattern from the prison gift shop or a combination or a cowboy or cowgirl, horse raring.

"Messed up my first one."

"They get testy you waste that leather, huh."

"Delpha's my name." The younger woman held out her hand.

Miss Doris wiped hers on the gabardine trousers and shook. She had to be in her sixties, but she held the squat limber as a frog. "Listen, look in the cart, get you out the blue blanket you can sit on it. It's got a down and a up side you can see."

"I need to be getting along, ma'am."

"Naw, stay." The deep furrows between her brows mashed closer.

"Well, I need to—"

"Just a little while. I'm a-feeling like the last pea at pea-time."

The younger woman's posture softened. "My mother used to say that." She hiked her thumb back of herself. "That place have coffee?" The sign on the building across the street from the alley read THE NEW ROSEMONT HOTEL $1 AND UP. The glass door top of the steps needed a cleaning.

A glint came to Miss Doris's eye. "They sure do. Ask Calinda, she'll sell you some. I want the chicory and get her to pour some milk and sugar in it."

"You wanna sit down in there?"

Miss Doris wrinkled both her nose and her pursed lips. "Got my valuables, honey."

Delpha crossed the street and climbed the steps, thinking *Honey*—how a tone of voice divided everything in the world.

The lobby was furnished with groups of chairs cushioned in a mix of middle-aged blue velour or spattered-flowers print. Old men and ladies sat in pairs or by themselves. One determined gent had his feet planted before a mahogany sideboard and was taking calculated hold of a water glass. He was beginning the delicate operation of pouring water from a pitcher.

"'Scuse me, where is it you buy the coffee?"

The pitcher lowered shakily until it achieved purchase on the sideboard. The process was repeated with the water glass, then, taking bitty steps, the man turned himself to behold Delpha face-on. "Well. Aren't you a purty thing? Calinda's there in the kitchen fixing lunch." The little steps began rotating him back toward the water glass.

In the center of a large kitchen, two women confronted each other over opposite sides of a wood chopping table. A white woman with a cap of gray hair, an apron, and judgment on her plain face loomed over a pile of naked chickens, which identified her as Calinda. She had a few years on Miss Doris and looked to be using a cleaver to illustrate some point to a cocker-spaniel-type thirty years younger than her. The cocker spaniel glowered from between two flaps of blond hair, crimped by a perm into a zigzag pattern to her shoulders. Second later, perfumey air from that direction radiated into Delpha's nose. *Gin.*

"...not true. I *do* take care of her most nights," that one said.

"When you can be bothered. Got one thing better to do, you're doing it, and she's just laying there alone, pore old biddy."

"Years, years, how many goddamn *years*! Pleasssse let's put her in Shady Lanes. They have nurses."

"Jessie knows Moselle. You wanna take Moselle away from her? Moselle and the house is all she knows now. Besides you and me. And sometimes I think I might as well be Eleanor Roosevelt."

"You look like Eleanor Roosevelt."

"You mean that as an insult, Ida, but I don't take it as one. Mrs. Roosevelt was a great lady."

"But Shady Lanes has an ice cream machine." When the ice cream machine produced no effect, the cocker spaniel growled, "A real estate man wants to buy the house. I want to sell it."

"You already sold everything in it wasn't nailed down."

"Hell's bells, it's *mine*!" The younger, shorter woman lunged forward, flaps flying back to show clenched teeth. The old one, hooded eyes narrowed in warning, raised the cleaver.

This was a familiar-enough scene. Delpha walked to within four feet of the table, no closer, and reserved room to move in either direction. "'Scuse me. Gentleman told me to come in here. Could I buy two cups of coffee from you, one chicory?"

Cocker spaniel wrenched up a naked chicken by both its wings and slammed it tailbone-first into the butcher-block table. "Eat shit and die, Calinda."

Delpha sidestepped as the woman stomped past.

"That's twenty cents." The old one named Calinda set down the cleaver and wiped her hands on the skirt of her apron. "Cream and sugar?"

A young black man in kitchen whites popped from a side room that might be a pantry, took up the cleaver and began swiftly cutting up chickens into eating parts.

Delpha handed over two dimes and took a paper cup of

black and one of cream and sugar for Miss Doris. She was thinking maybe she'd come back in and talk to this woman after they drank the coffee in the alley. After that. Half hour or so. She'd do it then. She would.

But she harked back to Joe Ford's hectoring and, goaded by two hands full of hot coffee, tightened up and asked, "You happen to have any rooms for rent, ma'am? And would you be innerested in trading some work for the room?"

The young cook shot her a look.

"Bookkeeping," she amended, so as not to step on his toes, though she had once been assistant-assistant-cook for nine hundred. Nothing anybody would want to eat, though.

"Hotel has a C.P.A."

Delpha edged over to a counter, and, still facing the woman, set down the two hot cups to cool off her hands. "Well, cleaning, what you got. I'm looking for office work, days, but I'd take some part-time to get started. You scrub your bathrooms at 'leven o'clock, they're nice and clean mornings."

The old woman's neutral expression soured at the idea of bathrooms. "Couple of 'em here wander nights. Shrunk old peckers miss the bowl half the time."

The young man snorted.

"Didn't mean to listen, but I heard you and the other lady. If you got a sick person needs looking after, I can do that too, got some infirmary experience. You think on it, ma'am, and I'll come back real soon to hear what you decide. Right now I got a appointment. Thank you much for the coffee. Have a fine day." She nodded, picked up the cups, and left through the tired velour lobby.

Gotta put on an act, do it, put one on.

II

TOM PHELAN HELD up his left hand, inspecting his middle finger. An aching stump shy of an inch tall. Could have been worse. Everything on an oil rig weighed as much as a greased Volkswagen, fifty billion mechanical parts to ram or slam, mash, whirl, fly off or collapse and fall. Lack of sleep, wee inattention to the makeup tongs, and now he had a ghost finger crowding his index.

He set his elbows on the *Beaumont Enterprise,* May 21, 1973 edition. They'd centered the ad announcing his new business, boxed it in black, and spelled his name right. The other ad in the Classifieds—Wanted: Secretary—had brought in two girls yesterday. He planned to choose the one with the coral nails and the Dusty Springfield voice. But just then he got a call from his old high school friend Joe Ford, now a parole officer, and Joe was hard-selling.

"Typing, dictation, whatever you need, buddy. She learned it in the big house. Paid her debt to society. What say you talk to her?"

"Find some other sucker. Didn't know you put yourself out like this. Since when are you Acme Employment?"

"Since when are you a private eye?"

"Since Worker's Comp paid me just enough bread to swing a lease."

"Thought you liked the rigs."

"Still got nine fingers left. Aim to keep 'em."

"Just see this girl, Tommy. She knows her stuff."

"Why're you pushing her?"

"Telephones don't answer themselves, now do they?"

"Thought I heard they invented a machine that—"

Joe blew scorn through the phone. "Communist rumor. Lemme send her over. She can get down there in two shakes."

"No."

"I'm gonna say this one time. Who had your back the night you stepped outside with Narlan Pugh and his inbred cousins stepped outside behind him?"

"One time, shit. I heard it three. Time you realized gratitude comes to a natural end, same as a sack of donuts."

Joe bided.

Phelan stewed.

"Goddamnit, no promises."

"Nooo! Course not. Make it or break it on her own. Thanks for the chance, it'll buck her up."

Phelan asked about the girl's rap, but the dial tone was noncommittal.

8:32. Footsteps were sounding on the stairs to his second-story walkup.

Wasn't skipping up here, was she? Measured tread. The knock on the door lately lettered *Phelan Investigations* wasn't fast, wasn't slow. Not loud, not soft.

Phelan walked out of his office, through the secretary-to-be's office, and opened up. Well. Not a girl. A couple crows had stepped lightly at the corners of her eyes. A faint crease of bitter slanted from the left side of her barely tinted lips. Ash brown hair, jaw-length, roomy white blouse, navy skirt. Olive-tinted skin overlaid with a jailhouse tan. Eyes gray-blue, a little clouded, distant, like a storm rolling in from the Gulf. This one wouldn't sit behind the desk blowing on her polish. The hand he was shaking had naked nails cut to the quick.

"Tom Phelan."

"Delpha Wade." Her voice was low and dry.

Delpha Wade. His brain racheted a picture toward him but not far enough, like when the Payday gets hung up partway out the vending machine.

They sat down in his office, him in a gimpy swivel behind a large metal desk, both included in the rent. Her in one of the proud new clients' chairs, padded leather with regally tall backs.

"Have to be honest with you, Miss Wade. Think I already found a secretary."

No disappointment in those blue eyes, no hope either. She just passed a certificate with a gold seal across the desk. The paper said she typed seventy words a minute, spoke shorthand, could do double entry. The brunette with the Dusty Springfield voice claimed all that too, but she'd backed it up with a giggle, not a diploma from Gatesville.

"Your first choice of a job a P.I.'s office?"

"My first choice is a job."

Touché. "What number interview would this be for you?"

"Number one."

"I'm flattered. Get off the bus, you come here."

The blue eyes let in a smidgen of light. "That doesn't count the eleven places I applied 'fore they showed me the door. And one other that didn't have what you could call an interview."

No wonder Joe was pushing her. "Had your druthers, where'd you work, Miss Wade?"

"Library. I like libraries. It's what I did *there*."

There being Gatesville Women's Prison. Now that she'd brought it up. "How many you do?"

"Fourteen."

Phelan quelled the whistle welling up. That let out check kiting, forgery, embezzling from the till, and dope. He was about to ask her the delicate when she handed it to him on a foil tray. "Voluntary manslaughter."

"And you did fourteen?"

"He was very dead, Mr. Phelan."

His brain shoved: the picture fell into the slot. Phelan'd been a teenager, jazzed by blood-slinging, and reporters had loved the story. Underage waitress in a bayou dive, waiting for the owner to collect the take. Alone. Two guys thrown out earlier came back. Father and son, that was the kicker. The son had beat her, raped her, cut on her. But surprise. Somehow the knife had changed hands. The father had got slashed and son punctured. When the owner's headlights showed, the father abandoned his son and peeled out in their car. Delpha Wade had not let nature take its course. She finished off Junior on the pine dance floor.

The Gatesville certificate was being fit into a stamped-leather purse, prison-made, durable and fashion-free. She gathered her feet under her. But didn't stand up. Those eyes got to him. No hope, no despair. Just a storm cloud back on the blue horizon.

The outer door tapped. A hesitant tap, like a mouse was out there. "'Scuse me," Phelan said and stood. His chair flopped its wooden seat upward like its next occupant would arrive in it via the ceiling. He wrenched it up. The seat surrendered again. "Gotta fix that," he muttered.

When he looked up, he saw Delpha Wade's straight back,

walking out. Funny, he'd had the distinct impression she wouldn't fold so easy.

"Forgot your purse, Miss Wade."

"No, I didn't." She shut the door between their offices— or rather, the door between his office and whoever got the secretary job's office—quietly. He heard "Good morning, ma'am. Do you have an appointment to see Mr. Phelan?" Her dry voice was smooth as a Yale lock.

I'll be damned. Phelan tipped the chair's seat into loading position and sat in it, like a boss should.

Mumbling. "May I ask what your visit is in reference to?"

More mumbling, a lot of it. Then—Phelan hated this sound—sobbing. Not that he hadn't prepared for it. He'd bought a box of tissues at the dimestore for the brokenhearted wives. Stashed it in the desk's bottom drawer next to the husbands' fifth of Kentucky. Had his .38 in a drawer, its license in his wallet, P.I. license on the wall, new-minted business cards. An ex-con impersonating a secretary.

Delpha Wade entered, closing the door behind her. "Can you see a client now, Mr. Phelan?"

"Bring her on." Despite the sobs, he was rooting for the Personnel Manager of one of the big refineries, Goodyear would do, who had a problem executive, thief or liar, and while she was here, she would see that new employees needed a pre-hire background check. Maybe the old ones too, say, couple thousand of them.

"You can go in now, Mrs. Toups."

A bone-thin woman in yesterday's makeup and rumpled shirtwaist took the doorway. Leatherette purse in her fists, little gold nameplate like a cashier's pinned over her left breast. The two slashes between her eyebrows deepened. "You're kinda young. I was looking for—"

"An old, retired cop?" Delpha Wade said. On "cop" her neutral voice bunched. "Mr. Phelan has a fresh point of view."

What Mr. Phelan had was a fresh legal pad. He wielded a ballpoint over it. "Please, sit down, Mrs. Toups. Tell me what I can do for you."

Delpha Wade scooped an elbow, tucked her into the client chair, at the same time saying, "Can I get you some coffee? Cream and sugar?"

Phelan furrowed his own brow, trying to grow some wrinkles. *Coffee*, he thought. *What coffee?*

"Take a Coke, if you got one."

The inner door closed behind Delpha Wade. He heard the outer door shut too. His first client stammered into her troubles, Phelan's ballpoint despoiled the virginal legal pad. The tissues stayed in their drawer. Caroleen Toups had her own hankie.

By the time his pretend-secretary returned with a dewy bottle of Coke, Phelan had the story. The Toups lived over on the north side, not far off Concord, nothing that could be called a neighborhood, more like one of a string of old wood houses individually hacked out of the woods. Her boy Ricky was into something, and she didn't like it. He'd been skipping school. Running around all hours. Then last night Ricky had not come home.

Gently, Phelan asked, "Report that to the police?"

"Six o'clock this morning. They said boys run off all the time."

Phelan silently agreed, having once waked on a New Orleans sidewalk, littered, lacquered, and sorry somebody'd pounded rebar through his forehead. "What does your husband think?"

"He passed last fall. Took a virus in his heart." Her reddened eyes offered to share that grief with him, but Phelan bowed his head and went on.

"Does Ricky have a favorite item of clothing?"

"Some silly shoes that make him taller. And a ZZ Top T-shirt says *Rio Grande Mud* on it."

"Would you know if those are gone from his room?"

"I would...Mr. Phelan." Having managed to bestow on T. Phelan's callow mug that title of respect, Mrs. Toups looked at him hopefully. "They're not."

"Have a piggy bank?"

She snapped the purse open and took out a roll, Andrew Jackson on top. "Till about midnight," she said, "I read the *Enterprise*. That's where I saw your ad. After midnight, I searched my son's room with a fine-tooth comb. This was in a cigar box under his bed. Along with some baseball cards and twisty cigarettes. There's three hundred and ten dollars here. Ricky's in tenth grade, Mr. Phelan. He doesn't have a job."

The phone rang in the outer office, followed by the light click of the reconditioned Selectric. "You wouldn't a brought a picture of him?"

Mrs. Toups dug into the leatherette, handed over a school photo. Fair and baby-faced, long-haired like a lot of kids these days. Grinning like he was saddled on a Christmas pony. *Ricky Toups when he still had a daddy.*

The mother's tired eyes held a rising rim of water. "Why I wanted you to look old and tough—you find Ricky, scare him good. I can't take anymore a this."

Phelan was jolted by a gut feeling, a pact connecting him to that haggard mother. He hadn't expected that. *Was that a regular thing? Who knew.*

"OK," he said quickly. While Mrs. Toups sipped her Coke,

he scrawled her address and phone number, then asked for an inventory of Ricky's friends. Make that friend. He jotted the name of a neighbor girl, Georgia Watson. School? French High, Phelan's own alma mater, an orange brick sprawl with a patchy football field. The legal pad was broken in now.

He wrote in her name on a standard contract and slid it toward her. He'd practiced the next part so he could spit it out without blinking. "Fee is seventy-five a day. Plus expenses."

Nobody was blinking here. Mrs. Toups peeled off five Jacksons. "Could you start now?"

"First day's crucial on a missing child case," Phelan said, like he knew. "You're at the top of the schedule."

He guided Mrs. Toups through the outer office to the door. To his right, Delpha Wade sat behind the secretary's desk, receiver tucked into her neck, typing. *Typing what? And where had she got the paper?*

"A Mrs. Lloyd Elliott would like to speak with you about a confidential matter. Says her husband's an attorney." Delpha Wade's dry voice was hushed, and she rubbed her thumb and fingers together in the universal sign for money.

Mrs. Toups stuck her reddened face back in the door, a last plea on it. But at the sight of Phelan taking the phone, she ducked her head and left.

"Tom Phelan," he said.

Local accent, bit of a throb in the speaker's voice, odd. But direct. The woman on the phone told him she wanted her husband followed and why. She'd pay a retainer. Cash.

"That'll work. I'll get back to you *very* soon, ma'am. Please leave relevant details with my...with Miss Wade. You can trust her."

And don't I hope that's true, he thought, clattering down the stairs.

*

The band was playing when Phelan pulled up to French High School. God, did he remember this parking lot: clubhouse, theatre, and smoking lounge. He lit up for nostalgia's sake.

A little shit-kicker perched on the trunk of a Mustang nudged back his Resistol. He had his boots on the bumper, one knee jack-hammering hard enough to shiver the car. Phelan offered him a smoke.

Haughtily, the kid produced some Bull and rolled his own. "Take a light."

Phelan obliged. "You know Georgia Watson?"

"Out there. Georgia's in Belles." The boy lofted his chin toward the field that joined the parking lot.

"What about Ricky Toups?"

The kid tugged down the hat, blew out smoke. "Kinda old to be into weed, ain't ya?"

"That why people come looking for Ricky?"

Marlboro-Man-in-training doused the homemade, stashed it behind his ear. Slid off the trunk and booked.

Phelan turned toward the field, where the band played a lazy version of "Grazing in the Grass." The Buffalo Belles were high-kicking, locked shoulder to shoulder. Line of smiling faces, white, black, and café au lait, bouncing hair and breasts, hundred and twenty teenage legs, kicked up high. Fondly remembering a pair of those white boots hooked over his shoulders post-game, he strolled toward the rousing sight.

After their routine, the girls milled sideline while the band marched patterns. Phelan asked for Georgia and found her, said he wanted to talk.

This is who Ricky Toups thought hung the moon? Georgia

Watson had an overloaded bra, all right, and cutoffs so short the hems of white pockets poked out like underwear. But she was a dish-faced girl with frizzled hair and cagey brown eyes. Braided gold chain tucked into the neck of a white T-shirt washed thin.

She steered him away from the knots of babbling girls. Her smile threw a murky light into the brown eyes. Black smudges beneath them from her gobbed eyelashes.

He introduced himself with a business card. "Ricky Toups' mother asked me to check up on him. He got any new friends you know about?"

She jettisoned the smile, shrugged.

"C'mon, Georgia. Ricky thinks you're his friend."

She made a production of whispering. "Ricky was helping this guy with something, but I think that's all over."

"Something?"

"Something," she hissed. She angled toward some girls frankly staring at her and Phelan and fluttered her fingers in a wave. Nobody waved back.

"This guy. Why's Ricky not helping him anymore?"

Georgia shook her head, looking over Phelan's shoulder like she was refusing somebody who wasn't there. "Fun at first, then he turned irritable. Ricky's gonna quit hanging out with him, even though that means—" Her trap shut.

"Giving up the green," Phelan finished. His little finger flicked out the braided chain around the girl's neck. Fancy G in 24-carat. "How long y'all had this irritable friend?"

The head shaking continued, like a tic now.

Phelan violated her personal space. "Name. And where the guy lives."

The girl backed up. "I don't know, some D name, Don or Darrell or something. Gotta go now."

Phelan caught her arm. "Ricky didn't come home last night."

White showed around the brown eyes. She spit out a sentence, included her phone number when pressed, then jerked her arm away and ran back to the other girls on the sideline. They practiced dance steps in bunches, laughed, horsed around. Georgia stood apart biting her bottom lip, the little white square of his business card pinched in her fingers.

11:22. He drove back to the office, took the stairs two at a time. Delpha handed him Mrs. Lloyd Elliott's details neatly typed on the back of a sheet of paper. He flipped the sheet over. Delpha Wade's discharge from Gatesville: April 13, 1973. Five foot six, hundred and twenty pounds. Hair brown, eyes blue. 32. Voluntary manslaughter.

"Only paper around," she said.

Phelan laid a ten on the desk. "Get some. Then see what's up in the Toups' neighborhood, say, the last three months. Thought this was a kid pushing weed for pocket money, but could be dirtier water." He told her what Georgia Watson had given him: the D name, Don or Darrell, and that Ricky brought other boys over to the guy's house to party. "I'm guessing Georgia might've pitched in with that."

Delpha met his eyes for a second. Then, without comment, she flipped through the phone book while he went to his office, got the .38 out of a drawer and loaded it. He glanced out the window. Calinda Blanchard, the New Rosemont's proprietress, rag in hand, shooting the glass part of the door with Windex.

When he came out, Delpha had the phone book open to the city map section. "Got a cross directory?" she asked.

Phelan went back and got it from his office. "Run through the—"

"Newspaper's police blotter."

"Right. Down at the—"

"Library," she said. She left, both books hugged to her chest.

Just another girl off to school.

The parole office faced the police station. His buddy Joe Ford was in, but busy. Phelan helped himself to a couple glazed donuts from an open box. Early lunch. Joe read from a manila file to one guy Phelan was related to and another he recognized on sight. That one took notes on a little spiral pad. Phelan, toting the long legal pad, realized he should have one of the little spirals. Neater, slipped in a jacket pocket. More professional. Joe closed the folder and kept on talking. One guy gave a low whistle, the other laughed.

Joe stood up, did a double-take. "Hey, speak of the devil. Tommy, come on down."

Phelan shook hands with Fred Abels, detective. Stuck his hand out to the other, but the man bear-hugged him. "Hey, Uncle E.E.," Phelan said.

E.E. boomed, *"Bougre, t'es fou ouais toi! T'as engage un prisonnier."* Which meant Phelan was crazy for hiring himself a convict. Abels, sporting a Burt Reynolds' 'stache and burns, only not sexy, studied Phelan like he was a mud tire track lifted from a scene.

Who said he'd hired anybody?

Phelan zeroed in on Joe, who raised his eyebrows, pulled down his lips, shook his head to indicate the purity permeating his soul.

"OK." Phelan set hands on his hips and broadened his stance. "All right. So my friend here appeals to my famous heart of gold. So I interview his girl. So she stuck some bad-doer. So what."

"Minced that one, yeah. I worked that case." E.E. wagged a finger. "I'm ona tell you, cher, lock up the letter opener." He punched his nephew's arm, nodded at Joe, and he and Abels ambled off, chortling.

"You loud mouth bastard," Phelan said to Joe. "Give me the dopers and perverts north side of town." Commandeering Joe's chair, Phelan reeled off some street names.

"That's confidential."

"Could have my secretary call you."

"Hand full a *Gimme* and a mouth full a *Much obliged*— that's you." Joe squinted, put-upon. "Not my territory, but old Parker lives in the can." Joe stalked over to his co-worker Parker's vacant desk, the messy one next to his clean one, and rambled through its file drawers.

Phelan phoned Tyrrell Public Library. He asked the librarian to get a Miss Wade, who'd be in the reference section, going through newspapers.

"This is not a bus station, sir. We don't page people."

Seemed like, Phelan thought while locating his desperately-polite-but-hurting voice, one bad crab always jumps in the gumbo. "I'm just as sorry as I can be, ma'am. But couldn't you find my sister? We're down the funeral home and our daddy's lost his mind."

Clunk. Receiver on desk. Joe was still pulling files.

Footsteps, then Delpha came on. "Hey, Bubba," she said.

Phelan grinned.

She told him she'd call him back from a pay phone. "Call Joe's," he said.

In three minutes, Joe's phone rang, and Delpha read out what she had so far. "Check this one from last night." A Marvin Carter, 18, wandering down Delaware Street, apparent assault victim, transported to a hospital. Then,

outside of husband-wife slug fests, thefts, one complaint
of tap-dancing on the roof of a Dodge Duster, she'd found
seven dope busts and a missing child report. She gave
him names and addresses, phone numbers from the cross
directory.

Joe set files on his desk, neatened them up, said "Vacate my
chair, son." Phelan ignored him, boring in on each mugshot as
he scribbled names on his unprofessional legal pad.

One of the names was a Don Henry. Sprung from
Huntsville two months back.

Some D name, Don or Darrell.

There you go. Cake.

No mud, no grease, no five-hundred-pound pipe, no lost
body parts. Man, he should have split the rigs while he still
had ten fingers.

2:01. He drove back to the office and hit the phone. Got a child
at the Henry number, asked for its mother.

"She went the store. Git away, Dwight, I'm on the phone."
A wail from the background.

"Honey, your daddy there?"

The child scolded Dwight. Dwight was supposed to shut
up while the child had dibs on the telephone. But Dwight
wasn't lying down. He was pitching a fit.

"Honey? Hey, kid!" Phelan hollered into the phone.

"Shut up, Dwight! I cain't hear myself talk. They took
Daddy back Satiddy."

"Saturday? Back where?"

"Where he *was*. Is this Uncle Merle?" The child yelped.
Now two wails mingled on the other end of the line.

A woman's harsh voice barked into the phone, "Low
down, Merle, pumping the kids. They pulled Don's paper,

OK? You happy now? Gonna say 'I told you so'? You and Ma can kiss my ass." The phone crashed down.

Saturday was six days ago. Frowning, Phelan X'd Don Henry. Next, mindful of the tender volunteers in pink smocks on the end of the line, he inquired feelingly for his cousin Marvin Carter. Baptist Hospital, strike. St. Elizabeth, long wait, transfer, and strike. Hotel Dieu, single to first.

He parked in a doctor's space in front of the red brick hospital by the port. Eau de Pinesol and polished tile. A nun gave him the room number.

The face on the pillow was white-whiskered, toothless, and snoring. A pyramid of a woman in a red-flowered muumuu sat bedside. Phelan checked the room number. "Marvin Carter?"

The woman sighed. "It's Mar-tin. Cain't y'all get nothing right?"

Phelan loped back to the desk and stood in line behind a sturdy black woman and a teenage boy with a transistor radio tinnily broadcasting the day's body count. The boy's face was lopsided, the wide bottom out of kilter with a narrow forehead. He nudged the dial and a song blared out. "Superfly." The woman slapped shut a checkbook, snatched the transistor, and dialed back to the tinny announcer spewing numbers and Asian place names.

"Jus keep listenin'. Cause you keep runnin' nights, thas where you gonna be, in that war don't never end, you hear me, Marvin? What *you* lookin' at?" She scowled at Phelan.

The boy turned so that Phelan verified the lopsidedness as swelling. He ventured, "Marvin Carter?"

The woman guided the boy behind her as she asked who Phelan was. He told her, emphasizing that he was not a policeman. He told her he was looking for Ricky Toups, kept his gaze on the boy.

The boy's eyebrows jumped. *Bingo.*

"Les' go." The woman pushed the teenager toward the glass doors.

Phelan dogged them. "Did that to you, Marvin, what's he gonna do to Ricky, huh? Want that on your slate? Could be a lot worse than the dope. "

The boy tried the deadeye on Phelan. Couldn't hold it.

"We talking *dope* now?" The woman's voice dropped below freezing. "You done lied to me, Marvin Carter." Her slapping hand stopped short of the swollen jaw.

Marvin grunted something that was probably "Don't, Mama," enough so Phelan understood his jaw was wired.

"Ricky got you there promising dope," Phelan said, "but that wasn't all you got, was it?"

The boy squeezed his eyes shut.

"Wasn't white kids did this to you? Was some grown man?" Marvin's mother took hold of his skinny waist.

"Listen," Phelan leaned in, "if he said he'd hurt your mama here, I'll take care of that. It's just a line. But Ricky's real. You know him, and he's wherever you were last night. Help me find him, Marvin."

"Eniss," the boy said.

"Ennis? The street near the municipal swimming pool?"

Shake from Marvin.

"That's his name? Ennis?"

Head-shake, cupping his wide jaw.

"Dennis?"

A shudder ran through the teenager. "'Sgot evertang dere. Air's a vig ache, man."

Phelan didn't press for a translation, he was scanning his list of parolees. One Dennis Deeterman. One D. Harold Holdrege. He squinted at his own handwriting. He'd jotted down an identifying mark for Deeterman. "Tattoo of a knife on his arm?"

Marvin lifted up his shoulders and let them fall.

"OK, OK. Concord Street? Lucas?"

A hard-K sound indicated Concord. Marvin muttered directions, minus some consonants. The mother glowered Phelan away. Marvin bent down and shook against her neck.

Phelan dashed back to the hospital's two payphones, called Delpha Wade, told her where he was heading. If she didn't hear from him within the hour, call E.E. Guidry down at the station. "That's G-U-I—"

"Know how to spell it," she said. "Got time for one question, Mr. Phelan?"

"Shoot."

Throat-clearing. "You think you might hire me?"

"Miss Wade, you were hired when you called me Bubba." He hung up the silent phone and jogged for the doors.

3:15. The house with the orange mailbox painfully described by Marvin was a dingy white ranch. It was set deep in the lot, backed up to tall pines and oak and magnolia, pockets of brush. Rusty brown pine needles and dried magnolia leaves—big brown tongues—littered the ground. With oil shot up to twelve dollars a barrel, somebody'd be out here soon, hammering up martin-box apartments, but for now wildlife was renting this leftover patch of the Big Thicket.

No car, but ruts in the grass where one had parked.

Phelan knocked on the door. Waited. Tried the knob, no dice. He went around the back to a screen porch that looked to be an add-on. Or it had been a screen porch before plywood was nailed over its large windows. A two-by-four had been pounded across the door; the hammer lying there in the dirt suggested that Dennis Deeterman might be recently away from his desk. Maybe. Phelan could hear something. He beat on the door. "Ricky. Ricky Toups, you in there?"

He put his ear to the door. *Something*. Phelan pounded again, louder. "I'm looking for Ricky Toups."

A low huffing, rhythmic. Intermittent creak. What *was* that sound? Like a rusted rocking chair.

He jogged back to his car, shoved a flashlight from the glove compartment into his pocket and snagged a pry bar. Ripped off the two-by-four. Opened the door. Directly across the porch was the door that led into the house. Phelan stepped over there, .38 drawn, and rattled it: locked. Already he was smelling piss in the hot, dead air. Then herb and cigarettes and some kind of dead-fish bayou stink. That creaky noise came from the far left, high up. He found a switch by the locked door and flipped it. Not a gleam.

He stuck the gun in his belt and strode into the dark room. His shin banged into something scuttling fast in the opposite direction. The thing slashed his calf shallowly and long, like a pissed-off girl keying her boyfriend's car, and rushed over his foot. Phelan yielded right-of-way, then bent down to rub his leg and felt the tear in his trousers. He craned back in time to see his assailant's ringed tail flee out the door.

A raccoon.

Irritable might not cover Dennis Deeterman. "Ricky Toups, that you in here?"

He shined the white circle up and left, to the source of the creaking.

Christ Almighty.

Phelan's jaw sagged. On the top of metal shelves was a half-naked gargoyle, perched there. No, clinging. Blue-jeaned haunches with a smooth, sheened back folded over them, fingers clawed around the metal, head cut sharply toward Phelan. Blinking eyes protruded from sunken holes. The down-turned mouth wheezed.

"You got asthma, right."

Ricky Toups' head bobbed loosely, flapping sweat-dark hair that had been dishwater blond in last year's school photo.

"What's going on, Ricky?"

"He got m-m-mad at—" The kid flung out a hand, pointing. Phelan heard a cat's hiss.

A cat, why not.

He zigzagged the light downward over matted orange shag littered with marijuana debris, the arm of a bamboo couch, crushed beer cans.

Behind came faintly from Ricky's labored breathing.

Phelan wheeled. His light fell on the toothy jaws flapped wide in another hiss. Damn thing wasn't but two feet long, but it meant business.

He flipped the flashlight to his left hand, his stump telegraphing a deep blue ache clear to his elbow as he fisted his hand around the flash's barrel. The little gator paddled forward and clamped his shoe. Phelan grabbed the spiked tail. It flung his hand side to side as it flailed. He yanked, its jaws dug in like a trap's. Phelan hopped for the door, dragging the foot with the gator. Once he was outside, he ripped the knot from his shoelace and kicked. Shoe and gator sailed off into the weeds.

Cussing, Phelan jogged back through the door into the black oven and laid a hand hard on what turned out to be Ricky's bicep. The boy slumped off the shelf into his arms. Phelan looped the boy's arm around his neck. They were hobbling toward the door when Ricky's ragged exhalation became a shriek.

The shaft of light from the door revealed part of a black pile that blended into the darkness. Phelan squinted at it. What? Most of him failed to make sense of what he saw. But not his skin—it was crawling off his belly, his nuts squeezing north of nutsack.

The pile shifted until only a tip remained. Then the tip disappeared into blackness. That it was heading toward him told Phelan enough. Most snakes light out for the hills. Cottonmouths come at you. Phelan ranged the light till it hit the bamboo couch and dumped the boy on it. "Keep your feet off the floor." He scanned with the flashlight. *Where the fuck was it?* Shag. Spilt ashtray. More shag.

Then the beam caught a section of sinuous black. He moved the light. There it was. Pouring toward him, triangular head outthrust.

Phelan fired.

The black snake convulsed, kept coming, tongue darting.

He fired again. Still the black form writhed on the orange carpet. He blew its head off with the third round. Phelan stepped wide of the quivering snake, wasn't dead enough yet to keep the head from biting. Ears ringing, he tossed the flashlight, pulled the boy's arm around his neck, dragged him out of that room into the daylight.

Bruises on the kid's arm, high up. Been grabbed, for sure. Held? Phelan draped him in his own jacket, stuffed him into the passenger seat, and peeled out onto Concord.

"He rape you, Ricky?"

Violent head shake. Negative.

"Hurt anybody else you know of?"

The side of the boy's head hit the window. The wheeze sounded less like creaking now, more like a tiny person lurking behind Ricky's teeth, whimpering.

Phelan blasted around Concord's tight curves, spun a right, a left, and gunned onto the straightaway of 11th Street. Delivered Ricky into the horseshoe entrance to St. Elizabeth's and used a hospital pay phone to call Mrs. Toups. Then he left a message for Uncle E.E. about the wild kingdom on Concord.

Mrs. Toups busted in the big glass doors, bony face lit up like stadium lights. She hurried off to her boy. Phelan limped to a chair in the waiting room, trying to remember when he last had a tetanus shot. He pulled off his sock. The front of his foot, tinged lavender with a garland of purple dents in it, drew two pig-tailed spectators.

"Ooo, what happen a you, Mister?"

"Look ug-lee."

Phelan shrugged. "Dragon bit me."

"No such thing," said the big one.

"Uh huh, look at his hand," squealed the little one.

He held up his nine fingers. The girls bickered while Phelan thought about half-naked Ricky Toups up on that shelf gasping his lungs out.

"Mr. Phelan…"

He looked up to see Mrs. Toups, petting his jacket.

"You saved our life, and that's the truth."

Phelan took his jacket, scrounged up a bent smile.

He opened his door. Delpha Wade sat in the secretary's chair behind an idle typewriter. She gave him a once-over, no doubt taking in the limp, the single shoe and the torn pants, the jacket wadded in his hand.

"Boy safe?" was all she said.

Phelan pressed his lips together, nodded. "Way past five. You didn't need to stay."

She pushed over his change, five ones and silver, and leaned over to pick up a sack from the floor. The brown hair parted. On the nape of her neck, an inch of scar tissue disappeared into the white blouse. She straightened, tugging up her collar.

"Didn't have a key to lock up. I started files on the Toups and the Lloyd Elliott cases. The phone call from Mrs. Lloyd Elliot, 'member that? Ran out and bought paper, carbon paper, and some file folders."

Phelan drew his key ring from his pocket. He jiggled off the extra office key, slowed down by the gouges from the baby gator's tail that were stinging his sweaty palm. He laid the key onto the desk.

"You sure you want this job?"

Her head lowered but not so far that he didn't catch the tint spreading over the jailhouse-pale of Delpha Wade's cheekbones.

Or maybe that was just the sunset squeezing through the window.

They settled the details of hours and salary. He listened to her departing footsteps, jingling the change in his pockets. He bent over and took off his lone shoe, chucked it in the wastebasket. He walked around his territory in his socks. After a while he leapt straight up and tagged the tin ceiling, locked his own door, and padded down the stairs.

III

TO CALINDA BLANCHARD, born the very last morning of
the nineteenth century, Delpha Wade was a girl who had to
toe the line. She showed back up in the kitchen after dinner,
presented a Gatesville Women's Prison release form for Miss
Blanchard to acknowledge privately, then folded it away again.
Stood there canvas suitcase in hand, leather purse tucked up
under her arm, deep pile of nothing on her face—waiting to
see if she'd be turned out or taken.

An idea glimmering twenty-watt in her brain, Calinda
took her.

"OK, I can give you your room and board free in turn
for taking care of my aunt evenings. Sundays off. You stay
with her from six-thirty in the evening to ten or till she's
sleeping. Sleeps a lot. Telling you now it's short-term. Jessie's
a hundred years old and when she passes, you got to start
paying for your room."

Color rose in the girl's pale cheeks. "I can pay. Found a
day job today."

Calinda's estimation of her hiked a notch. She explained
to the girl that her aunt Jessie needed a dinner she could eat
with five teeth. Needed dishes washed, kitchen swabbed, sheets
changed, and personal hygiene care that meant muscle and
fortitude. There was a nurse-aide, Moselle, until three in
the afternoon. After that, her care fell to her granddaughter,

Calinda's cousin Ida Rae, who lived with the old woman when she wasn't shacked up with some lizard. Calinda was stepping in now, given Ida's personality deformities. Not to mention the gin.

Miss Blanchard went on to say that her aunt had recently had a stroke, and a few days afterward began to cry and say she wanted to leave Calinda something that was in her room. Cousin Ida had interrupted to ask what it was.

"Jessie said Tiffany something or ruther. Couldn't hardly understand her, but Ida and me both made out that Tiffany name because Ida stared blue murder at me. Moselle heard too, she surely did, and Moselle's got no use for Ida. Couple days later, Jessie had an even worse stroke than the first one."

Calinda paused, narrowed her gaze on Delpha. "You know what Tiffany is?"

"No."

"Jewelry. Know what kinda box it comes in?"

"Nice, I 'spose. Not cardboard."

"Just keep an eye open and tell me if Ida's poking around and gets excited all of a sudden. Maybe I can catch her fore she sells it off. Don't think about cutting a deal with her. It wouldn't occur to Ida to keep a bargain. Besides that, I copied down your parole officer's name. Steal from me, and I'll put you on the bus back to Gatesville."

"I'd be glad for evening work, Miss Blanchard, and the free room, I sure would." No tone to her voice.

Studying the neutral, respectful face before her, Calinda felt medium perked-up about this tit for tat. She gave Delpha Wade a key and her aunt's address on Ashley Avenue. Also gave her a key to Room 221 at the New Rosemont Hotel.

The offer of a free room induced stillness in Delpha. She liked stillness, liked quiet, but she thought best when her body was in motion, busy, occupied so that her mind, left alone, could feed her the tricks that might lurk behind such a proposal. For now she just listened to Miss Blanchard talk.

"Couple days later, she had an even worse stroke than the first one."

Aunt tells niece she has something in her room to give her. Tells her it's some valuable piece of jewelry. Then she up and suffers a stroke. And not her first one either. Delpha saw that Calinda Blanchard wanted her to understand the connection between the stroke and cousin Ida. Yeah, Delpha understood night followed day. What she pondered was how the cousin had given a hundred year-old woman a stroke without killing her. Some miscalculation going on there.

"Ida stays juiced up," Miss Blanchard said next.

Well, there you go.

Then the threat, ever the same, evergreen as the middlemost pine in the piney woods:

if you _____

if you _____

if you _____

or dare to _____, you're screwed, got it?

Delpha expressed her interest carefully. Excitement would not suit. *Gotta put on an act, do it, put one on.* She accepted one key to Ashley Avenue, one to her room, and an invitation to fix herself a peanut butter sandwich.

Oscar, the young cook, stopped her from uncapping the 32 oz. jar of Welch's grape jelly from out of the industrial-size refrigerator. He ducked into the pantry and brought out a Mason jar.

"Mayhaw," he said, "my gran put it up last summer. This is the last one."

Her mother used to make jelly from mayhaw berries. The

sweet-tea smell of the jelly rose. Tears sprang to her eyes. Dipping her head to blink them away, she murmured thanks.

She carried her suitcase and a plate with the sandwich out of the kitchen. The residents turned her way. She nodded vaguely toward the old men and one old woman, drawn into a forward tilt by a pair of watermelon bosoms, a pink cardigan sweater tented around a humped back. "Hello," called the woman, wiggling her fingers. Delpha managed a smile and climbed upstairs, where she found the bathroom mid-way down the hall. She lowered the suitcase sideways to the floor and set the plate on it, used the toilet, and scrubbed her hands and face. Then she retrieved the plate and the suitcase, sacrificing teeth brushing so that once she entered her room, she could stay there.

She had thought this out many times.

She opened the door to #221, put down the suitcase and plate as before. Swiveled and locked the door, set the key in clear view on a chest of drawers. Then she picked up the plate and looked around. Moss-green walls. Window facing an alley. Single bed with a chenille spread, dusky rose. Bedside table, lamp. Chest of drawers. Chair. Closet. That picture of two kids huddling on a bridge, wide-winged angel flared up behind, enough to scare the tar out of them. She'd count on a Gideon in the night table.

Delpha unpacked her four pairs of white cotton panties, her extra brassiere, also white cotton, a sanitary belt and box of Kotex into the chest of drawers. Hung two skirts and blouses and a dress in the closet. Unzipped her navy blue skirt and hung it up too, shed her shirt, bra and panties, and kept on the white nylon slip. The old hotel had been refurbished with central air but a measly amount circulated. She raised the window for fresh air. Switched on the ceiling fan, but not the lamp. She took her sandwich to the side of the bed, where, sitting down, she ate it slowly, holding her head over the plate so as not to drop crumbs onto the swept wood floor. Fragrant, that mayhaw. She sopped up the crumbs with a damp finger. Then she pulled down the covers and lay down, stretched out her legs, her toes spread against cotton washed two hundred times, drew the sheet up to her shoulders. Laying her head on the flattened pillow, she felt, then savored how the door was locked and she was alone.

The door was locked. She was alone.

Nobody was in this ten by twelve space but her. No other breathing, gabbing, farting, pouting person. Everybody, everything else shut out. Locked out, on the other side somewhere. No one could walk in. She was not counted. She did not have to speak. She did not have to share or to hoard, yet. She had to hear no one, except an occasional door shutting, a word or two from down the hall whose meaning she was not obliged to heed. She lay inside this idea for an indecipherable while, breaking the spell periodically to check the key up there on top of the chest of drawers. Still there.

Light had faded from the window, and the dark had come in to hang beneath the ceiling.

She breathed up the quiet, the silence—substance, balm, flower, fruit and medicine. She was taking it inside of her, where it expanded, filling scores and pits. The silence of the people who were not here. Silence of the bureau. The single bed. Silence of the empty places where the furniture was not. Silence rose up from the corners of this moss-green room like clear walls. Silence of the curtains riffled by a breeze. Silence of the lock.

The next morning, a Saturday, after a shower she took alone, Delpha sat for two morning hours in a chair outside the New Rosemont. She sat in the humid, roofless air, uncontained, unsupervised. The sun rose and took hold of the sky, and she drank coffee. Cars and buses rolled down the street without halting at gates, without showing manifests or I.D. cards, as a few people passed north, south, east, and west. Greeted or ignored each other, jaywalked, dawdled, hurried, trudged. They wore white and yellow and red dresses, prints and stripes, black skirts and white blouses, blue jeans. They wore lipstick and rouge on their cheeks, and their hair was teased, twisted up with ornamental clips, hung down. They wore suits and khakis and delivery and mailman uniforms. The few children wore shorts on their knobby legs. Birds tattled on the power lines. They hopped jerkily on the sidewalks, ruffled and flew off to trees. Other ones flew down.

At ten o'clock Delpha walked over to Tyrell Public Library, a downtown standout. Formerly a church, which explained the arches and the stained glass windows, the building was a sand castle dripped from medieval gray stone. She signed up for a card and checked out an art book. Turned its pages in her room. Delpha turned the pages all over again the next morning, in Sunday's sultry breeze. Streets wet from rain in the night. Only a few cars hissed past and not near as many buses. Birds fussed over an alley cat crouched on the sidewalk, gnashing his teeth at them. Bells rang.

Tiffany & Co. had made more stuff than jewelry.

IV

"MORNING, MISS WADE."

"Morning, Mr. Phelan."

Monday, Delpha Wade wore the same white blouse as on Friday but with another color skirt, green print, kind of swirly. Well, it was swirly when she walked but when she stood still, putting her purse into a desk drawer, it hung straight down.

This morning, awkwardness presented itself. Until the business got established, got rolling, him going in and out, her taking calls and writing notes on office paper—they would sit around, wouldn't they? Him in the boss office and her in the secretary office, him reading the paper and her—what would she do? The two girls he'd interviewed before her, they could have sat out here without a thought from him, why not her?

There was one thing to start with.

"Why don't you call me Tom?"

Miss Wade sat down in the secretary chair and scooted up to the desk. The rosy grace on her cheeks he'd spied Friday was banished now. The woman held herself like she wore strands of invisible barbwire, even though she knew she'd walk out the door at five o'clock, not in five years.

"First names maybe doesn't look so good for your clients," she said, indicating the door, as if clients were piled up on the stairs, clutching little paper numbers in their fists. She took a couple sheets of paper out of a side drawer, slipped a carbon in between, tapped all the edges even against the desk and carefully wound them into the typewriter.

What did she plan to type?

"Well, using last names sounds so *old*. And when there's no clients here—if we're just sitting here by ourselves saying Miss Wade this and Mr. Phelan that, I'm gonna feel like I'm back in homeroom." He shifted his shoulders in the suit jacket, just that little bit too tight. Maybe he should have bought a 42. But then it would have hung in the belly section.

She took in what he had to say, nodded and began to type. She stopped when she noticed Phelan looking at her. "Bill for Mrs. Toups," she said.

"She paid me a hundred to start and rate's only seventy-five a day. I owe her."

Miss Wade pushed a button and the typewriter zinged back to another line.

"What?"

"Well, how much that flashlight cost that you left at the house where you found the kid?"

"I don't know. Maybe three dollars."

"That's an expense, Mr. Phelan."

So much for the informality angle.

"How far you say you drove? Gas high as it is, that's an expense you always charge for."

She was right. Phelan estimated the distances: the high school, the port, Dennis Deeterman's menagerie house, the hospital, back here. No, he shouldn't charge for driving back here. He subtracted those miles and gave her the total.

She pulled out a desk drawer, took a pencil and a ten-cent sharpener, sharpened and did the multiplication. Typed it in. "Now what about your pants?"

"What about my pants?" Phelan looked down. The suit came with two pair, and he didn't even have to get them hemmed. Thirty-two waist/thirty-four length, they were OK as far as he could see.

Miss Wade suppressed a smile. "The ones the raccoon ripped. You get them fixed, that's an expense, too." She spoke a silent word to herself, squinted, spoke another and hit the keys five times.

Phelan was losing the loft he'd earned last Friday evening. He felt like they were writing a treaty.

"Now at the beginning, I'll put what you did, like a summary of how you found that boy. Then the rate and the expenses. What do you want me to write at the end—'Thank you for your business'? Or something like that. 'Your business is appreciated'?" Her eyes tightened as she considered.

He understood then that the gold-stickered certificate from Gatesville's business training course that she'd slid across his desk was no light thing to Delpha Wade. It was her get-out-of-jail promise card, her elevator out of the dungeon, and it came with standards, rules, and obligations.

"I don't know about that *Thank you*. You were selling pipe or hardware, OK, but not in this business." Phelan walked over to the secondhand plaid couch in front of the secretary's window. No Rosemont gents taking the air, just the downtown regular, skinny Miss Doris with her sacks and bags and her little gray goatee, resting her restless self.

He turned. "I guess what I mean, that release letter they gave you from Gatesville—they didn't end it with 'Y'all come back now'."

The gray-blue eyes lifted. The storm—the one far out on the Gulf that he'd seen in her eyes when she first presented herself, that had moved a ways out to sea by this morning—it was back.

For a minute. Then her lips pursed. "So...being as Mrs. Toups' business was her kid getting messed up, you don't wanna thank her for that."

Phelan spread his hands. "What I'm thinking."

"You're the boss." She figured again and typed in a total, removed the sheets and carbon. Handed him one of the sheets.

"Mrs. Toups owes *me* seven dollars?"

Proper as a witch-candidate soft-talking a Puritan elder, Miss Wade explained that Mrs. Toups owed the business seven dollars. He should start thinking that way because *Phelan Investigations* wasn't the exact same thing as Thomas Phelan. It had a mouth, and it had to eat too. And some more things, she said, flicking him a glance.

Phelan nodded for her to go on.

Number one, he really ought to have letterhead. It was classy. Number two, the Toups boy might be messed up, but Phelan didn't do it. Phelan had given Ricky the only chance he had to get on with his life again. And number three, she had called Mrs. Lloyd Elliott and suggested a ten a.m. appointment at the office on a day convenient to the client. Next week, Mrs. Elliott had said. But she preferred ten at night and Leon's, a bar down on College.

Phelan appreciated item number two. As for the postponement, the ten p.m. appointment, he shrugged. "Next week. Her bucks, her say. What?" he asked when he noticed the little shake of her head.

"Oh, nothing."

"No, what?"

"Never mind."

"Can't leave me hanging, Miss Wade. I'm the curious kind."

"Just that...used to know a girl had worked for an oilman's wife. She told me that how that woman spent her days was choosing. Furniture for a beach house, color of a new car, where to go on a vacation. Kinda funny, huh?" She reached for the phone. "Choosing all day."

Choosing. He hadn't ever thought about it, but now he did. Considered his years on the rigs, slipping in mud, twelve-hour day then dragged out of bed, get your ass out there, boy, zero to ninety in no seconds, get ahold of this pipe. Didn't like it, he was free to quit. Not so in the army. Neither did Miss Wade there have the option to quit Gatesville. Some people'd see it different: she'd had the option not to slice up a bleeding man.

Phelan didn't know if that was true or not.

At noon he needed to get out. Miss Wade was eating a sandwich at her desk, studying pictures in a book. Phelan glanced at a colorful one. "Looks like a glass jigsaw puzzle."

"Dragonfly wings. And"—she smoothed over a page like it might shatter—"here's a vase like a peacock feather." She looked up. "See why I like libraries."

"Cause you can go anywhere free?"

"Huh. They let you take stuff. And when books talk, which they don't unless you want 'em to, you don't know what they're going to say."

He went off to the printer where he'd got his business cards and did some choosing: typeface and layout for letterhead. Then he went over to visit the *Beaumont Enterprise*'s archive and asked the clerk barricaded behind a little television to pull any article or photo she could find on Mr. Lloyd Elliott. Miss Wade could have done it for him, but he didn't feel like sitting. The pretty, gray-haired woman had to wrench herself from the TV.

"You're not watching this?" she asked. "I can't take my eyes off it."

Her back was crooked. She hobbled off and pulled articles. Phelan stepped around to check out the television. Right. The Watergate hearings. Bunch of suits crammed together at a long, paper-littered table, everybody with their own silver microphone. Glarey lights. Phelan fiddled with the antenna. The black and white picture sharpened on Sam Ervin reading from a sheaf of papers and, down the way, some politico trapping a pencil between his upper lip and his nose.

The gray-haired woman handed over a file and hustled behind the TV.

The business-section articles were sparse-written. Near as Phelan could understand, Lloyd Elliott, attorney-at-law, had just handled an industrial espionage case. A small outfit called Daughtry Petrochemical had sued Enroco Oil over a formula brewed up in their meager Research and Development department. That formula had allegedly ducked out of Daughtry and snuck into the broad back door of Enroco Baytown. Little Daughtry's lawyers, Lloyd Elliott in the lead, hollered. Enroco thundered back. Dinwoodie, Blanchette, Elliott, and Klein conferred, schemed, burned the green-shaded law lamps late into the night, aiming to knock mammoth Enroco to the ground and blow on their slingshots. Enroco, brandishing sword, spear, and legions of lawyers, raised up on giant thighs.

This is where Phelan got lost. Enroco didn't, for some reason, bestow the death stroke. As far as he could tell, the colossus had lumbered down the slope to hunker with the runt. There was an abrupt end to the lawsuit. A settlement, must be. The amount didn't make the paper, but one third of whatever-it-was would have settled into the bank account of DBE&K. Case closed, champagne flutes overflowing, on to sticking it to somebody else.

Which was why Mrs. Lloyd Elliott wanted to talk to him. Lloyd was sticking it to somebody else.

May and still under ninety. He slung his jacket over his shoulder and walked down past the City Auditorium—where red, white, yellow, and pink rose buds conspired, getting ready to riot together—to the police headquarters. The senior sergeant on the desk buzzed Uncle E.E. and then sat grinning at Phelan.

Phelan said, "What?"

The alarm should have rung on the sergeant's retirement right around 1964. The shaggy gray eyebrows rose, innocence descended. Phelan had already experienced the look from Joe Ford down at the parole office. The previously unconsidered possibility of Joe mentioning his job referral to E.E. and E.E. gabbing it around the station hit Phelan, presenting itself as a crimp in his temple. *Forever hold your peace, buddy,* he thought, and did an excellent job of minding his own business.

The grinner busted. "Delpha Wade," he said. "Boy, you got two large ones, you."

Another member of the Napoleonic brotherhood. Mildly, Phelan said, "What God give you, you got to bear."

"Put 'er here, son. George Fontenot." The old cop stuck out his hand.

"Tom Phelan. Good to meet you, sir."

"I know who you are, cher. I worked that case. 1959. You know what was the fatal flaws?"

"Miss Wade and I hadn't exactly discussed it."

"What was wrong was this." He held up two fingers. "She didn't take out the old man, and they sent her to the Do-Right. That girl'd already done right."

"Sure handed her a jolt. Anything to do with her finishing off a dying man?"

"Hell, everbody has their bad days."

"Did you tell me E.E. was in, and I missed it?"

"Come to think on it, that one's right down the hall." He pointed the way.

"Genuine pleasure to meet you, Sergeant."

"Cain't argue there." Fontenot winked.

Uncle E.E., tugging at the knot of a splashy tie, beckoned him in. Phelan took the chair in front of the desk. For a few minutes, they exchanged sad information about Phelan's grandmother, E.E.'s mother-in-law, who was fading from cancer. Then E.E. cleared his throat. "So I got to hear 'bout my nephew through the grapevine. Whyn't you come tell me you wasn't going back to the rigs?"

"Because lemme tell you how that conversation woulda gone. 'Ride that G.I. to college, Tom. Get yourself a banker job, Tom.' If I'd asked you about joining the force, you'd of hemmed and hawed. 'Well, what about the Forest Service, E.E.?'—that woulda got a horse laugh." Phelan did his E.E. imitation: "'Hide out in the Big Thicket? Look for fires in all that swamp wawtah? That sound like *le bon temps* to you, Tom?'"

"Aw." His uncle spread out his elbows on the desk, pretended to consider. Then said, "Yeah, you got that about right."

"You been good to me, E.E. Don't think I ever told you that before."

His uncle blinked at him in surprise. Edouard Etienne Guidry, solid-built, silver-haired, creased olive skin, deep blue suit and a tie like a light show behind Jefferson Airplane. "I stole the angel in your family, Tom. I don't be good to you, who gonna be, tell me that." E.E. laced thick fingers. "Private investigation. You takin' on bitter stuff and stupid stuff and dirty-nasty stuff. I know what I'm talking about."

"You the only person I know personally knows what he's talking about. You telling me none a your day is bitter and stupid?"

"Bitter and stupid with a pension, cher."

Phelan held out his right palm.

For a moment, he thought he might just sit there, ear-rims burning, palm extended. But after a noisy sigh, E.E. slapped it.

Blessed, Phelan left his uncle's office and gave a see-you-later salute to George Fontenot. "Gonna catch Dennis Deeterman, Sergeant?"

"*Tracasse-toi pas. Chaque chien aura son jour et son jour vient.*"

"Swear, y'all speak more French than English down here. All I got out a that was *dog* and *day*."

"Said that dog, his day is coming. When your uncle gonna learn you a language with some culture?"

V

SHE GOT OFF the bus too soon, down at the wrong end of
Ashley Avenue. Walked past an array of two-story mansions.
Stared through the wrought iron fences at red brick and
white brick, white pillars and black shutters, gracious wide
doors, a crystal chandelier lit behind a picture window. Yards
like the green felt of pool tables, shiny cars parked side-by-
side in the driveways.

Addresses on the black mailboxes told her how many
blocks she had to go. After four or five, the mansions began to
drop off in quality and size, the yards in neatness. She came
finally to a high hedge, past which she could see no more
houses at all, just land and a tangle of trees, and—a block
farther on—cars driving by. Miss Blanchard's aunt might
live on an avenue with many mansions, but she owned the
puttered-out end of the street.

A driveway disappeared like a footpath into the wild
hedge. Delpha could see no house at all. But it was a driveway
because she walked on it through the hedge, and an unwashed
Cadillac was parked in it.

Lions in the wilderness.

That's what the place looked like. The grounds a thicket
of bushes, sticks and rotting leaves, canopied trees, straggling
flowers. She climbed concrete steps that lofted up to a pair
of guard lions, the one on the right missing the claw part of

his foot. Delpha used her key. The door swung open. Marble foyer, no chandelier though there was plenty height for one, grand staircase laid with a carpet runner held in place by tarnished brass rods.

Delpha walked down a passageway, snapped on the light. *Look at this.* Her Rosemont room would fit three times into this kitchen with the black and white checkerboard floor. Ten foot ceilings. White enamel wood-burner converted to gas, glass-front white cabinets holding shelves of silver-ringed china.

She went closer to the cabinets. Plastic water glasses, paper plates, twenty cans of Campbell's soup. Some shelves empty. Drawer of dimestore forks and spoons.

She took down a Cream of Mushroom out of a row of them, found a saucepan, mixed the jellied soup with some water, and lit the gas with a wooden match.

Mr. Phelan's job. This job. She had work.

That meant a door to close and a lock on that door, a shower with hot water twelve steps down the hall. Meant Miss Blanchard's fine biscuits and gravy and Oscar's pie, it meant all right. That burst on her, and Delpha held in her mind one of the three picture shows she'd ever seen on the outside, *Cinderella*. She'd been eleven years old, bug-eyed as singing birds and rats with clothes on sewed that girl a pink and white dress and tied bows all over it. That girl had danced. Delpha did a thing she used to do in the dark of her cell: she petted her own head, petted it and crooned some nice words that never really came out of her mouth.

"Who are *you*?"

Delpha's head snapped up. She backed to the sink, hands down and visible. The cocker spaniel woman, a pair of white patent leather boots dangling from one hand, moved a highball glass from her forehead, so she could squint through damp blond bangs.

"Calinda Blanchard hired me to stay with your mother evenings, give her some supper and all."

"My *mother* ran off with a morphine addict when I was four years old. Jessie is my *grandmother*. Jesus, how old do you think I am?"

The blue-jean miniskirt said twenty, but a sag at the knees admitted to forty. This was Ida Rae the cousin, second cousin, whichever. Delpha nodded to her. "Grandmother, sorry. 'Bout my age, I guess."

"And how old are you?"

"Thirty-two."

The woman skated over on stocking feet, boots flapping, and attempted to hug Delpha, tipped some gin onto her blouse. "Oops! Thank you, sweetie pie. You and me'll be friends. Will you be my friend, please?" The cousin's head tilted to the side as she smiled, in a pose that must have been adorable thirty-five years ago. The gin protruded like a blade from her face.

Delpha leaned back.

"Warning you, you're gonna get tired of her fast." Ida pinched her nostrils together and rolled her eyes, gave a little trill. "But you—" She touched her head, slopping her drink from the glass. "Who rubs their own head? That was so *cuuute*. I'm Ida Rae. Tell me your name. Oh, wait, you know...doesn't really matter. Watch out for Moselle, the day nurse. No matter how nice to her I am, she never likes me."

Blandly, drunkenly pleasant, Ida's face crumpled for a second, as though crushed by a huge hand, and then expanded back into blandness. She didn't seem aware of the change.

Delpha continued to stand stiffly as the woman veered close and breathed into her face. "And don't—do *not*, you hear?—be poking around my house. Bye, sweetie." Ida Rae skated from the kitchen and collapsed into a bowlegged chair in the hall. After tugging the boots on, she clopped toward the marble foyer.

The heavy front door shut. Delpha carried a tray up the broad stairs. She looked in the first bedroom, spied a spurt of white hair above a gullied forehead, cheeks grooved vertically, fretful little eyes and plucking hands. The sewer smell greeted her as soon as she entered. Delpha toted the soup back downstairs and returned with a rag soaked in warm water. She opened the large oak cabinet that served as a night table, found a set of sheets from one side, and a fresh diaper from the other, put these on the marble top of the cabinet, and closed up its two doors. She searched out a nightgown in a bureau drawer.

"Roll on your side, Mrs. Speir." Delpha helped her. "Hold up your arms now. Hold 'em up."

She peeled off the soiled nightgown, gathering it in her fingers so she didn't spread the shit.

"Stay rolled now, Mrs. Speir."

Slid the diaper from between her legs. Look like a girl front side, hairless, white, sealed as an angel. The other side, no butt at all. Yoke of bone, puddle of skin from it.

Jesus God, let me not live one hundred years.

Took forty minutes moving slow to fix her up again, positioning, swabbing, drying, maneuvering on the diaper and the sheet under her. The nightgown. Then clean in a clean bed.

Delpha bundled the dirty clothes and stuffed them in the washer downstairs, hit the button, and scoured her hands and on up her arms. She sniffed herself. Nope. Washed and sniffed again, still smelled shit. Washed each fingernail separate, knuckles, palms, inhaled up to the elbow, ah there was a smear on her rolled sleeve. Took off the blouse and scrubbed out the spot, buttoned it up, folded the sleeve higher, washed her hands. Done. She reheated the soup, carried it up on the tray, and set it on the broad old night table.

The outer corners of Jessie Spier's eyes, calm now, were wreathed in powdery, finely-crisscrossed skin. Thin lips, harshly downturned on one side, parted, and she let out garbled phrases.

"My name's Delpha. Brought you mushroom flavor but if you like some other kind, you just say."

The forehead wrinkles deepened. Delpha repeated herself, but her patient scowled at her until she finally hollered, "Is mushroom soup the kind you like?"

It was or it wasn't. Mrs. Speir delivered her opinion in such shrewd, definite syllables that Delpha believed she could understand if only she strained sufficiently. Couldn't. Offered spoonfuls of soup, which were accepted until a hand began to spider toward the nightstand. She set down the bowl, picked up a pair of cat-eye glasses lying there, stroked back the white topknot, and fit them on the old woman's head.

Said, "Hello there."

Ten thirty on a hot May night. Block east of the New Rosemont, Delpha got off the bus to the distorted chords of pedal steel. She sat down on the bench, slid around to face Crockett Street's yellow party-glow. Surge of guitar, thump of drum, again the twang of pedal steel. Not a tune she recognized, but then she didn't know many of them now. The Beatles, The Beach Boys, The Supremes, she'd missed all that. The last honkytonk song she'd heard blaring across a dance floor might have been Elvis' "Hard-Headed Woman" or Johnny Cash's "I Walk the Line."

A distant crowd clapped and whistled. Delpha stood up from the bus bench and walked on to the New Rosemont's steps, picked up an empty of Night Train and, swinging it by the neck, carried it in to throw away.

VI

HANK AARON WALLOPED his 685th homerun—just thirty more to beat The Babe's record—and next week was here.

Phelan strolled out onto Leon's pine floor at quarter till ten, taking inventory. Two young pool players were having their fencing match refereed by a red-faced man in a bar apron. Three guys sat at the bar, across from the neon Jax sign, heads angled to view baseball on the corner-mounted TV. A twined couple whispering in a booth. Pack of women past forty who seemed to be laughing with genuine pleasure. Few tables of Monday night spouse-avoiders with half an eye on the Astros game and a jukebox urging them to "go home to the armadillo."

"Tommy Phelan!" A pointy-chin waitress might have flung herself on him if she hadn't been toting a tray of longnecks and a dish of peanuts.

Behind the Max Factor and the red lipstick overlaid with Vaseline for shine, Phelan picked out the freckled face of his junior prom date. The one he didn't know he was supposed to get a corsage for until his grandmother Lila had sent him off to buy a white carnation dripping with ribbons.

"Patty Peavey. How you been?"

"It's Johnson now. I got two kids, a divorce, and this new job. Just a minute."

Patty dealt the round of beers to a table of raucous guys,

slipped out from under one of them's grabbing arm and returned to Phelan.

"Tommy," she said seriously as she took in his suit, "who died?"

Phelan fingered a lapel. "Just business."

"Heard the army made you a medic in Vietnam. Then you went off to the rigs and hadn't heard nothing since."

"Came back. There a lady in here by herself?"

Patty glanced around. "No, all the crazy people are where you can see them."

"If one comes in, I'll be in that back booth. Send her over. I'll take a Salty Dog, and...you liking this job, Patty?"

"Tell me what likin' has to do with workin', baby."

Phelan smiled, passed the line of unoccupied bar stools, saluted the three occupied ones, and paused to take in the score: Astros tied in the bottom of the ninth. He slid into the back booth. Smell of frying hamburger, maybe a little catfish wafted from behind the swinging doors to the kitchen.

He unfolded the sheet of paper Miss Wade had given him: available info on Mrs. Lloyd Elliott.

"You want me to research the client?" Miss Wade had asked.

"Cover all the bases," Phelan'd said. Why not? Might be something useful there. Besides, Mr. Phelan and Miss Wade had *beaucoup* time on their hands.

"Isn't much there," she'd told him as she set the handwritten sheet down on the desk beside the Selectric. "Pictures, but you'll have to go see those." She typed up her findings, Phelan noting that the sound of the typewriter going made him feel like his business was going.

He swallowed some Salty Dog and read it all again. Mrs. Lloyd Elliott had been Neva McCracken, daughter of R.J. and

Tillie of Dallas, Texas, president of McCracken Investment Management and homemaker, respectively. Neva had married young attorney Lloyd Elliott in 1952 after graduation from Texas State Women's College in Denton. Attended by eight bridesmaids in her chosen colors, rose and pink. Phelan didn't get that part. Rose, pink, what's the difference. Miss Wade had sketched a picture of the full-skirted bridal gown—a yellow, stripey one, since she was using pencil on a legal pad.

The next paragraph detailed a society dinner and a gala attended by Mr. and Mrs. Lloyd Elliott. Phelan skimmed it and went on to the last paragraph, which summarized mentions of his client during the late '50s and early 1960. Mrs. Lloyd Elliott had given generously to the Neches River Festival and opened her lovely home for a fund-raiser for Senator Richard M. Nixon.

Putting the paper away, he wondered how she felt about her boy Nixon now that he'd acquired his own special prosecutor. Phelan had had one of those in third grade, until he cracked the fifth-grader's head with a Davy Crockett lunch box. Maybe Nixon'd try that.

Last ten years, no more pictures of Neva McCracken Elliott. No dinners. No galas. Galas—everything Tom Phelan knew about that subject, he could record on a grain of Uncle Ben's rice. Boards, she sat on boards for this bank and that foundation and Lamar College's Building Fund.

The heads at the bar turned as a dark woman in three-inch black heels entered Leon's. Two turned back to the game. Patty balanced a tray of highballs while she bent her head to listen to the tourist. Then she brought up her right hand and shot Phelan with her index finger.

Mrs. Lloyd Elliott wore a suit no gala had ever seen. Charcoal gray and boxy, covered buttons, skirt past her knees. Didn't go with the high heels and the fashionable tips of glossy brunette hair lofted and feathered around her face. Hair and shoes were here in 1973, but the suit was strictly Mamie Eisenhower. Given the paint-black sunglasses and Leon's romantic lighting, Phelan wasn't surprised when her toe snagged the leg of a barstool. He was on his feet at once, caught her before she stumbled.

The black lenses fixed on him. "Thank you."

Patty, bearing a clean ashtray complete with matchbook, came to take her order. Mrs. Elliott stationed her index and thumb four inches apart and said, "The least disgusting scotch."

Patty's gaze floated past Phelan's without landing on him.

Once the waitress was out of range, Phelan's client cut short his attempt at a friendly introduction by removing the sunglasses. Her eyes were reddened and glassy with tears, and the pupils were unusual, an unattractive, boggy brown, focused on him like an X-ray machine.

"How old are you, Mr. Phelan?"

Phelan offered his hand. "Glad to meet you, Mrs. Elliott. I'm twenty-nine. I hope you're well this evening."

"That ad announcing your business and now, seeing you—you're new to the profession." She switched her car keys to her left hand, wrung his hand and dropped it.

"Why don't we sit down? Yes, I am establishing my business. Is that a problem?"

The stare had not left him. "Not necessarily. But you have no experience at all?"

"Nothing in this world can take the place of persistence, Mrs. Elliott."

It was curious to watch. The X-ray machine shut off slowly, from the inside. The ugly brown eyes did not become friendly, but they lost their penetration.

"Of all things. Quoting Calvin Coolidge. Is that normal for a detective?"

Phelan smiled. "Just something my grandmother says. A less educated lady than yourself might not have recognized old Cal, and that might have made me look good."

She laid her car keys on the table and sat down. Finally.

"I happen to like Calvin Coolidge and especially that speech of his. You couldn't have known that, Mr. Phelan, so that makes you lucky. And luck can be better than experience."

Patty returned with Mrs. Elliott's scotch and a new Salty Dog for Phelan. Mrs. Elliott stared at the drink.

"I can get you something else," he offered.

She put the glass to her lips, tipped her head back, and half the scotch was gone, languidly. She was here at Leon's and sort of not here, as close as he could figure it. The woman had sounded so contained on the phone that this change in composure now interested him. He put it down to her being already blasted. That could be 90% of it. But there was something else, he felt it.

She slipped the glasses back on and became very here. "All right, what I want is quite simple. Photographs of my husband with his girlfriend. His car is a black Cadillac Seville, license J5489. I know they went to the Holiday Inn once. I'm not certain they go there every time. You'll have to find them. Take some pictures of them and give me a call on a Tuesday or a Friday at eight in the morning before I leave for work. Your secretary has the number. I'll meet you somewhere to pick them up and settle your fee. This is a retainer."

During this rapid speech, the Texas in her voice dried up. She pushed an envelope toward him. "Is there anything else I need to tell you?" She edged a knuckle beneath a black lens. It came away wet.

He took out his small notebook, jotted the license number

and make of car. "This is fine. I'm sorry, Mrs. Elliott. Anyone in your place would be upset. I take it that the photos will be used in a divorce proceeding."

Her top lip curled. "I think that's likely." She picked the matchbook from the ashtray and idly struck a match. Her head tilted as she studied the fizz of ignition. "Don't you think that's likely?"

Phelan lifted a hand. "Excuse me. Whatever you want the pictures for is your business."

"A divorce is painful. You'd agree that a divorce could be extremely painful." The blackened match dropped and a second one flared. "It would hurt."

"I'd be unhappy."

"Unhappy." Her voice was distantly puzzled. "You'd be unhappy."

"Sure. Anybody would."

"The loss of your wife, your mate, that would be ungood, it would be unpleasant. Un-nice."

"Mrs. Elliott—"

"It wouldn't be..." She lit another match. Behind the yellow flame, the woman's lips parted and her brow squeezed. The muddy eyes must be squeezing too beneath the black lenses. There was some panting noise caught between her throat and her teeth that did not release, that held itself at bay like a bleeding animal in the dark of a cave.

Phelan sat up straight and got his feet under him.

The noise stayed back. Her voice switched on. "That loss wouldn't be...wouldn't be, oh, say...eviscerating for you? You wouldn't feel lacerated into parts that can't recall how they were ever joined?"

The black matchstick fell into the ashtray. It had burned her skin. He smelled it.

"I don't know," he said. Hairs on his arms shifted.

"My blessing on you, Mr. Phelan, twenty-nine years old—may you never know." She vanished the other half of the scotch.

"Can I get you another drink?" Phelan asked.

Mrs. Elliott flicked away water on her cheekbone. "No, thank you. And don't get up. Call me when you've got the pictures, please. And only then. My time is dear." She slid from the booth and walked off, trailing a hand against the backs of the empty bar stools as she passed them.

Phelan sipped his grapefruit. This woman considered divorce eviscerating, yet she was engineering one. Must be the betrayal she was talking about. Easier now to understand why her social life had dwindled in the past ten years. Imagine tipping a glass of pink champagne with Neva Elliott. Like trading banter with a bandsaw. Phelan couldn't figure if his estimate of Lloyd went up or down.

All in all, he thought, *up*.

He laid down a couple bucks for the drinks. He folded a ten, just about enough for a sack of groceries, by the far side of his glass. Maybe he'd piss off the freckled girl who'd worn that white carnation corsage. Maybe not.

The three guys at the bar were leaving. Astros must have wrapped it up. The lunkhead pool players and the middle-aged ladies had already taken off. The bartender reached up and dialed the channel to an *I Love Lucy* rerun. Except for the table of beer-drinking grabbers, Leon's was deserted.

Patty cruised by. "That suit's doing strange things to you, Tommy. Your type has changed considerably."

"Professional meeting, darlin'."

"Well, as I recall, you used to beat 'em off, not drive 'em off. You make that poor woman cry?"

"Not on my account. You gonna keep this job?"

She whispered in his ear. "Just till I find a suitcase of money."

Phelan kissed Patty's Revlon-coated cheek. She grinned, licked her thumb, touched it to one hip, and hissed, "Sssssst. Still got it."

VII

A THURSDAY EVENING and Depha got on the bus at two
minutes after six with a pair of rubber dishwash gloves in
her purse. Shared a flick of eye contact with the woman
in the first seat, pocketbook and sacks, brown knee-highs
wilted at her ankles. She was your average six o'clock rider:
that is, homebound, black, and tired. But there could be the
rare downtown-bound rider, too, and the second had to be
one of those. Unusual to see a white boy on the bus; his car
must be broken down. Longish dark hair around a surly
face, beads showing in the neck of an oxford shirt, one knee
hammering.

Did a boy wearing a necklace mean he was a hippie? The
Summer of Love had not ranged so far as Gatesville.

The kid jumped up at the next stop and sailed off the bus,
swinging out from the handrail by the door. Another stop and
a muscular boy whose Afro had a comb planted in it spanked
the pert butt of a girl in an orange mini-skirt. She yelped.
They chased each other halfway down the street. Delpha
marked each bouncy step they took—the way hands kept
grazing bodies, how the girl whirled and buried her face in
the boy's chest, walking backwards—until they disappeared
around a corner.

She heated up a can of Vegetable Beef, took down the
clean tray from the shelf she'd left it on. Servant serving.

Carrying and setting down before. Beers. Tubs of powdered mashed potatoes, tubs of over-floured gravy, canned carrots, tubs of hot washing. Basins of piss, bloody sheets, towels, pillow cases for the infirmary. Finally, last three years, cart of books, library desk, best of all.

Delpha had promised herself patience. Get used to all the clear air around her, the streets stretching out, doors that open open open. Couldn't come all at once. Come slow. She'd have to get used to wearing sky over her head. Would get used to it, like everybody else so used to being free that it didn't even enter into their calculations. But promising and doing were two different things.

She was grateful for Tom Phelan. Polite to her, and it felt genuine. Noticed he was a nice-enough looking man, yes, she did, the minute he met her at the door. The dark hair that was kind of long on his collar had some deep auburn when the light hit it. Seemed like he was used to moving or not as he chose. But these observations she folded away. Without Tom Phelan chancing on her, she'd be eaten up with the problem of keeping herself and dwelling in a world of old people. New Rosemont rented to retirees. Ida Rae topped 40, Miss Doris in her far sixties, Calinda, 70-something. Mrs. Speir, queen of the boardwalk.

Delpha, carrying and setting down before. Right now maybe but not forever. And a *free* handmaiden, remember— she was getting paid for her work.

Don't overlook that, Delpha.

Don't think you got nowhere. You got where.

A radio played at the end of the hall, farthest room from Mrs. Speir's. Oldie, *A little bit of soap will never wash away my tears.* Who sang that? Couldn't remember, but she'd heard it. Might or might not mean Ida Rae was at home.

She fed Mrs. Spier every last spoonful of the Vegetable Beef. It was a record player that was playing and a 45 because after the song ended there was a silence then it started again. Ida Rae could have turned off the damn thing before she went out. No more thought than a red-headed woodpecker.

Mrs. Speir's eyes closed. Her knees drew up and her chin curled into her neck.

As Delpha strode into the room where the record player was repeating, her toe kicked an empty bottle, spinning it aside. Large room, chandelier, main feature dead ahead: a brass bedstead fit into an alcove, sheets twisted off onto the floor, pink lightbulbs in the fringed lamps casting a rosy glow. The air smelled like gin, sweat, and...yeah, cum. Delpha did recognize that sea smell. Ida Rae lay splayed naked, letting it air out beside some hairy-butt snorer wearing only striped crew socks dirty on their soles.

Ida had slim white legs but was carrying some thick in her middle from the gin. She raised sleepy lids. "Night nurse, my friend, sweetie, what're you doing in my room?"

"Your grandmother wants me to shut off the—"

Ida Rae pushed herself up. She plucked at the sheet, but it didn't move. "Oh. I'm lying on it. What'd you say you were in my room for?" The man turned over on his side and cupped his balls.

"Just came to turn off your record player. Watch." Delpha crossed the room to a table by the window and yanked the record player's cord out of the wall. "See?"

"Oh. OK." Ida Rae knocked the fellow beside her between the shoulder blades, causing him to grunt. "Get dressed. Let's go out." She reached toward Delpha. "Hand me my robe there, would you? You know, if you have some better clothes than that, we could go out and have lunch sometime."

Delpha handed over the robe, went back to Mrs. Speir. *Nekkid people night.*

Ida and her companion finally exited. The front door shut, a Cadillac engine turned over. Telling herself maybe she could spy the Tiffany for Miss Blanchard, Delpha pulled on rubber dishwash gloves and searched.

She rolled up the carpet and the pad beneath. No trap doors there. Delpha knelt to see under the bed with the flashlight. She ran her hands between mattress and box springs. She lifted the gilt-framed paintings, craned up the chimney of the tile-front fireplace, pushed on the oak mantelpiece. Genuine horsehair settee beneath the long window, hard as a pirate's plank. She took off her black flats and walked it, weighing down each section. No bulges or corners or lumps.

Delpha plunged her hands into bureau drawers containing Mrs. Speir's old-lady underwear and nightgowns and fresh sheet sets. These were to be moved, for convenience sake, to the bottom shelves of the bedside night-cabinet. She did this now, transferring one set of flower-sprigged sheets into the lower shelf of the night table so they would be to hand when next she needed them. Sliding out its single drawer, narrow and deep, she saw clippers, Q-tips, Vick's Vapor Rub laid out before an army of plastic pill bottles.

She sat on the chipped-gilt bench at the vanity table to study the sepia photograph of a bride and groom. Ramrod back, cascade of veil, high lace collar, she had a swan's neck on her then, didn't she—young Jessie angled away from the new husband, offering him a chiseled cheek. Young Mr. Speir—high shine to his shoes, boutonniere—had a forward nose and receding chin that might have made him look rat-like if it hadn't been for his thick legs, the shoulders far wider than the upright chair he sat in.

The old photo was in a black dime store frame. Delpha bet it had replaced a silver one.

Her own face in the three-way mirror. Tired, lines at her eyes, both wary and calm. Way different than a horror-struck girl's mug shot in 1959.

She unscrewed a jar on the mirrored vanity table, cold cream dried to a solid white paste. Pulled open the top side drawer to sniff at the faint sweet of face powder. Peeled off a clumsy rubber glove and slid her flat palm along the ceiling of the drawer, make sure nothing was taped up there. There was a powdery coating over the items in the drawer: lipstick tubes, a deep red called "Honor Bright," scattering of bobby pins, tweezer and dull brow pencils. Heavy gold compacts with their tiny latches—one containing pressed powder, in the other a crescent of rouge. She bent sideways, peering in. Pushed to the very back, a round box. She grasped it, knuckles grazing the drawer-back, and brought the box out.

It was cardboard but look, painted on its lid—oh, she liked it. Still a bright, cheerful orange, the women drawn on it so clear, a ruffled lady at a vanity and her sharp-nosed hairdresser. Delpha had met those two in prison more than once, the privileged bitch and the sly suck-up you keep your front toward.

Three Blossoms Face Powder, shade *Naturelle*. "Naturelle," she said aloud, "naturelle." Pretty word. Reluctantly, she set the box back, feeling the powder-dust rub between her fingers. Below, in the lower drawer, a comb, a brush, and four jewelry cases, one for a ring, three rectangular. Green leather.

She held her breath. Pried them open, one by one, to satin and velvet. The only gold inside was lettering: *Tiffany and Co. 550 Broadway New York.*

Had Ida sold the jewels or kept them? Sold, according to Miss Blanchard.

The mantel clock read 10:03.

Got her handkerchief out of her purse and wiped the lipstick tubes, the compacts, the jewelry boxes, drawer-knobs thoroughly. Not great but better than her prints on them—she'd be blamed for anything that went wrong here.

Then her fingers darted back in for the pretty *Three Blossoms* box that nobody had used in decades. Her knuckles knocked *tock* against the drawer-back, which fell over them. She froze, the thin piece of wood lying over her fingers.

Delpha reached them both out, the powder box and piece of wood. She set the box in her purse. As for the drawer-back, it was a shorter square of wood that must have been wedged or lightly glued in there. She got down on her knees and craning, saw the true back of the drawer.

Things in front of it.

She reached in and took out a small pad with marks on it. *Grandma*, line down the middle, *Ida*. A scorepad, pencil hatchmarks on it. She peered in again. Pair of dice and a light-colored pouch. A white scrap.

Could put jewels in a pouch.

Her hand stayed where it was, and her stomach hitched. Find a necklace in a nice leather case, she'd tell Miss Blanchard. That was big, and her connection with it would be big too, if anyone went looking. Find a handful of loose gemstones, well, a problem. A situation. Was that the right word—a dilemma, maybe.

There could be one ruby less inside a pouch somebody'd hid away.

She would not go back to prison. Would not go. That prohibition sharp as a whack to the jaw, real as a concrete floor under a pair of bare knees. Pawnbroker give her a penny on the dollar for any diamond she'd set on his counter, and he would learn her face.

Delpha's hand moved. She rolled the pouch until she could grasp it and lifted it out over the dice, all the time her fingertips were squeezing the loose-weave burlap for stones. Felt none. When she got a close look, her breath freed itself in a rush. She sat back on her heels. A damn tobacco pouch. Somebody hiding their smokes in a secret place. That's all it was.

She loosened its yellow drawstring, stirred her finger around inside, sniffed again. Its faint odor spoke of age, this was old leaves, and not tobacco exactly—she guessed dried hemp. Wild hemp grew in the Big Thicket, but this had to be the kind made reefers. Explained the hiding. She'd known a woman in Gatesville serving seven years for it, and five kids at home.

Little orange paper glued to the pouch held the rolling papers. RizLa+. Lacroix Fils. 24 papers. Some left. The loose scrap back there—she plucked it out—yep, it was a rolling paper too.

With handwriting on it.

Don't smoke all this without me sunshine.

Sweet. Mrs. Jessie smoking reefer. With her husband, Mr. Sunshine Speir the stockbroker. The thought tickled Delpha.

Moselle, the day nurse, bored out of her mind?

Smart money would be on Ida. The scorepad, the dice, the pouch, Ida must have known about this compartment, maybe fixed it up herself. Forgot about it. Shorted out the brain cells that remembered this hidey-hole.

But wait, what Ida said about her mother. Went away with a morphine-fiend. If the couple liked morphine, might have liked reefer too. And *sunshine*—sweet on each other, sweet on hemp, not enough sweetness for their baby daughter.

All happened back in the shadows of the long ago. Shame that shadows were so damn long.

Delpha fitted the *sunshine* paper in with the others in the orange placket and replaced the items in the drawer. Wiped off the wood piece, tapped it in, closed up the drawer. She straightened and leaned over the vanity table. Who'd care if she touched the prickly-glass atomizer. Be more *naturelle* if she had—she squeezed its bulb. She expected it to be dry, but a burst of flower petals picked sixty years ago bloomed out, rich, oily, diffusing over the stale room. Delpha sprayed her wrists, then rubbed them together, sprayed a blast toward Mrs. Speir, bless her old heart, curled like a shrimp drying on a plate.

She dropped the handkerchief in her purse, then snatched up the rubber gloves, which she stowed away under the kitchen sink, and left.

VIII

PHELAN MADE THE rounds of the motels, looking for
the black Seville. Nothing the first few nights, but he felt
useful, employed, and he kept circling, following the list Miss
Wade had typed up, starting with the ones closest to Elliott's
office. Beaumont, smack on I-10 between Houston and New
Orleans, had a shitload of motels. Tonight he'd found three
black Sevilles but not with the right plate. On the whole,
he preferred cruising the tourist courts where people had
their doors propped open, some standing outside swapping
cigarettes, beer and conversation, ice machines doing a steady
business. The pricier the place, the quieter, except for kids
hooting in the swimming pools.

He got a burger at the Pig Stand, grease soaking through
the crinkly white paper. Lined his lap with napkins and ate.
Made a pit stop at a 7-11, came out keys in one hand, large
coffee in the other, package of dessert Twinkies clamped in
his teeth.

Two empty spaces over, a pudgy teenager jawing into the
passenger window of a Dodge Coronet bellowed, "You know
what. Just forget it, Diane." He straightened, then bent into
the window again and shoved the girl's head. She pitched
toward the steering wheel.

Phelan detoured over and booted the guy in the ass, at the
price of jogging hot coffee over his left hand. Dropped the

Twinkies into his key hand and said, "Cut that shit out. Mean little turd. You're embarrassing yourself."

The teenager twisted around to him, the surprise on his face giving way to the death stare without any matching death moves.

Phelan found Lloyd's car at 8:09. The red brake lights of a black Seville. J5489, *jackpot*. The driver was alone, arm stretched over the seat back. Just sitting there, windows rolled up, AC deployed. The Seville was parked in front of room number 111. Phelan circled around, parked by the office with the Caddie in view.

At 8:30, Lloyd put it in gear. So...they must have a plan in place. Didn't get here by 8:30, she wasn't coming. Lloyd didn't seem devastated. His lips were moving. Practicing a speech?

Phelan had his info—Holiday Inn for sure, approximate time. Jazzed, he watched as Lloyd drove past him. Guy was singing.

Phelan turned the opposite direction, took a right, was passing St. Elizabeth Hospital's bright ER entrance when he heard the whoop of a siren. Firing closer. He nudged over to the shoulder behind a pickup and monitored his rearview.

A shrieking vehicle charged into sight, red lights flashing. Pontiac station wagon painted orange and white busted a sharp left into the horseshoe drive too fast to hold the curve leading to the ER doors. The ambulance took out a corner of a concrete bench, tight-spun in the opposite direction as the driver overcorrected, and plowed—bull's-eye—into a pillar of the port cochére. There was a bang like a transformer had blown, a rush of steam, and the bent pillar slumped.

Phelan slammed out of his car and ran the twenty yards. Pulled up when, like an afterthought, the port cochére gently shifted downward.

He was wary of the structure collapsing but he circled

round and peered through the driver's open window. The man's bald head had spidered the windshield, which had returned the favor probably a quarter-second before the steering wheel crushed in, hooked him under the chin and rammed upward. Slack as a sack, no gasp, no shudder, no blink.

Phelan loped to the ambulance's back door window. On the gurney lay an elderly man wearing a useless black oxygen mask—its hose was torn loose. The attendant, on knees and elbows, had snagged a shelf on the way down and was bleeding from temple to jaw. Shiny stripe of blood dividing off into separate rivulets.

Phelan opened up the back door. "Y'all all right?"

"Scraped the side of my head off. Fucking Marshall. You hear me, you wino son of a bitch cocksucking bastard."

"Your driver's wasted," Phelan said, climbing in and bending over the old guy on the stretcher.

"No shit, Sherlock," the attendant snarled. He crawled over to the window to the front seat. "You just got us both fired, Marshall. I told you—"

Phelan said, "No, I mean he's wasted."

The attendant jerked around.

"Look, get the head, I'll get the foot." Phelan leapt lightly out of the ambulance. His fists closed on the gurney rail like they used to on stretcher handles dozens of times before, and he was sliding it out, unsurprised at the weight of the emaciated man, knowing bodies were heavier than they looked, specially the ones he was used to, the bony ones that belonged to boy soldiers. The only different element here was this gurney's undercarriage, wheels and crossed metal legs like at the bottom of an ironing board—handy, these'd pop down and turn hefting into rolling. Could maybe manage this by himself, which was a good thing because the idiot attendant, apparently not believing Phelan's call, was jabbing his index finger into the driver's pulseless neck.

A tiny nurse, long hair escaping from a bun on her neck, appeared at the back of the ambulance. She turned a scrunched-up face to Phelan. "Who are you?"

Phelan's chin jutted toward his car. "I was driving by."

Her face scrunched further, but four hands got the gurney land bound. Then, as Phelan pushed, she latched onto the gurney and guided its foot-end over the threshold.

Inside the ER, genuine medical personnel relieved Phelan of his temporary job. He lingered there, watching the elevator after its doors closed till he got a gleam that he was waiting for it, like a Huey, to lift off into the sky.

Numbnuts.

He eased onto the freeway and drove. By the glittering refineries with their smoke and fiery flares, by the low ricefields, down reedy back roads leading to the bayous. Turned and headed for the neighborhood off Concord, beginning a ritual he would keep.

Drove by Deeterman's house near the woods, the dingy white ranch that he was convinced Dennis Deeterman could show up at sometime. He wanted to check. Establish a baseline. See if there was any sign of habitation.

Orange mailbox under the streetlight. Police tape across the door. Same grass and weeds grown up there and on the path back into the woods. Longer now. The tire tracks could still be picked out.

House was dark.

Phelan drove by the Toups'. Light on in the living room.

He got home to a ringing phone, chose to get a beer from the icebox rather than answer it, and snapped on the television. Fred Astaire and Rita Hayworth, all elastic and firecrackers, skipping and sliding loose-jointed, twirling and tapping in two-tone shoes. He answered the phone a half hour later. His older brother Fuller, pissy because he'd been calling all night, barked at Phelan that their grandmother Lila had passed.

IX

A MUSICAL BLOCK remained of Delpha's walk to the New Rosemont, the katydid and cricket orchestras assembled and fiddling in the humid summer night, high...low...high, trail off and rest, surge again. Gold moon had cooled to silver. Sidewalk still radiating heat. A hunched figure lurched out of a doorway, hand covering mouth and nose like a robber too cheap to buy a mask.

The fountain pen was out of her pocket and in her fist, nib forward.

He flinched back. "Hey, don't. I'm just looking for a tissue or something. Do you have any I could borrow?" The muffled voice was nasal and earnest.

Feeling with her left hand, Delpha located her handkerchief above the *Three Blossoms* box and held it at arm's length. "Keep it."

He reached for it, exposing a swollen, bloody nose.

Looked a little like the boy on the bus earlier but no, not wearing any hippie necklace.

Delpha was about to pass him when he said, "Wow. Even like this"—he lifted the handkerchief, grimaced into it, returned it to his nose, winced—"I can...you smell like a Persian garden."

She stared at him.

"Can I..." He tipped his head at her.

"Can you what?"

"Smell your perfume. That's all." He held up the palm without the bloody handkerchief.

She waved the perfumed wrist in his direction.

The kid, the young man, stepped forward into the area her wrist had occupied. Beer, that's what she could smell. He *was* tall, more than six foot, but he stooped. Bad posture, or he'd have been even taller. He blew his nose into the handkerchief and grunted in pain. "No, really, I can do this." Bending his head, the dark hair tumbling forward, he moved the cloth away from his nostrils. He shut his eyes. As he took long, slow breaths, one of his eyes shut tighter in concentration.

Slowly, deliberately, as if naming people picked out of a distance, he said, "Lavender...citrus...and that's...it's...vanilla. That powdery, musky, maybe it's amber, that's what it smells like. What's the perfume?"

"Belongs to a lady I work for. How you know what flowers it is?"

"Family thing." He smudged off the blood, but his nose was still leaking. His chin needed a shave, just his chin, cheeks were smooth. The nose had a curve a school bus'd run off of.

"I got in a fight tonight."

"See that. Your nose is broke."

"I don't care. I'm OK. I was kinda out of it before. Then this guy hassled me, about"—his hand pawed his bare neck—"never mind. He just shoved me. I'd have left the bar, but he wouldn't let me by. Obliterated my nose. So...I mean, I don't mean I...I didn't do great, didn't knock him out or anything. Not sure where I hit him, jaw, I think, but he actually fell down. On the floor. It's starting to hurt a little now."

He ran his middle finger across the knuckles of his right hand. "It's just, you know, when you're afraid of something, and...it's like this boogeyman you obsess about all the time, that you're this inadequate wimp and then it actually happens and you do OK and then it's, holy crow, you did that, what were you so afraid of? And so it's...really neat. This is a good night for me."

He smiled, front teeth outlined in blood.

"Sorry for startling you. You don't have to stab me with whatever that is. You're probably nervous, huh? Oh, wow, you probably have somewhere to be." He stepped back to clear the way, so that she could hurry off to her pressing appointment.

She had a room to be in with a single bed, a chest of drawers, a chair, a framed picture of two kids on a bridge and an angel. She had a locked lock on the door, and a few weeks ago, in some perfect cascade of moments, she lay on the bed, her head on a flat pillow, and marveled at the fact of her possession of this room. It was safe. Soundless. Complete. She had wanted to be this room.

That was then. Nothing had changed. But things move, they just move, can't stop them.

"What's that mean, *out of it*, what were you out of?"

"Can we sit down on those steps over here for a little bit. Not the bus bench, people'll sit there."

Delpha glanced at him, deciding. Nothing surly about the boy now. Here came the bus lumbering down the street passing a lame man with a lunchbox who got his elbows working and followed alongside it.

"I'm shit, sorry, crappy at talking to girls. But you're not one. I mean...you're a woman."

The wistful tone was what allowed her to sit down on the steps. He might have been identifying a fairy-story creature. His innocence—wasn't that what it was, this quality he had of lacking in threat—made *him* the fairy-story creature.

A couple clipped by in high heels and cap-toed shoes, the man eye-measuring at the tall boy, running tongue around his lips at her, and the regular world was back.

The bus squealed to a stop. The man with the lunchbox hauled himself on. In the wake of the bus's diesel departure, the boy sat down beside Delpha. Knee to ankle, length of leg on him.

He puffed his cheeks, making a kid's drawn-out explosion sound, which sprayed out some blood. "Oh, gross, god, sorry. Sorry." He wiped his nose and went on, rounding his hands like they contained a cloud. "That's what I felt like when I came down here. Maybe *out of it* isn't the right words. I wanted to nuke something."

His name was Isaac. In answer to her question, he said he was twenty and amended that to "Well, close enough." They talked for fifteen minutes or so mostly about him, which was all right with Delpha because the conversation, the steps, the sitting down beside were tumultuous and exotic.

Isaac had been away at college, but might not go back right away. Yes, he had really liked his college but he might not go. He might enroll at Lamar or maybe work construction. A friend's dad had offered to get him a helper job tile-setting— and anybody could frame or drywall. Conscientiously he asked Delpha a question (Where did she work?), and bowed his head as he listened to her answer about old Mrs. Speir. The boy's nose had to hurt, but his mood appeared lighter as the minutes went by, like he was filling with happy gas.

Delpha too was enjoying herself, and it was almost like a hallucination. It had to be caught up and handled and verified and thought about.

"Well. I'm going home," she said, gesturing. "Block up that way."

"Oh, sure." He popped up, holding out his hand for her. "Man, thanks for talking. And not stabbing me." He moved his left fist back and forth like it clutched a knife, laughing.

She'd been going to take his hand, but he shredded, thinned apart. Her brain had protectively interpreted for her the improbability of believing herself to be about to shake the hand of a young man on a street on a summer night, and the young man was not in prison, and she was not in prison, and she had, in addition to her black flats standing on the warm concrete sidewalk, a room, two employers. In a bit the shreddedness reformed into a smiling young man who was losing the smile, slipping hands in his pockets, and he and the yellow streetlight and his blood-spotted shirt returned to color and fullness.

She blinked against the lost moments and said, "Stand down there off the steps. Stand still and look here."

That choppy hair, falling back from his upturned face, mess in the middle of it. He looked up with wide-open eyes. Twenty years old. She put her fingers on either side of his nose, one high, one mid-ways, feeling where it was off its place, said, "This might help you breathing on the way home. Can you stand it?"

"Yeah."

She guided firmly with both hands, feeling the pop. He reeled away groaning, panted like a winded dog, fanned a hand in front of his nose without touching it.

"Your parents should carry you to the doctor tomorrow. Night, Isaac."

He managed to stop the panting though his watering eyes dumped out on his cheeks, drew himself up, dignified, gentlemanly. Did well enough, considering the stoop and the tear-tracks.

"I'll watch till you get in. Delpha."

She smiled. Polite kid. Be a handsome man.

She could have said, *Sometime, like you told me, you might have something you're scared of, then that thing happens, and it's not* neat. *It's the wrong angel, Isaac, it's the Prince of Hell, the Spoiler. Ever day you wake up with him and what makes him scary is that you're so, so tired of him, and he might never go away.*

What for? She said, "Thank you."

X

PHELAN'S MOTHER DOLORES picked his grandmother
Lila a pine coffin shellacked so high it shined like a plastic go-
car. Thibodeaux the mortician battered the mourners with
"A Mighty Fortress is Our God" on the eight-track, though
church songs ran contrary to Lila's taste. Why couldn't they
have had "Won't You Come Home, Bill Bailey?" or "The
Big Rock Candy Mountain"? Thibodeaux'd get his money
whether he played John Wesley or Johnny Cash.

Phelan shifted his shoulders uncomfortably in the suit
he'd bought, dark gray. He'd ironed a blue shirt, wrestled
with a plain navy tie, left off the aftershave.

"Man, who wears a blue shirt to a funeral," his brother
Fuller whispered loudly. "Look like a mailman."

Phelan glanced over. Fuller's new white shirt bore folding
creases. His jacket had to be a relic from his brief working
days, before he gave up on employment and moved in with
Dolores—it was an inch shy of his wrists. Wouldn't have
buttoned if wrestlers Brute Bernard and Skull Murphy had
each grabbed a lapel and run for the middle.

"Didn't know you had shoes covered your toes," Phelan
muttered.

"Don't y'all start," Dolores said, sniffling.

Rain fell on and off during the graveside part of the
funeral. There wasn't much loitering afterward. The family

was headed back to Aunt Maryann and Uncle E.E.'s house. Neighbors, Maryann announced, had just buried the dining room table in casseroles and congealed salads. "Oh," she winced, " that was the wrong word to use."

Phelan wasn't ready yet to desert Lila's ground. He turned up his collar and took a walk among the damp stone angels and their stone houses, remembering, humming under the vast green umbrella of the live oaks.

In the Big Rock Candy Mountains,
The jails are made of tin.
And you can walk right out again,
As soon as you are in....

He'd found his heroes in his grandmother's stories, in people battling what they couldn't beat. Davy Crockett. Coxey's Army, marching ragtag on the White House. Clyde Barrow and bony little Bonnie Parker. Those bank robbers weren't outlaws back when three quarters of the country could put themselves, a shotgun, and a bank vault in the same picture.

Up ahead was another canvas canopy with rows of folding chairs and a mortuary van crunching toward it down the oyster-shell lane in unseemly haste.

A long-legged young man in a narrow beige suit flew out of the van, speedily unloaded flower sprays, tall white gladiola spears, an easel of peach roses, mixed bouquets, some potted plants. He darted around, placing arrangements, switched the gladiolas and the easel, stood back, index finger poked in his cheek, switched them back. He was wiping down the folding chairs when a black procession nosed down the lane, followed by a string of cars with their lights on. The young man started, dove into the van, and drove away at two mph.

The black procession began its caterpillar-like halt. Lights flicked off. Men in suits deboarded the coffin and rolled it to the front of the green tent. Might be a porter or a gopher, but in the funeral business you wore a suit to push and fetch. The coffin-deliverers piled into the hearse when they were done. It crept out into the cemetery lane toward Phelan, passed him trailing strains of Archie Bell and the Drells' "Do the Tighten Up."

Meanwhile, back in the bereavement realm, Thibodeaux was bending toward the family's limo with a black umbrella. First person out, a man, brushed past him. The mortician extended a hand, and a widow appeared, black hat with a net veil like fine chicken wire.

A grizzly bear in a gray Stetson lumbered up to her at the limo. He removed the hat and palmed it at his chest, showing a head of sparse white strands on downhill retreat from a Rock of Gibraltar forehead. He stiffly offered out his hand, said a word to the widow.

Phelan had already lost interest in the scene when she opened her purse and extracted a black glove. She pulled it on, not a pair, just the one, held out her gloved hand to clasp the big old man's. He was trying to say something, but she put a finger none too gently to his lips. She then pinched the glove by its cuff, pulling it inside out, and dropped it into her purse. She showed him her back.

Whoa. No green pastures for you today, Mister. No still waters. Just a widow's message you're something she wouldn't touch with a bare hand.

The old man plodded grimly back to a car down the line.

Family grievances, who didn't have those? Phelan considered his older brother. Take some restraint to make sure his own family's reception went off without minor violences. Phelan flicked the leaf of a live oak, scattering raindrops.

'Member that rainy eve that
I threw you out,
With nothing but a fine-tooth comb?
I know I'm to blame,
Well, ain't that a shame
Bill Bailey won't you please come home.

The usually reticent phone rang as Miss Wade walked in the next morning. Her pleased glance met Phelan's relieved one, and they exchanged the triumphant look of parents whose three-year-old has bellied up to the toilet rim and peed all by himself.

She answered with "Good Morning, Phelan Investigations. How can we help you?" and handed it to him.

The excited lady on the other end suspected a devious neighbor, Juanita Martin by name, of poisoning her Laddy. See, they had worked in the same building until Juanita retired and sat around all day, while she herself still had to go to work. And Juanita had always been a rotten—Phelan interrupted. To his questions, she answered that yes, Laddy was a dog, a wire-haired fox terrier, AKC, the client went on—and she had a fenced yard. She left the dog out there daytimes while she worked, brought him in at night. How was he sick? Well, twice now he had upchucked and staggered and then laid around all evening, wouldn't play or eat at all. Had she seen any food in the yard that she hadn't fed him herself, say, a little steak, piece of bone or gristle from one? Of course she hadn't. If she had, she wouldn't be calling him. She'd have called the police on that white-walled bitch, Juanita Martin.

Phelan recommended she keep Laddy inside until he could check out her yard for any action of a suspicious nature. Just how much would that cost her, the woman asked. Phelan yielded the call to Miss Wade, stood there while she delivered the bad news.

Miss Wade did, listened a while, came back with, "Yes, ma'am, I surely do understand. Not everybody can afford a crack P.I. And as lovin' and faithful and precious company as a little dog is, well, it's just a dumb animal, isn't it?" She held the babbling phone out from her ear for a while, then said, "Well now. All right. Will you please hold and let me see what I can do." She covered the receiver and they contemplated each other.

"You wanna make some paper-rustling noises while you look through our calendar," Phelan murmured, raising his eyebrows.

Her mouth pulled down at the corners. After a few more seconds, she said, "Ma'am, we might could fit you in this morning, seeing as it's a matter of your poor dog's health. Maybe even life or death. We could do that for *you*."

"Good work, Miss Wade," he said when she hung up. "You got us a dog stakeout." Then he wondered about that "us." He shouldn't be expecting her to feel the same urgency he did about his new business.

But she took a breath of satisfaction and let it out. "Thank you, Mr. Phelan."

At 9:30, he pulled into the Minglewood subdivision and parked to the side of the client's house so he could watch the terrier behind the chain-link fence. The subject did not look either wiry or foxy. He had white, curly-looking hair with a black saddle and a tan face shaped like a shoebox. The dog had a hut to keep him out of the sun, but he didn't venture near it. Cars passed. A bus or three. A siren wailing in the distance brought Laddy to attention. He threw back his head and bayed like a hound until the siren faded. Then Laddy settled himself by the fence and watched Phelan back.

Subdivisions in the mornings were like the woods. You knew there were animals lurking, but they hid themselves. The rows of houses just sat there, green yards and a tumped-over sprinkler, chain link and parked cars and basketball hoops, sunlight shifting on leaves. Breeze. Birdcalls. Phelan puzzled over the Elliott case, silently recited state capitals, relived a few romantic intervals and a couple of outright bangathons. Now he was horny. And hungry. And he could have used a cup of coffee with cream and sugar.

A squirrel spiraled around a tree and down. Laddy chased after him, barking to break the sound barrier, front legs straining onto the tree. The squirrel spurted up to a branch and leered, mixing its paws together like it was making evil plans.

The barking continued full-throat until a woman in a housecoat stalked out into her yard next door to the client's and screamed "Shuuuuu-ut up, you little shit!" Juanita Martin, Phelan presumed. The poisoner? She glowered while the squirrel retreated to a height Laddy considered unthreatening. The dog's front feet hit ground. He wandered over to a flattened ball and tussled with it. No poison hamburger sailed over the fence that Phelan could see. The alleged poisoner, arms tightly folded, ducked past a hanging plant into her back door. After a while, Laddy stopped lipping the ball and went back to watching Phelan. Another hour passed. His first stakeout, this was it. Phelan cursed himself for not setting up, bringing a newspaper, a coke, that cold meatball sandwich pining away in his fridge.

A mailman came along sorting envelopes. He shortened his stride and soft-footed it up to the porch's mailbox. The growling dog pressed its face sideways to the chain link until the guy's foot hit the porch, then he combined growling with wild barking and dancing. The postman slotted the mail. When he drew even with the dog, he feinted once, tantalizing Laddy from the safe zone on the sidewalk, and went on his way. The dog almost fell over backward barking. A door across the street flew open, and in it, a woman in curlers, her mouth moving. She was making some kind of pissed off voodoo signs toward his client's yard.

Phelan thought he had the story. Dog acts nuts all day, barks itself sick. Owner comes home. It throws up and collapses. End of case. Advice to owner, *lagniappe:* obedience school, give the dog a bedroom, take it to work. She was lucky nobody had tossed a grenade in her yard.

He was about to start his car when a man with roostered hair, wearing white boxers with enough storage space for three butts, a T-shirt, and house slippers came out of the garage of the house in back of his client's. He had a sack under his arm and was carrying a kid's toy, one of those paddles with a ball on a string. He wasn't alone. Tottering after him, one stiff step at a time like a wooden dog, was a gaunt, faded golden lab, its muzzle as white as Colonel Sanders's goatee. The guy motioned. The dog sat.

Being in underwear near a public street at eleven in the morning didn't seem to bother the man. He plodded toward the client's fence, where he set down the little brown sack. He hauled back the paddle and whapped the ball so that it zoomed into the terrier's air space before rebounding. After a couple bobbles, he got a rhythm going.

The terrier began leaping for the ball, snapping air, howling and yodeling until he matched the paddle's rhythm. Up, down, up, down, snarl, bark, howl, a spit-spraying, ear-flapping, jack-in-the-box frenzy. The woman next door tore out of her house again, this time dressed in a pantsuit, a hairbrush in her hand. The electric-chair look on her face crimped into a mean smile.

Hand over an ear, Phelan checked his watch. Three minutes, four. How'd the old guy keep it up? Boxer, maybe, once upon a time. Still had shoulders, though the bicep flesh was bouncing. *Smack smack smack smack.* Berserko dog freakout inside the fence. The old lab sat behind the man, head cocked, Tony Bennett taking in a Jerry Lee Lewis show.

Laddy started missing the rhythm now and again. One jump instead of four. Finally the man in the underwear quit and massaged his batting arm. The hairy terrier collapsed, heaving, four legs splayed, like somebody had stepped on his back. Foam rimmed his mouth. The man bent down, skinny white legs bowing out, fly gaping, and snagged the paper sack. Phelan stepped out of the car.

"'Scuse me, sir," he said.

The man pulled a marble out of the sack, leaned over the fence and drew a bead on Laddy's panting head.

"Sir," Phelan said louder, jogging up to him.

The man jumped. "What do you want?"

"You planning to bean the dog?"

The guy squinted, creasing the considerable bags under his eyes.

"I said—"

"Wait a minute." He turned his head and pinched inside his ear to remove a plug. Then the other, dropped both earplugs in the T-shirt pocket. "Wasn't for these sons a bitches I'd be dead. What'd you say?"

Phelan smiled and introduced himself. "Your neighbor," he hiked his chin toward Laddy's owner's house, "hired me to make sure nobody was hurting her dog."

"That's not a dog. That's a broke-dick yapping machine."

"Call the police on him for disturbing the peace?"

"'Bout ten times. They don't come anymore." The man backhanded the air disgustedly.

"I could sure understand it, but I don't suppose you fed that dog anything dangerous?"

"Dangerous." The guy blinked crusty eyes at Phelan. "You mean rat poison. Strychnine. Arsenic. Insecticide. Cynanide." He thought a second. "Brass tacks."

"Something like that," Phelan said.

"Naw, that'd be against the law. *Which* I know. I'm a security guard, work the eleven to seven. Listen, dogs are better'n people any day. Find a bad dog, you find a stupid, selfish bitch-face owner."

The man shot Phelan a sly glance, brought his hand up to his mouth and ate what was in it. Phelan imagined molars cracking on the marble. *Ow.* Going pretty far to prove a point. The old guy was wearing the same crimp-smile as Juanita Martin. He bent and fished out a couple more marbles, tossed them into his mouth.

"Want some grapes? More in the sack."

Phelan commanded himself to maintain a professional attitude. Which, as far as he understood it—and he had understood it since he was ten—meant tough and knowing. Tough. Knowing. Couldn't hold it—he laughed. Told the neighbor what he was going to recommend his client do: keep the dog in the house, send him to obedience school, etc., etc. "For the good of everybody, including the dog."

The man bent and fondled the neck of his mannerly lab, who craned to lick the guy's whiskered jaw. "Yeah? I'll believe it when I see it. *This* is a dog, by the way. Ain't ya, old boy? I was gonna poison somebody, I'd poison *her*." He stabbed toward the client's house. "And I tell you just how I'd do it, too—"

"Don't tell me."

The man stared at him, nodded. "Good point." He headed back to his garage, slippers slapping. The old dog followed him.

Phelan squatted and examined the contents of the abandoned sack. No marbles, nails, capsules, or razor blades. Unripe-looking red grapes pulled off a stalk. He rolled them around, checked for needle sticks, none he could see. He sniffed one. Grape.

Back at the office, Phelan gave Miss Wade his hours for the bill. His secretary left for a late lunch and when she got back, stuck her head in his office and said, "Grapes."

"What about 'em?"

"Them and raisins are bad for dogs' kidneys. Don't know how many it'd take to kill one, but a bag of grapes didn't help Laddy out any." She put her purse in a drawer and took out some typing paper.

"You eat at the library, Miss Wade?"

"They don't notice, you sit at a back table and keep a sandwich under it."

At 5:20, Phelan called the client and gave her his report absolving Juanita Martin. Despite her pestering, he declined to reveal the identity of the neighbor whom he called "the chief complainant" and read out the two numbers of canine obedience schools listed in the Yellow Pages. Mentioned her other options. The client protested that Laddy was a sweet dog, and she didn't need him to tell her different.

Mindful of his fee, Phelan countered softly, "Ma'am. You ever eat at a nice restaurant and have somebody let their kids run all over the place, yelling and screaming and knocking into your chair?"

"I sure have!" The client hated that and said so, anecdotally, for one and one half minutes.

"Ma'am, Laddy's that kid, and your neighbors are the people at the restaurant. You might just be the most popular lady in the neighborhood if you were willing to fix the situation."

Silence. She offered grudgingly that she would think about it. "I don't have to pay you for a whole day, do I?"

"No, the bill will be for half plus expenses. That's how long it took to...*find out anybody within a hundred yards of your house was a suspect for dogacide*...isolate the problem."

When the painter blocked out *Phelan Investigations* on his door, Phelan had envisioned complex, strung-out cases that took weeks. Good he had the Elliott one.

XI

DELPHA STEPPED DOWN onto the street. The bus door
exhaled air behind her. A young guy with tangly hair, a
rolled-sleeve shirt, and a deep lavender eye sat there on the
bus bench. He held up a white rectangle. Around 10:30 at
night, breathless hot, two people clattering by on the sidewalk,
a car's headlights.

Her handkerchief was washed, ironed, folded. He dashed
his top lip with the back of his hand. Sweat ran from Delpha's
temples.

He followed her into the New Rosemont's kitchen that
smelled like Twenty Mule Team Borax and fifty years of
bacon grease. Delpha waved toward a stool at the wood table
Calinda Blanchard and Oscar the cook chopped on, got two
Pearls from the icebox and popped their caps on the church
key bolted to the wall. Streetlight from a parking lot, security
light over the back kitchen door kept the room from being
black dark. Delpha set down the bottles, one in front of Isaac,
one across, then walked over to the counter behind his back.
But she watched him.

"Hey, thanks." He fit his hands around the bottle and
upturned it. Looked to drink most of it in one go.

She smoothed out a five-dollar bill on the linoleum
counter and slid the top edge of it under the corner of the
big tin breadbox, where you could see the full Lincoln. Then

she sat on the wooden stool, rolled the cold glass bottle to her cheek. After a while, she drank. Beer. She'd only missed it because she couldn't have it.

"How's your nose?"

"Sore. My doctor said it'd be OK. So, did you work both your jobs today—the office job and the old lady?"

Mouth full, she nodded.

"Long day. Why do you do it?"

She swallowed. "Saving up."

"For what?"

"Something I want."

"What do you want?"

I want a life I want. "Don't know yet."

He smiled. Straight teeth. "C'mon. Don't you have an idea of what it might be?"

"Something different than anything I had before."

"That's cool. Saving up for a mystery."

"Don't believe a person could be hell-bent on having something they don't know what it is yet?"

"I don't know. But I know what I want."

"What?" She'd known one thing he wanted when she saw the ironed handkerchief.

He looked away from her. "I want to be older, finished with college, making money—"

"You gonna be older. There you go, your first wish's granted now."

"Albert Einstein said there's not any now. The past and the future and the present are all happening simultaneously. Linear time, hour after hour, day after day, it's an illusion."

Delpha's brow ruffled. "You believe that?"

"Think it's possible. And another scientist says that for one place in time there're all these possible directions to go, and each one has a certain amplitude, and when added, the sum is zero—"

"Lost you."

"OK, OK, wait. Our kind of time, one o'clock, two o'clock, summer, fall is just the most probable direction, the most probable path in space out of lots of other paths, the one the most people take."

"A path."

"Yeah." He lifted his eyebrows. "Time's a dimension."

"OK. So on one path, you lived this life. Or you could of took another road and lived in China."

"Or Africa or Chicago. If I had taken a less probable path."

"Well, there's the deal, isn't it? The scientist should have told us how you change paths. Plenty people would."

"I would. My mom keeps going on about how these years are precious, but I just want to rocket forward. Does that make sense?"

"Wantin' years to be minutes? Oh, yeah. I can understand that."

Very small smile. "I *knew* you could."

"Why?"

"Just knew." He couldn't hold eye contact and chugged the last of his beer.

The conversation stalled.

Didn't bother Delpha. In all her life to come, no matter how long or how short, there was no way sufficient quiet could accumulate to balance out the years of noise. The light fell on his face, bony now, the kind of face men grew into. She put stooped Isaac in a brick college, tie, hair trimmed up, touch of gray, professor like Dr. Einstein. Made him stand up straight. Gave him a tall blonde wife with glasses, kids.

She got two more beers from the icebox. When she put

down the bottles and sat, Isaac broke the silence. "Education is…was this huge deal to my parents. Man, talk about saving. By the time I was eight, they'd saved up my whole college tuition so I could go to anywhere."

"So, why aren't you going anymore?"

"Oh." He looked down at the scarred wood table. "I will. Just not right now. My mom thinks she doesn't need any help but she does."

"What's your dad say?

His lips mashed in. "My dad's…he passed away."

"Oh. Sorry to hear about that. Boys need their dads."

He didn't look up. "Girls too."

"That's true. Just, boys that didn't have a daddy, they're either searchin' or taking it out on a woman lotta their life."

"Oh, great."

Delpha pressed the barrel of cold bottle into her forehead and counted *shit, shit, shit*. She cleared her throat. "Know what. I can run off terrible at the mouth."

They sat there. He glanced up at her through his lashes, long lashes for a boy. "No, wait. Guys that didn't have a dad, did they tell you that?"

She shifted sideways on the stool so that she faced the refrigerator. "No, Isaac, and that's what I mean. Bunch of women told me that."

"Oh." He nodded. They sat. After a while his fingers tapped her forearm. "So, did you go to college?"

She didn't laugh. "No."

"Would you have liked to?"

"Yes."

"What would you have studied? I mean, like your major?"

"When I know the answer to that, I'll know what I'm saving money for. What are you studying?"

"Science. The only other thing I ever liked as much was mythology." He shook his head. "I was this dorky kid. Not the biggest Superman fan, surprisingly. Well, not true. *Superman's Return to Krypton* was cool. But Theseus, Perseus, Dedalus, they're major league. And Zeus and Thor. I wanted to hurl lightning on people." A pause. "I sound five years old, right?"

"Some people need lightning. Tell me 'bout your dad."

Isaac leaned his forehead between index and thumb, so that his fingers shaded his eyes. "He's...He was"—huge, soft, helpless smile—"the best." He sniffed and gave his head a couple of hard shakes.

"Like how?"

"We used to run. Sometimes jump the hurdles if they were left out on the track. He could still do that. Every night until he... We used to go canoeing up in the Big Thicket. In spring when the creeks were high. Know how many bugs live in the Big Thicket—like a million to the 10th power?—but Dad made this stuff we rubbed on our faces and hands and necks and we were fine. It's peaceful in there on the bayous just gliding along. It's like time travel. You don't see anyone and it could be 1700 or it could be 600 B.C. Dad knew the name of a lot of the flora. Like *Ilex Vomitoria*"—Isaac grinned—"that one used to crack me up. Old vomitoria—it's yaupon, and it *can* make you throw up...and, let's see, Chinese tallow, that's *Sapiem sebiferum* and... did you ever go to the Thicket? You must have."

She angled herself around again, almost facing him. "Orchids, pitcher plant, loblolly, magnolia, holly, cypress slough, moss, willow, thick old vines like ropes. Don't know those names you said. My mother and me lived the edge of the Thicket. I moved to Beaumont after she died."

"With your dad?"

"He came round once. He wasn't like your dad."

Isaac looked at her face for a while. "You should have had a dad like mine."

Delpha pushed her beer bottle over to clink the base of his.

The lights snapped on. Isaac jumped off the wooden stool. Once Delpha stopped blinking against the glare, the scarecrow form of Calinda Blanchard appeared in roomy pajamas, gray hair rumpled. No eyeglasses, no teeth.

"Ran outa aspirin. Got a new bottle in here." The New Rosemont's proprietor stretched out her corded neck and squinted toward the four brown beer bottles, then her gaze scraped fiercely up and down the length of Isaac, who'd clasped both hands over his crotch. She set a fist on her hip.

"I have rules in my place."

"Under the breadbox, Miss Blanchard. Ain't nobody mooching here."

Calinda stared at Delpha before slapping over to the counter on wide, bunioned feet. She pinched the five-dollar bill up in front of her nose, turned it over, made sure both sides were green. The pajamas had a breast pocket, Calinda tucked the five in there.

She raked a glass off the shelf, filled it with tap water, took a little white bottle from a drawer and fiddled with its cap, muttering irritably. "I be dog." Calinda made a threatening face at the bottle, then planted her bare feet and wrestled with the cap. She banged it on the counter several times. Brought it up close to her then, to glare it off.

"You fool little punk piece of plastic, get offa here."

Isaac looked at Delpha, whose fingertip rose from the table.

"I don't know what they think they're doing, making a aspirin bottle that doesn't open less you're a go-rilla—" Miss Blanchard gave it two more whacks against the counter.

Isaac said, "Here, let me get it for you." He went over, twisted his palm against the cap, twirled it off, and held it out to her.

"Keep it." She sprinkled out several aspirins and tossed them in her mouth. Swallowed some water. "Just throw that son of a gun away." Her elbow pointed toward the bottle cap in Isaac's hand. She opened the breadbox and snugged the white aspirin bottle into a back corner of it, and then carried the glass of water with her to the doorway. "G'night," she said, flipping the light, throwing them back in the dark.

She padded away. A door shut.

Wooden legs slid on the linoleum as the stool was pushed to the table. Isaac was walking over. "Delpha—" his voice said. "Jeez I'm glad she turned off the lights. I want to ask you... would you ever consider...you could think about it, I don't need to know right away...but maybe going out somewhere with me, I mean to the movies, what kind of movies do you like? Or out to eat somewhere..."

She could see him again now. His shoulders were rounded like an old man's, his fists punching inside the bottom of his jean pockets.

"You have any idea how old I am?"

He bent forward and his lips collided with the side of her cheek, but they slid over and found her mouth, he breathed inside, touched her lips with his tongue.

She tilted her head so their noses fit right.

His other hand fumbled on her arm, and she stood up.

"I couldn't care less how old you are. Does it matter all that much?" He dipped his head and kissed her again and drew her to his chest, leaving air around her, rather than trapping her backward against the table. Her arms went around his ribs and up, climbed till she was holding his shoulders, pushing up on tiptoe to kiss back. The deep root inside her strained outward, feeding the veins to all the rest of her body, forcing arms, waist, thighs, fingertips, toes, to stretch and bend and open. Heat rushed her cheeks.

Delpha murmured, "You have protection?"

White in his eyes. Frozen in place.

She'd scared him. Pushed him down one of those other paths in time, one that led to a cheerleader, ribbon in her hair and sticky panties, he was probably backpedaling from what he'd started with that kiss.

"N-not with me," he said. "I have the car, but drug stores are closed." He brought his watch up to his face to confirm. "It's, yeah, it's eleven thirty-seven, and they're locked down but the bar, in the bathroom, they have machines...Change, change, do I have enough change?" Quarters bounced out on the table. He was counting them, not touching her.

She caught the chest of his shirt before he could break into a sprint.

"Isaac. Wait a minute. You sure about this?"

He started to answer, choked and had to cough it out, "Wait," forearm covering his mouth. He hauled breath in. "Incredibly sure. I want to do this more than I want to be twenty-one. I don't want to be twenty-one without doing this. I don't want to *be* without doing this."

"Then OK. There's not just the one thing. You know that, right?"

Wonderment bloomed on his face. "Well, yeah. Sure, I..." The wonderment wilted. "Theoretically." Isaac touched her hand that held his shirt. "Promise me you won't leave. That you'll be here in the kitchen when I get back. That you'll let me in that door." He pointed at it, as if there were three or four doors, and she might make a mistake.

Delpha held up index and middle and crossed them.

Her clothes were draped over on the chair, and his lay on the floor. Ceiling fan was spinning. He came with only the sight of her standing there. She squatted and put her mouth on it so he wouldn't be alone in the finishing. When she lifted her head, he was slack-mouthed, head lolled back. She sat beside him on the bed, their bare feet on the floor like two people on a bus seat. It was kind of funny and for the most part not real, which made it easy for her. It was like a picture show, except the moment kept stubbornly going on instead of shredding or winking out.

Delpha turned sideways, jutting her knee out onto the bed, and she angled him around. Looked into his face, skin like a kid's. Too dark to see the shade of eyes but the nose straight enough, ran her finger down it, light, so it wouldn't hurt. Flat cheeks. Had a good jaw. One of those Adam's apples that stuck out.

"How'd you get such broad shoulders. That a family thing?"

"Swim team." He was gazing at her breasts. His lips were open. He smelled like sweat and soap and beer and some kind of aftershave but not Old Spice.

Her skin must be whiter than this bed sheet, white as cornstarch.

He reached.

"One second, OK."

He looked in her eyes then. She looked back. They said something, on her part it was verifying: this kid, this man, this male person, there was a message but she didn't know what he said, guessed he didn't know either. She touched his chest. Few hairs round the nipples. Muscles on his flat belly.

Felt the ribs. No gut at all, inward curve. He was circumcised, first one she'd seen. She touched his wet dick, and it moved in her hand, and he groaned. She let go, and he groaned again. Ran the heels of her hands down the long, long length of his thighs to the muscles above the knee, then back up the taut sides of his legs. He was hard again.

He opened his hand so she could have the foil package with the rubber. She took it. "You got huge feet, Isaac." She grinned.

"Thirteens. Don't expect me to know anything. I don't—"

"Yeah, you do."

He was quiet for a while. "May I touch you now?"

Listen to that, *May I*.

He did what she had done. His hands hovered on her breasts, not squeezing or pinching, letting his palms graze her nipples, then he rounded his hands and contained them. He bent and rested his face, then his lips on them as his hands traveled the curves of her waist and the flare of her hips and the insides of her thighs. He put a finger inside her and exhaled choppily, avoiding looking at her. "It goes in so—"

She rolled down the rubber, hoping she'd got it on the right way, scooted back and brought him with her. The second time didn't take long but long enough for Delpha's body—and not solely her brain—to confront a proposition: that the present was recording a piece of time she might want to keep rather than stack up and dismiss. That she was not in Gatesville Women's Prison, favoring Rita who had a pretty face and poor table manners and would always take up for her. Or Rita favoring her. This was a new piece of time.

XII

AT 6:30 ON a Thursday, Phelan parked in a space near the Holiday Inn office where he could monitor arriving guests. Tonight he'd gotten it together enough to equip himself with a thermos of coffee, a Mounds bar, and the evening paper, in addition to the camera with fast film. He sipped the coffee slowly.

At 7:10, the coffee and coconut long gone, a woman in a green Ford Maverick parked in a slot near the office but did not get out. Phelan jotted the plate number and noted the McGovern '72 bumper sticker, *Put A Human in the White House*. Five more minutes and a black Seville, license J5489, coasted to a stop by the motel doors. The man who got out automatically buttoned the second button of his jacket, as though preparing to step up to a witness stand.

That was his guy.

Lloyd Elliott was maybe five ten, with a little paunch and hair combed straight back. Not a lot of it on top and not trying to hide it. Late middle-age. Furrowed brow, worry lines all over the map. The woman in the green Ford waved to him. He raised a hand to her. As he stood there, hand up, twenty years tumbled off him. A younger, taller man entered the lobby to sign in Mr. and Mrs. Jones.

Phelan snapped a photo as Elliott leaned into the Ford, probably giving her the room number. The woman touched his chin, and he smiled. *Snap*. Phelan gave the Ford and the Seville a long lead, then carefully followed them around to the backside of the motel. The woman who got out was brunette, around five three, regular weight, pretty but not beautiful. Her tip-tilted nose was shiny, lipstick pale if any. She wore a billowy-sleeved flowered blouse and maroon pants, a modest bell to them. And boom, ring on the left hand. They entered Room 162, Elliott unlacing his fingers from hers to hold the door for her.

Snap.

Phelan needed one of those zoom cameras so he could find a slit of curtain to shoot through, get some flashes of the action. His opinion was that that's what the husbands would be looking for, the nitty gritty, but being as this was the wife, a clench might do it. Hadn't got that yet, and he wanted the smoking gun. Like the reporters these days, sniffing around for Tricky Dick Nixon's smoking gun. Hadn't unearthed it yet.

Figuring the clench was most likely to happen when they left, Phelan settled in to wait some more. Maybe Lloyd was a two-minute kind of guy. Thing was, the coffee had backed up on him. He should have thought of that. Phelan had to take a leak, and he had to stay where he was. He toughed it out for twenty-seven minutes then got out of the car, leaving the door open a crack, and walked behind the trunk. Looked around, unzipped.

They came out of the room.

Phelan slithered back into the car, leaving the door quietly open. But he could have slammed it and popped a wheelie for all the couple out in front of 162 would have noticed. The woman was barefoot and crying, Lloyd Elliott in his shirt sleeves trying to surround her with both arms, all the worry-lines back on his map. Slouched in his seat, ear out the open window, Phelan listened. If only he had a drive-in speaker clipped to the window. But theirs was a silent movie.

The woman put both hands over her face, her shoulders shaking. The billowy blouse was untucked, little strings that tied at the neck untied. Lloyd reached out to her but let his arms fall back helplessly. She turned to him, gazed up into his face. Then she put her arms around his neck. His hands closed on her forearms. They looked at each other for a long moment, leaning toward each other until their heads touched. Then they went back into the room.

Phelan'd got a shot with the hands to her face, starring the wedding ring. He recorded that tender stare-down.

After searching around under the seats for an old cup or coke bottle, he sacrificed his thermos by taking a piss in that. Thing had the benefit of a cap.

He waited another hour, jacket off, sleeves rolled. Alternately he stifled in the roasting car or rolled down the window for a breath of air, an invitation to the mosquitoes, which exulted in on him singing and stinging. A few minutes before too-dark-to-see, Lloyd Elliott and his girlfriend walked out of the room. Phelan held the camera tightly to his head to keep it steady. In between the black Seville and the green Ford, the couple embraced, they kissed, the lawyer clasped the woman to his chest, his chin on the top of her head, his eyes closed like he was standing in the parking lot of heaven.

Snap. Snap.

Smoking gun.

Soon as they'd gone, Phelan chucked a perfectly good thermos in the Holiday Inn's dumpster. One expense Miss Wade would never hear about.

XIII

FIRST THING FRIDAY morning, he put a rush on the film by slipping the technician a five, but *Ha-ha on you, Tom,* all that really bought him was the first call when the photo packages rolled in Monday. Tuesday, he loomed over Miss Wade's desk and had her set up a meeting to deliver the photos to their client.

"So when and where do I meet her?" he asked as soon as she hung up, but the phone blared again, startling both of them. Phelan heard her assuring Joe Ford that yes, she was at work, and yes, she remembered her appointment this evening. She was about to hang up again when Phelan said, "Lemme have him."

She handed him the receiver. Phelan asked Joe if anybody they knew had taken up the law.

"Son, I work with the ones that took against it."

"I know, smartass, but what I'm wondering is—"

"Miles Blankenship."

"Who?"

"Drum major with the funny hat. Valedictorian."

"Him? That was Miles Blankenship that gave that speech?"

"Yeah, saw him at the ten-year reunion, the one you didn't go to. Drives a Lincoln Continental. His wife's homely, though."

"And you got yourself one beautiful Amazon. How're those twins of yours?"

"Future Hall of Famers. I tell you Kathy's 'bout to pop out another one? We're working on the starting lineup."

"That's some easy work. Thanks, Joe."

Phelan flipped through ATTORNEYS until he found Miles Blankenship. Same business address as...he licked his fingers and turned the tissue-like pages until he matched Miles to a law office ad. There it was, Griffin and Kretchmer, Miles' top dogs. Here Phelan's trunk held a P.I.'s toolkit—pry-bar, wrenches, hammer, rope, twine, Baggies, flashlights heavy and slim, change of clothes, raincoat, couple hats—and turned out the Yellow Pages were his best friend.

Phelan pondered how to approach his old acquaintance. He could buy him a drink, but it was weird asking a guy out for a drink unless you'd already drunk with him. He shelved that idea and just phoned him, prepared to remind Miles they'd gone to high school together.

But Miles recalled a little matter of a couple tackles lifting his tall drum major hat after a game. They had squeezed him out, played catch with it until Phelan snatched the hat from its flight plan and tossed it back to Miles.

"Hmm." Not something that had stuck with Phelan. "All I remember is you giving that speech in the city auditorium."

Miles Blankenship coughed. "Sure thing. You and my mother. She thought I should have used fancier language."

"No, it was good. 'We've inherited a crummy world. But we can fix it.' You were right on about the first part. Hope the last is true."

Silence on the other end. "Thought you were blowing smoke."

"Nope, you got my attention." And Miles had too. For Phelan, the lines were a showstopper. He'd been struck by the foreign notion that anything he might do could repair crumminess. Had not fit himself and fix-the-world into the same toolbox before, but he savored the idea.

Nothing was forthcoming from Miles. Probably surprised to hear his eighteen-year-old self quoted back to him ten years later. Phelan felt like a prize wuss himself. He launched in on what his new business was and what he needed: details on the Daughtry-Enroco case that a lawyer named Lloyd Elliott had handled. If Miles knew anything. If lawyers all talked shop at some lawyer bar.

"Some do. Not me so much. But here's what I heard." The case was over a formula. Daughtry developed it. Allegedly someone slipped it to Enroco, Daughtry caught wind of that and sued. Enroco claimed simultaneous discovery in its own Ph.D.-packed R&D, but after some negotiating, the lawsuit went away.

"Kind of an unusual outcome," Miles said. "Enroco hoisting the white flag."

"Suppose so. Daughtry still in business?"

"That, I couldn't tell you."

"What's Elliott's rep among you men of the bar?"

"Standard enough, earned his partnership, not a hotdog. Does well for himself when he could be swinging in a hammock."

"Meaning what?"

"Well, the wife."

"What about the wife?"

"You have been out in the bay, Tom. Hadn't heard of Neva Elliott."

"Yeah, well, you lawyers want oil in your cars, I was doing my best to help you with that."

"And my car is damn grateful. But Neva Elliott...ever heard of Midas?"

"In Mrs. Fortner's English class, I think. Changed everything to gold just by touching it. Married to the woman with snakes for hair."

"Hey, now there's a stand-off." Miles laughed. "The Elliotts don't have kids. But whatever Neva and her Wall Street partners touch turns to gold. Lloyd Elliott could twiddle his subpoena all day if he cared to."

Phelan dotted his ballpoint against a notepad. Neither one of them needed money. But then, nobody minded having too much money, and the wife's pile might be motive for Lloyd to hang on to the marriage. Just, he hadn't looked like a man who cared about cleaving to any woman other than the one with her arms locked around his neck.

So why not just split? Why rub Lloyd's nose in the pictures and humiliate yourself doing it? Peculiar. Unless the Mrs. was after his girlfriend. Stir up shit, kill off the girlfriend's marriage as a token of her appreciation to Lloyd.

Even that didn't—Phelan pulled himself up short. There was a business opportunity in this phone call. He offered to help Miles out if he ever needed some investigation and in return, could he call Miles when he was looking for info about legal cases? Asked if Miles would be a contact.

"Sure, as long as they're not our cases."

"Great. Appreciate your time."

"My mother would appreciate you remembering my speech."

Swathed in pink ribbons, Phelan hung up. "OK, back to Mrs. Elliott," he said to Delpha. "Where does she want me to bring the photos?"

"J&J Steakhouse. The restaurant has a museum called The Eye of the World. You know about that? Tomorrow night at ten."

"Now that is one supremely odd choice. What'd she say to you?"

Miss Wade's brow creased. "Mrs. Elliott talked like she needed to convince somebody. Educated woman—she used a word I had to look up in my dictionary." Delpha slid out her top drawer and showed him a miniature book with a red plastic cover so, Phelan guessed, you could consult it in the rain or the bathtub.

"I just agreed with her. Sounded to me like she wants to make Lloyd think more than twice before he cheats again— she said him getting your pictures would be a *deterrent*. Now, that particular word, I didn't need to look up. It's big around Gatesville."

"She's also a very wealthy woman, according to my old friend Miles. So rich her husband probably wants to keep being her husband."

Delpha frowned. "She seem high-strung to you?"

"Among other things. Night I met her down on College, I didn't see her mouth move, but her scotch disappeared. Like drinking with a ventriloquist."

Phelan already knew the strip-like museum tacked onto the J&J Steakhouse was not a comfy spot for conversation. Parents went on in to order their T-bones, get some peace while kids gawked at The Eye of the World, a boggling display of miniature people, animals, and architecture whittled by one of owners.

He siphoned himself off from the entrance with its smiling hostess and stepped through a door labeled Museum into a corridor two feet wide. One wall was the showcase: dioramas behind plate glass. Two rows of Bible stories enacted by orange-crate-wood figures, topped by other cut-out citizens along with non-scale birds, camels, and sheep populating the Statue of Liberty, the Parthenon, and the

Tower of Babel. Spires, cupolas, domes galore. Mrs. Elliott was standing, arms folded, by a grand nativity scene arranged in an Alamo-style manger. She wore the charcoal suit and sunglasses. A girl of maybe eight or nine was down at the end, forehead plastered to the glass.

Phelan handed over the envelope with the photos and studied Mrs. Elliott while she opened it. Same brunette hair with a high sheen, bangs, feathery curls. Straight nose, strong chin. Thick make-up, oranger on her jawline than her white neck. No perfume. In fact, little whiff of anti-perfume, doctor's office, maybe. She tilted the 8x10s left and right, brought them forward, briefly tipped down the sunglasses. He caught a glimpse of the swampy brown eyes, their rims puffed and redder than before and thought about Lloyd and his girlfriend's clutch in the parking lot. He felt sorry for her.

She lifted a briefcase from the brown carpet and put the photos into it. The little girl squeezed by them. Mrs. Elliott waited for her to leave, then held out a white envelope, a notable quiver in her grasp. "Your secretary quoted me the total amount owed. It's all here, rounded to the dollar. Thank you for your services."

The sunglasses confronted him until he understood he was dismissed.

Wham, bam, you're welcome, ma'am.

He nodded and walked past *The Last Supper* and *Solomon's Temple*, out the restaurant's entrance and into the steamy night.

The woman he'd met last time had been in a way different mood. Feverish, talky. This one was the curt woman who'd called up their first day. He'd always been fair at reading faces, knew when a guy was likely going to start something or back down—knew without much thinking—and his body readied itself accordingly. Thought everyone did it. Was harder with the dark glasses but what he was reading with Mrs. Elliott was not distaste or disappointment. It was impatience. She wanted to get this picture show on the road.

He slid into his car and waited. She'd have to pass him to get back out on the street.

Families went by, couples. Car doors slammed. She never came out.

He got out, smiled at the hostess and scanned faces in the restaurant. Exited and strode behind the J&J to a dumpster and some patched blacktop. Flatbed parked back here. Crates and boxes. Weeds. Line of woods directly to the west and damned if there wasn't a cut for a street that ran off through there.

Ditched me. Do I not like that.

He stood sweating behind the steakhouse. A short guy in an apron banged out the back screen door, cigarette already in his mouth. Slapped his pockets then raised his face to Phelan as if to a deck officer passing out life jackets.

Phelan tossed him a matchbook from Leon's.

Well. Unfair as it is to you and misguided as they are, everyone cannot love Tom Phelan. Your second case is finished. Get the money to the bank.

In the morning, Miss Wade counted the bills in the envelope Phelan handed her and block-printed a deposit slip for State National Bank. Then she looked up and listened to the story of the payoff.

Phelan strolled around a while and came back. "Know anything about wigs?"

"Little."

"'Scuse me, but how?"

Her eyes flicked toward him then away. "Woman I knew,

her hair came out in fistfuls. She got her mother to send her a wig cause she didn't want a answer to Cueball or Baldylocks."

"Tell me how a wig looks different than real hair."

"Well, less they're wore out, they look shiny. And all the hair's one same color, no streaks or anything." She ran a hand through her own ash brown hair. Some of the strands were lighter, sunnier than others. Phelan leaned over. Her hair smelled like lemons.

"You don't see any scalp, just this seam of hair, and it's better they have bangs cause if they don't the hairline looks like the end of a kitchen table."

"Mrs. Elliott has brunette hair like that. Bangs. Very shiny."

"And?"

"And...and I don't know. You just have the phone number for her, right?"

"Yeah. That one she'll answer on Tuesdays or Fridays at eight in the morning. Before she has to go to work. She says. We got no address for her."

"Lloyd'll be in the book." Phelan strolled a few more steps, stopped and glanced back at her. "Thanks for saying 'we.' "

He got a stare followed by a nod. He hesitated, feeling on delicate ground, tapped his pencil. After a while, shooting her a glance, he asked, "You know any blackmailers, Miss Wade?"

She'd been starting to smile, but her head went down then. Silence floated like a buoy between them.

"Of the people I meet these days, Mr. Phelan, you and Joe Ford and Miss Doris and Calinda Blanchard know I been in prison. 'Cept for Mr. Ford, that has to, they hadn't found more than one occasion to refer to it. You need to know something I learned from my past, ask me straight out. I'll tell you. Just don't act like my slip is showing."

If Phelan'd had the hammer from the P.I. kit in his trunk,

he'd have whacked himself with it. "That's a pact," he said softly.

She looked off toward the window as she spoke. "We're dealing with a wife don't trust her husband here but, in case she's taking somebody else for a ride, you don't want it to be us."

Phelan raised his index finger together with the one middle finger he had left and tipped them both toward his secretary.

"OK then," she said. "Blackmailers. Some just see a chance. But the other kind think you got something that's theirs. May be true. But it don't have to be, that doesn't matter. May be some piddly thing. In prison it gets real piddly. May not even be a thing, just your attention or some favor they think they deserve. What matters is they get what they want. They win. You don't. You do not win. Only thing that matters. Understand?"

"Got it. Thanks. Mrs. Elliott's out to win, I can believe that. It's what she wants to win that I'm not too clear about." He was walking around. Stalling. Why was he doing that? He slipped his hands in his pockets.

"OK then. Say hello to Debbie at the bank."

"Think Debbie would ruther you say your own hello's. Just a idea I got."

Debbie had greeted him the day he went in to open a business account, and Phelan had recognized her right away, bleached hair and all. After the army, Phelan had spent a lot of down time with Debbie McClary, partying across the Louisiana line at The Oaks or The Pelican Club or lying zonked on Crystal Beach. In those days her dark hair had been stiff with salt water. Him with sand in his crack, a cooler with beers bobbing, the waves rushing like erasers over Phelan's mind.

"Debbie's an old friend from a lost time," he said. "Why don't you take the rest of the day off, Miss Wade. I'm going to."

XIV

HAVING A DAY, and having the day off—like having fudge
icing on top of pecan pie. Back at the New Rosemont, she
asked Calinda did she have anything to fish with. Calinda
went and pried open a door at the end of a corridor, rooted
around. The storeroom inside was a treasury of broke-down
furniture and headless lamps, lame floor sweepers, yellow
stacks of papers jumbled one over another—could have been a
lease for the Lucas gusher itself in there somewhere leveling
up a bedstead that last saw happy action during Prohibition.
The rattling and prying went on for some time. Finally,
batting webs out of her stubby hair, she heisted out a pole
with some line on it.

Held out the keys to her '55 Ford, too. "Bus doesn't take
you to fishing holes. You know how to drive?"

Half-smile from Delpha. "I can't wait to remember. You
got a hat, Miss Blanchard?"

Miss Blanchard did, a straw with a wide brim for shade.
In return, she wanted Delpha to do some grocery shopping for
the hotel.

Delpha considered driving all the way down to Rollover
Pass, putting her cane in the water and letting the Gulf's salt
air soften her thoughts. But she ended up rubbing 6-12 on
her arms, hands, neck, and face, rolling down the long plaid

sleeves of her Goodwill shirt and heading for a bayou. She bought a container full of worms and three hours with a squat little boat and outboard.

A lank-haired white woman wearing overalls over a tank top took her money, then plopped down in an aluminum lawn chair, hauled up onto her lap a blond thumb-sucker with a doll, and turned back to the black and white TV flickering behind the counter. Another blond girl, older, maybe ten, jumped up from behind the counter, flapping a coloring book and crayon, making sounds at the woman, who raised two fingers and snapped them downward. The girl's face crumpled. She made a fist and rolled it repeatedly at the woman. The thumb-sucker copied her sister, letting go of the doll in order to wiggle her fist in the mother's face.

The mother snuck a sideways glance at Delpha, mumbled, "They cain't hear." She made a waving-off motion. The older girl imitated that, her face questioning. The mother rolled a fist at her. The blond girl grinned. She and the coloring book disappeared behind the counter. Delpha said, "Bye-bye," made her own wave. The littler girl popped the thumb from her mouth and waved bye-bye, big, open-mouthed smile. Nothing from the other one.

Delpha walked out to the dock and chose a boat. None of them looked perky.

She yanked the cord, and the Evinrude bucked up. Hadn't known if she could stand being out here, but now—just riding over the brown water eased a clench in her stomach. She wound around the channels, minding her direction, the bowing willow there, stand of reeds and cattails, ahead some cypress she veered right to avoid. She cut the engine and as the boat eased on a ways of its own silent accord, the insect-singing—the bugs, the frogs, the locusts, the whole chittering, clicking, sawing, whirring choir—descended over her like a lofted sheet on its airy way back down.

Delpha let out a breath that felt fourteen years trapped. May be that these bayou channels weren't wide as two-lane. May be the trees folded over and clutched, paring the sky to a high blue strip, thickening the green shadows. She could hear laughter floating back over the water, a kid's yell. Didn't matter. She couldn't see them.

Alone. A better alone even than in the hotel where there were walls and people noise. Noises everywhere out here, but they added up to one big quiet. There was no next cell, next door, next hall, line up, count off, lay down, shut up, lights go out, lights flip on. No concrete in sight, no khaki guard with B.O.-black armpits, no potato peel to scrape off linoleum with your thumbnail, no reek and burn of bleach. Nobody griping, fighting, crying in the night, lying, spinning such backwards bullshit sometimes you'd wrap your arms around the poor woman and hold her until she just ran out of it. More times you wanted to bust her skull with a ladle for the soul-nourishing crunch of it. Make her quit that sweetie wishy voice or the chin-out bragging one. Man got her in here would not be shifting one foot to the other waiting for her when they let her out. Kids she hadn't seen in seven years wouldn't holler Mama and come flinging to her. Hell, they grew up without her and they got accounts too. God, no thigh fat jamming hers on a dining hall bench, no screaming overhead light, no used Kotex smeared across a bathroom wall so a finger could write in it.

Delpha opened the cardboard container full of dirt and reddish veins. Pulled out a rubbery worm and dropped it into the bayou. Little fish head appeared, big old mouth, nipped it down. If she'd stayed in her room, she'd have paced around.

Here she could breathe air. She dropped in another worm, to see the splash and the rings. Did this for a while, fed the fish.

Fourteen years without touch save a few women with chapped hands, a shoulder-patting chaplain, and a fat guard captain who liked to make her lay over a desk in the furniture supply room, liked to say, *What you gone do, kill me?*

She set the faded orange life preserver down in the boat and sat on it, leaned her elbows back on the wood seat. Drifted some, paddled a couple times so the line would drag the water. Sky and water and the keening of presence. Pole-tall pines and bending willow and the yaupon and the slim grasses of the land were here, grasses that bowed and nodded and stood. The stirring water and all the swimmers singers flyers burrowers and twiners, sun spot prying through the brim of Calinda Blanchard's straw hat. A splash and rings of water.

Eventually she threaded a worm on the hook. Careful not to hang up in the reeds, she tossed out her line. By the time the sun was slanting, she had dropped back a few baby bream and caught three fair-size bass. Plastic bucket in the boat. She put them in that. She was sitting top of the seat by then, water sloshing in the boat bottom had soaked her tennies. Egret in the reeds. Mosquito whine. She was about to start the Evinrude when a broad stick drifted by. Only it wasn't a stick, it was a gator submerged past the eyes. She jerked the cord, the motor ground, sputtered and caught, loud. The egret lifted off flapping, coasted to another landing farther down the bank. The stick put on a spurt of speed, away down the brown channel.

End of her fishing day. Two dollar deposit for Delpha to collect, somebody's kids popping up and down hollering *RC Cola* and *Eskimo pie*, a teenager and a couple of sweaty men with six packs weighing down their arms. The woman with the deaf kids was not behind the counter.

It was an old man in stained khakis, a flat ball cap low on his forehead.

Not long after somebody hits you in the mouth, your lips swell tight. Maybe the skin splits, maybe it holds, but it burns so that every second you are aware of it like you are never aware of skin. That was happening to Delpha, all over.

The old man yawned in her face as he pushed her deposit across the counter. To a fisherman blustering about having to bail his leaky boat, he said *You knew it was a piece of shit you got in it. Git outa here, pal, go git you a ocean liner.* His hand ranged under the counter and the customer left grumbling but the counterman's voice—which Delpha, stepped back, the two bills crushed in her hand, had been waiting to hear—was bored. Bored, the threat in it a tired habit. She stepped back up, scooped a peanut patty from the shelves underneath the counter. Eyes rolling past her, he handed her ninety cents change. There was the scar. Where it should be, starting at the wrist and rising, the way the veins ran. Where she put it.

He stooped to get some Redman for the teenage boy. The back of his neck was crosshatched, cheeks flabby, neck skin dragging. His speckled arms were burned brown except for the raised white scar underside of the arm.

This old man had claimed he tried to stop his boy from hurting her, got cut for his efforts. His word against hers. The cops, the judge, the jury—he pissed down their backs and told them it was raining. What he had done was slammed Delpha's face into the plank floor, raped her and turned loose his son. That son. The son straddled her back, gripped up her hair and carved into her neck. Each line a long sting that did not abate and a warm falling off to either side. Punched her in the head when she struggled. Did that till he was hard enough, flipped her and climbed on top. Bucked and slammed but he couldn't come, couldn't come.

Then finally a stuttering grunt burst from him and his eyes rolled back. Fingers slacked apart, and he lost his hold on the knife. Delpha had had to skin it across her throat to grip it in her right hand. The blade was facing toward him or she'd have cut her own throat.

Headlights raked across a window. The old man'd jumped after the knife. Blade up like that, she'd dug, opening his arm wrist to elbow. He'd lurched back, and the son rared up—she stuck it into his chest. The young man made that knuckly fist again, but he was only swatting. Rolled onto his back, said "Daddy." The old one looked at him, but then he ran.

There are true words for a place and a time—like funeral words, promises, gratitude, apology words. Remorse was a parole-board word. Those two men'd had a gun, she'd have been in the bayou fifteen years. There was nothing in her world truer than that.

She was in the old groove, the old *When* and *How*. She turned the Ford into Weingarten's Grocery, harked briefly to a voice coming from a car in the next parking space, jawing about owning a '55 Ford too, and how it ran for a hundred forty thousand miles…Delpha walked off. The three fish she caught were wrapped in newspaper on the front seat: she couldn't tarry.

Five loaves of Rainbo bread, four dozen eggs, margarine, four packages of bacon, two giant-size cans of Folger's. She pulled it all off the shelves like she was fighting somebody for it.

Her arms were full with the two sacks. Out by the store doors, a little girl in dirty pink shorts and impetigo legs was parked on a galloping horse machine still pretending to ride the thing after her quarter was spent. Leaning toward her was a smiler in a short-sleeved shirt offering out a box of gumdrops.

"This your child?"

The guy straightened up, gripping his affable expression, his ground. Thought maybe he could smile her by, let him get back to it.

"Have some gumdrops 'fore they all stick together, young lady."

Delpha's head was shaking No.

"All y'all," she said. "Ever goddamn one. Playing like you ain't a rattler. You just ain't been stepped on yet."

His nice smile flatlined, and he slid away down the sidewalk.

She set her brown paper sacks down on the hot concrete, lifted the little girl off the saddle of the butterscotch-colored horse with the bucky teeth, carried her on her hip into Weingarten's. She seated the child on the Customer Service counter and told the manager to call the mother on his loudspeaker. The young man plucked a quarter from his pocket, said, like it was bonus points for her Green Stamps book, "On us. Let the little buckaroo ride some more."

"Call her," Delpha said.

His undershot chin moved back into his neck. He made a production out of returning the quarter to his pocket. Then he flipped a switch and picked up a microphone on a short gooseneck. "Will the mother of the little girl out on our hobbyhorse please come get her at the Customer Service Booth?"

Delpha stretched tiptoe over the counter to get into the vicinity of the microphone. Raised her voice.

"Before another pervert tries to lure her off, you stupid bitch."

Rung out good.

The checkers and shoppers snapped around. Depha

strode out the door again, snatched up her groceries by the riderless horse. The crown of her head was afire. Her mind was burning. Not just with the old man back at the bayou, but—how's she sposed to not see this stuff? People preying on kids, preying on other people. Others of them act surprised, act scandalized. *Oh, that's just terrible, that's a shame*, and then they go their way. The girls at Gatesville would agree with the terrible, with the shame, but surprise—c'mon. Who hadn't been messed with there, who hadn't been broke?

Car smelled like a dead whale.

She carried in Calinda's groceries, filled the refrigerator. Leaned over the sink and gutted the fish, went out the hotel's alley door and dropped the slimy mess on yesterday's newspaper. Cats already galloping, necks stretched, as she turned to go back in, the tan ones that would have been white if they got a scrub, the one-eyed tom.

What was she going to do about that old man? She had meditated on that question since she was eighteen years old. Each answer had been handled and put back tattered. The first answer, move away from Beaumont, move up north or to California and never come back—she'd blown that one. Now she knew he was still alive, knew where he worked.

Forgive, like the chaplain explained to her?

"I'm just advising you to let it go. Not to turn the other cheek."

Good he wasn't because those two made sure Delpha had done that.

"Your problem is a conundrum."

Several chaplains rotated through Gatesville, but Delpha cared to see only this one. His harelip repair looked to have been sewn with twine. His shirt was pressed even if the collar had creases ironed in it. He'd shaved, his nails were clean; he didn't come through the gates like this was some backyard crawdad-boil. Delpha credited him for that. During her next visit to the prison library, she lingered over that word, *conundrum*, in the donated Webster's Dictionary with the loose spine. She credited the chaplain for that too, because of how it made her feel—changing the sound *co-nun-drum*—into a word, into a meaning that stopped, for a while, every noise and movement around her while it told her a secret about her life.

The chaplain said, "Miss Wade." That's what he called her. Not Wade. Not Delpha right-off, before he'd been invited to. "Miss Wade, the forgiveness is not for his sake, it's for yours. As long as you allow yourself to harbor hate, you're the one it hurts."

She'd flared at him. "That hate was rammed into me."

He held up his hand. "Far be it from me to argue. But here is the point. That man doesn't have the hate now, does he?"

"I don't know. Probably not."

"Who does?"

"Me. So."

"It is poisoning you. Not him. You."

She'd understood that, but had not been able to use it.

Some of the cops had been on her side. She remembered that well. Fontenot. Merriweather. They couldn't do anything. Her word against the old man she had cut, father of a murdered son. Sat up in the court alongside the deceased's drooping mother and a little sister attached like a tick to the mother's side, that was how it'd been. A crime long judged, bought and paid for.

Delpha took Calinda's paring knife and scraped silver scales from the gutted fish. Always came down to the one thing, always did.

She could kill him.

XV

PHELAN HAD IT in mind to score some tacos al carbon and watch baseball on the couch. Atlanta was scheduled to play, and Hank might just smack another homerun. Phelan's '69 Chevelle though, that car suffered from steering issues. It passed the taco place and meandered him out to the refinery part of town, where he located Daughtry Petrochemical at the edge of the industrial zone. Welders, pavers, concrete guys bordering the refineries themselves: great gray cities of pipe, tanks, burning flares like flags flying, acres of cars and pickups in the lots fronting the office building. Blacktop in summer was gummy tar, heat from the operations combining to offer a hundred-twenty degree blast coming at you up down and sideways.

The address he had matched a long low brick building, probably twenty, thirty years old. A faded red on white sign reading Daughtry Petrochemical hung half off its uprights, two workmen lowering it down. Out of business?

He knew it. Enroco killed Daughtry, and they just didn't say so in the paper.

He parked the Chevelle a fair distance away from the only two cars in the blacktop parking lot. Both Ramblers. What were the odds? One was a plain old two-door, but the other was a '58 wagon with braided chrome trim, be flashy if it'd been washed within the last decade. Maybe employees were inside cleaning out their desks. Or their lockers or lab or shop, whatever was left of Daughtry.

Phelan thought he caught a glimpse of someone by the Rambler wagon, but when he turned to get a good look, there was nobody.

He entered to find an office, wooden counter running across the front. Framed pictures of the place hung on the wall leading up to it. A stout, late-middle-aged woman behind the counter leaned over a desk, setting file folders in towering piles. Boxes sat on the floor around her. Cleaning out her desk sure enough. Daughtry Petrochemical was finished. Mentally, Phelan bent his right hand fingers, blew on them, and buffed his lapel.

She looked up and frowned. "Oh, I wasn't 'sposed to unlock that door. But I'm so used to unlocking it every morning, I forgot. I'm sorry. We're closed today." The woman wore a black suit, sheened polyester, over a white blouse tied at the neck in a floppy bow. Black patent leather shoes with gold buckles. Pretty formal outfit for packing up.

"Closed," Phelan echoed.

She wrenched open a sticky desk drawer, rummaged. The motion unbalanced a precarious stack of folders, which began to slide. "Oh no. No, don't you dare." She threw her hands out, rescuing the top one while the ones below splatted onto the floor, spilling out sheets of paper.

"Oh, my goodness." She started to kneel down.

Two seconds, and Phelan was through a little gate and behind the counter. "Lemme help you," he said. "You'll get yourself dirty." He squatted and stuffed pages back into the manila sleeves, handed them up to her. He smiled while noting file titles—lengthy, nonsense words that might be names of chemicals.

"Aren't you sweet? Wait, let me get a box." She took the

folders as he handed them to her and set them in the box. "Should of done it this way in the first place, Margaret, you goose," she said.

"That your name, Margaret?"

"Margaret Hanski, yes."

Phelan stuck out his hand. "I'm Tom."

"Nice to meet you, Tom. You didn't come to see Mr. Daughtry, did you? Cause he's not here."

"No, just intended to check out your products for my company. Maybe meet some personnel. We're branching out down this way."

Margaret scalded him with a glance. "You from New Jersey? You don't sound Yankee."

A crash came from somewhere beyond the wall, glass breaking, some muffled exclamation. Phelan turned toward the sounds, but Margaret didn't.

"No, ma'am. Beaumont boy."

"Thought so. It's just lotsa the big companies have headquarters up north, and they just barge down here and tell people what to do. Mr. Daughtry would never have let anyone tell him what to do with his company."

"You sound sad about Daughtry's closing."

"Oh, just the lab's closing. Not the office. We're moving the office over to Broadway. Old house that's been restored— my lord, the woodwork! Oh, I meant to give you this." She plucked a card from the drawer.

"Then, would you say...business is booming?"

Her chin turned. "Yes, moving. I already said that."

"Booming," Phelan said, louder.

"The business is doing very well," she said stiffly. "We're becoming more financially-orientated. It's just that it's happening so fast."

Phelan unpatted his own head. Daughtry not slaughtered. Moving. Figure that.

The folders were boxed. Phelan stood up. "Can I help you with anything else?"

"Oh no, thank you. I'll be leaving soon for the reception. Let me give your card to Mr. Daughtry. I'll make sure he gets it," she said. "And I'll tell him how helpful you were." She smiled.

"Thank you, but I'll just catch him at your new...place," Phelan said, tucking the card into his jacket pocket.

"No, please. I'll be glad to do it." Her hand was out.

Phelan tried a charming smile. "Don't bother, ma'am."

"No bother at all." Mock-sternly, she said, "Just give me that card, boy."

Fake cards. Damn, he should have thought of this situation before.

Her hand kept reaching toward him.

"You know, that's a handsome suit. Elegant."

She looked down, spanked on a piece of skirt that covered her thigh. "Thank you. There's the reception this afternoon. Plato and I're going—"

"Plato?"

"Plato Willis is our assistant chemist. Little smart aleck's somewhere round here." Focusing on the black suit darkened Margaret's chipper mood. "You know, they say bad things happen in threes. We lost our head chemist, Mr. Robbins. Terrible. Been expecting it for some time. Then my daughter-in-law just up and lost her baby, like to cried her eyes out and me with her. I swear. They got all boys, and they just knew this one would be a little girl. Samantha, they were going to call her."

"I'm so sorry. Was there a third sorrow?"

"Well, yes. Mr. Daughtry's been under the weather, and a few days ago, just like that, he's gone. You hadn't heard that?"

Phelan hadn't. "My condolences, ma'am. What was it that...what did Mr. Daughtry die from?"

"Oh, he's not dead, he's in Arizona. With his daughter. I would've heard if he'd died, why, John Daughtry and I have worked together thirty-four years. He's always suffered from sugar diabetes, and when he got this awful bug that swam out of his stomach into his bloodstream, his daughter moved him out there. John's wife's passed, you know. His son—" Flick of her eyelashes. "And with us so depending on foreign oil. This gas crisis we have. You know how much oil this country is importing now? Thirty-six percent from foreign countries and Mr. Daughtry—"

"And Mr. Daughtry sick, you say. Must be tough for him."

"After forty-two years in his business, business he built with his own two hands, well, I shouldn't say this, but he handled it better when Marjorie died. That was his wife. Having to leave the business broke his heart in two."

"Since the company is relocating, you said"—he didn't want to bring up the card again—"who's taken over for him? Not that anyone could fill his shoes but..."

"You don't know? Mr. Wallace Daughtry." A hitch of her upper lip. "He restored that place on Broadway to live in, piled it full of pricey antiques. Now he's decided it's going to be his office. And his father's chair still warm." Margaret shook her head. "Excuse me, that was uncalled for. Now, I know I was about to do something, wasn't I?" She narrowed her eyes.

Before she could remember his card, Phelan formed a sandwich of the secretary's hand between his. "Thank you for your time. Privilege to meet you, Margaret."

She was responding "And you too," when a car braked hard outside, making her startle toward the window.

The man appeared in the office so fast he might have *Star Trek*-teleported. Lanky guy, 30s. Bolo tie with a hunk of turquoise. Western-cut suit, tight to the butt and a flare to the trousers. Looked like he was sewed in it.

"I thought I told you to keep the office locked today."

Margaret blinked rapidly, her lips parted. Her jaw moved a couple times before she said, "I'm sorry, Wallace. I just forgot for a minute."

"A minute. Only takes a minute to lock the damn door. The files are sensitive stuff."

"I am really sorry." Her miserable expression lightened momentarily. "Oh. Oh, I forgot. I had copies cut of your new office keys, like you asked me to. Didn't know exactly how many you wanted, so I had Sears cut—"

"You keep saying *forgot*, Margaret."

"Only twice," Phelan put in quietly.

"Who's this joker?" Wallace hooked his thumb at Phelan, who smiled and stuck out his hand, murmured an indecipherable company name.

"This is a salesman happened by—" Margaret trailed off.

"And waltzed right in the front door. A salesman." Wallace Daughtry had eyes like black ball bearings. He head-butted the air. "Hit it, buddy. Plato back there?"

"Yes, he's in the lab. I *do* apologize, Mr. Daughtry, for forgetting to—"

"You still have all our keys, don't you?"

"Course I do. In my purse like always. Including those spare keys for the new office, like I just said. Or wait, maybe I put those ones in my top desk drawer. Surely not. Oh dear, I know it's one or the other. Let me look—"

"No."

The snapped order stilled Margaret.

"Later. You know, Margaret, your game needs upping. You—" Wallace Daughtry glared at her. "Oh, never mind." He spun on a boot heel and went out the door again, passed in front of the window. There was the sound of a door opening and some voices.

Once Phelan had determined that he couldn't make out the men's conversation, he turned to Margaret, who stood precisely as she had when Daughtry, Jr. had spoken to her, pale, her neck above the floppy white bow beginning to blotch in squarish red patches. He said a quiet "Thank you again, ma'am," lightly touching Margaret Hanski on the shoulder, and navigated his way outside, where he cut around, taking a last survey. The Daughtry Petrochemical sign lay prone in the parking lot. But out front of a house on Broadway Avenue, there'd be a new sign.

A side door was propped open, and Wallace in his tight Western suit was haranguing into it in a low tone, index finger out, arm chopping. Phelan slipped into the Chevelle and started it. Messed with the visor and a polishing rag on the inside windshield until young Daughtry slammed himself into a shiny Datsun 240Z, metallic blue, and did as he'd advised Phelan to do—hit it.

Phelan climbed out of his car and walked over to the side door. A small man with his arms around a cardboard box was backing out. He turned, breeze scattering his pale, flyaway hair, and Phelan caught a startled glint behind the wire-rimmed glasses before the man scuttled back over the threshold.

Janitor, mover, assistant chemist, first name Plato? Phelan shaded his eyes to peer in at the man hugging the box. Wallace must have scared all the blood south to this guy's Earth shoes because he had the chalkiest face Phelan had seen outside of a Johnny Winter album. Sweating too.

He offered his hand. "Good afternoon. Plato Willis? Assistant chemist, right?"

"You are?"

"Salesman. I was sorry to learn John Daughtry was sick, but my time's not lost if I make a few contacts. That was Mr. Daughtry's son that just left, I take it? Man in a hurry."

"Yeah, that was Moondark the Soulless." The guy studied Phelan's hand, looked him up and down and said, "Salesman? And I'm John Carter, Warlord of Mars." He kicked loose the doorstop and pulled the metal door shut.

Phelan slipped his spurned hand into his pocket and walked back out to the Chevelle which, surely now, would agree to stop at the *sabroso* Tacos La Bamba. He just might get home in time to watch Hank hammer number 690.

XVI

DELPHA, SHOWERED AND dressed for Mrs. Spier's house, met Mr. Rabey slogging up the stairs. He stretched out a hand to peck her arm. As this right hand spent its day caressing his pants' zipper, she took her arm back while lowering her ear to him.

"Today's Hettie's birthday," he said direly. His eyebrows perked with significance.

She understood she was tipped. "Well. All right."

"Delpha! Delpha, come here." Mrs. Bibbo was waving from the sofa by the television. Delpha swerved from her route to the kitchen and went over to her.

"Evening. How's the hearings?"

Mrs. Bibbo was the New Rosemont's Watergate expert. Banks of men in suits filled the screen. A young man with a steep forehead was bending his neck to a microphone.

"Nothing new. But...thirty-five times," said the old lady, shaking her head tightly.

"What?"

"That's what he said all last week—thirty five times that young man there talked with the President about covering up the Watergate break-in. That Nixon says he never heard of even once. Not even Al Capone's mob was as bad as this gang. Capone was just bootlegging liquor. This is not whiskey. This is America the brave! These men lie, and they cheat, and they show no shame. Just so they can have all the power. Every one of them will tell you they deserve what they have. But when they're alone in the dark"—Mrs. Bibbo tapped her own chest, the gentle slope above the magnificent breasts at her waist—"they know."

The young man's top lip glistened in the TV camera.

"Oh, and,"—now her finger wagged like a teacher's—"it's Hettie's birthday."

Delpha nodded gravely.

Mr. Finn and Mr. Nystrom, at the game table, had already put aside their playing cards and were waiting, bright-eyed and courteous, for Delpha to draw even with them. They both cleared their throats, then glanced at each other with irritation.

"Afternoon, Mr. Finn, Mr. Nystrom."

"Afternoon, Miss Wade. Did she tell you? You should know."

"Well, I hear it's somebody's birthday today."

"She heard, Harry. No need to chew her ear off," said Mr. Finn, but that answer did not stave off Mr. Nystrom.

"Are you hungry? Because we have some cheese and crackers in our rooms. Simon and me'll share with you. Cheddar cheese. Not that Swiss stuff with holes."

"That's nice of you. You two not eating dinner?"

"There's no dinner. It's Hettie's birthday."

She had to ask but experience had taught Delpha that, with these two, asking beckoned to a herd of randy stories. Some were even worth hearing. Mr. Finn there had been a high school science teacher become doughboy in the Argonne Forest. But Mr. Nystrom had sold restaurant supplies, napkins, forks, eggbeaters, what have you. Never knew which one would get the floor—and she had her heart set on a cup of coffee before catching the bus out to Mrs. Speir's. Nothing out there but instant. She thanked them and headed toward the kitchen.

Oscar burst out of the door still in his cook's whites.

Dapper type with a solid fan club in the sisterhood, Oscar liked his bellbottoms, his broad lapels and cologne. Now he was booking for the street wet, in a sudsy apron.

"Any coffee left?" she asked him.

"Everybody for their ownself." He untied the apron behind his back. Mrs. Bibbo scatted her hand at Delpha, who almost followed Oscar out the door. No, she could just run in and get a cup. She'd be quick. Thinking about the four hours at Mrs. Speir's mausoleum, she turned back and entered the kitchen.

No electric lights on, just the slant light of a summertime evening. The kitchen was black and gray and yellow-white, the grill and stove cold. Ten-inch bread knife lay on the floor not far from her shoes. Delpha angled back to the kitchen door, then to the knife again. Could have been thrown, bonked off the door, landed where it was.

On the chopping table, a low-tide bottle of Four Roses and another lined up touching, its bosom friend.

Delpha surrendered the coffee idea.

Down past the end of the table, between it and two refrigerators, Miss Blanchard was folded over a guitar, playing a melody on the bass strings and strumming on the high ones. Delpha had heard the tune—even before she'd listened to the Grand Old Opry broadcasts with a bunch of other women at Gatesville, carried on the radio. A voice rumbled, and she wouldn't have recognized the blue of it for Calinda Blanchard's had it not been that this here was her kitchen, and there she sat on a kitchen stool.

I never will marry or be no man's wife
I expect to live single all the days of my life
My love's gone and left me, the one I adore
She's gone where I never will see her anymore

Mother Maybelle's song. Miss Blanchard sang the tune even lower, but with more breath than lift on the high notes. The guitar stopped as she came up for a swig of bourbon.

"Can I make you up a plate?" Delpha murmured, careful to put no more tone in her voice than a stray gust of wind. "Sandwich? Leftovers? Get you anything?"

The old woman reached, tilted the bottle long and banged it back on the table, wiped her lips on the shoulder of her shirt. "Yeah. 1942. 1943. Go get me 1944, how 'bout."

Dim light. Dark of the open pantry stretched back without end.

"If I could fetch back missing years, Miss Blanchard, I'd do it for you. Fetch back fourteen for me."

Miss Blanchard was peering toward Delpha, but it didn't seem like she was seeing her. The old woman finished the bottle and heaved it straight-on at Delpha's head. A rush of air riffled the hair by her left ear. The bottle smashed on the kitchen door, Delpha raring back from its flying glass. She slid on shards as she scurried from the kitchen.

Mr. Finn and Mr. Nystrom were standing shoulder to shoulder outside, out of the range of the door. One clutched a white sleeve of Saltines and the other a block of orange cheese. "We told you," Mr. Nystrom scolded.

"Hettie was her sweetheart, huh?" Delpha said.

Mr. Finn said, "Jack that used to rent #313 told us she was a service pilot, or training to be, over at Ellington Field. During the war. There was a fire." Mr. Finn's head was lowered. "C'mon, Harry. The girl didn't know. It's her first birthday here."

To a one, the inhabitants of the New Rosemont's lobby stared toward her balefully. Well, she'd drink instant tonight. She called up Isaac on the pay phone and put him off till tomorrow.

*

They had drunk two plastic water glasses of beer apiece, she and Isaac, because Oscar had been running out to the store for butter, and Delpha had held out two dollars and asked him to buy some Pearl.

"Correct me now, baby, but I'm believing you old enough to buy beer," Oscar said.

So Miss Blanchard had not told her cook about Delpha's record. That was an interesting thing to know about her landlady. She extended the dollar bills.

They looked each other in the face until Oscar's chin went up and his eyes half-closed like a cat's. He took the money.

Delpha and Isaac had done it three times, the second time pulling and shoving, and the third, just as they started to get up from that fight, they went back down. He lay flat on his back when they finished, breathing so you could hear it. Delpha slid off and over sideways. Tears bolted from her eyes. There was no stopping them, the way there would be no stopping if you stumbled into a hole you never saw as you approached it, a hole wider than your own flailing arms, that offered no handhold, no ledge to hinder your fall. Delpha rolled and buried her face in the pillow, pressing the flat thing to her ears with both hands, helpless as the surge pumped through, as it poured.

Isaac was kneeling on the bed, trying to turn her around. "Did I do something wrong? What can I do?"

She shook her head, rubbing her face against the pillow.

"If it's me you can tell me, and I'll try to fix whatever it is. But if it's something else, let me help, OK? Is it your family? You never talk about them. Is someone sick or in trouble?"

She pushed the pillow up to her forehead. It was OK now. Gone. "It's not you."

"Delpha. Delpha, turn over. No lie, I would do anything for you. Or for anyone in your family. I have some money saved. You can have it. I'd do anything."

Delpha turned toward him. He was looming over her, all that dark hair tumbled around his smooth, bony face, the wide shoulders caved in.

"Thanks."

"Tell me."

"I don't know, I can't really. Lemme up."

"Wait. Go somewhere with me. We're always here in this room. Not that it isn't my favorite place to be. But I want to take you somewhere. Wherever you want. I don't mean right now but another time."

"You hungry?" Delpha rose, took the slip from the chair back and put it over her head, pulled on her dress.

"I'm not three and distractible, I'm twenty. And capable of helping you. If it's something that can be helped."

"It's not, Isaac. I'm hungry. Be right back."

Fifteen minutes later, Isaac had his jeans on, and they were sitting on the floor of her room with forks, eating out of a saucepot of spaghetti and meatballs she'd heated up in the kitchen. No use in dirtying up two plates to wash, she told him. He twirled the spaghetti, stuck mounds of it into his mouth. Starving, naturally. He talked about where they might go. He could take his mother to work and have the car all day. Or he could drive his dad's car.

Something after two in the morning, in a room in the New Rosemont Hotel. Crickets singing through the screen. Spaghetti a mite gluey. She ate the last spoonfuls of Oscar's savory, garlicky sauce, licked the spoon, and smiled at Isaac's offer. "Your dad's."

Dark, but she could see, and he could see, they were used

to it. She and him had traded bodies, given them, taken them, she'd unburied an old channel of sorrow that opened up, that poured, and she wasn't acting.

Hesitantly, Isaac asked her about the scars on her neck. Delpha swallowed a mouthful of sauce and replied that they were from a childhood accident.

XVII

"HEY, TOM, HOW'S the investigating business?"

"Doing all right, Miles. How's the lawyering?"

"Besides the eighty hours a week, I can't complain. Listen, you still on that case with Daughtry?"

"No, but it's still on me, if you know what I mean."

"Well, I heard something last night that called our conversation to mind. I was at an Oil and Gas Development dinner. My brother-in-law, the Ph.D., was getting a plaque for some sort of packaging design."

"Like Christmas wrapping?"

"Near enough. Couple guys hanging out in the bar mentioned your case. They were skipping the speeches—"

"Since you weren't giving one."

"Bull-shitter. These guys were three, four sheets to the wind. Talking about the deal Daughtry and Enroco cut on a formula for a new oil-based drilling mud. I got my bourbon and just stood with my back to them. These guys were slinging terms around, diesel, additives, those're easy ones, but couldn't help you with the particular emulsifiers, polymers, whatevers. Want the scuttlebutt I *could* understand?"

"Lay it on me."

"I had to bend over backward. All this time I'm thinking, *What, what's so hot about it, man, what?* Then the first guy said a mud not made out of diesel but ordinary old vegetable oil."

"Talking Crisco."

"Not a clue. But they had a hardon for this formula."

Phelan knew why. Contamination. Of water, fish, wetlands. Hell, dry land. But he let Miles tell him, people liked to tell things. And part of what Miles said surprised him, after all.

"Diesel'll kill fish. If it runs off into fields, it'll kill the crops. They're not too worried about that. But whatever this vegetable formula is, it *fertilizes* crops."

Neither Miles nor Phelan said anything for a while.

"OK." Phelan cleared his throat. "So Daughtry had this vegetable formula. Enroco got ahold of it somehow, Daughtry sued. How are they gonna prove who had it first?"

"Besides testimony from the guys who invented it? Notes. Logbook. Chemists keep a log of their development process. All down there. Day by day. Year by year."

"OK, and a logbook could be copied."

"If someone had the original to copy from."

"Right. Maybe there were dueling logbooks. Maybe just one. Whatever—either Enroco's lawyers or Lloyd Elliott managed to broker a deal between them and Daughtry. A payoff. Or percentages of a future product. Or both, how the fuck would I know?"

Phelan caught himself—shouldn't say stuff like *How would I know* out loud. Private eyes were supposed to know or find out.

"How much did Lloyd Elliott get out of it?"

"All negotiable. Everything would be on the table."

His adrenalin had risen, stupid, given the zero peso return. This case was dead as a crab in crude, but it wouldn't stop skittering sideways.

"Just thought you might like to know. And, well, I'd like to throw a little business your way."

"All ears."

"We settled a case for a guy a while back, and now he's bugging me with some family problem he's got. Calls every day."

"What's he want?"

"A leg. Here's the phone number."

Phelan wrote it down. And waited.

"Don't let him play poor on you, he can pay. And how. Make him lose my phone number forever, and we're square for a favor in advance."

"I'll take the deal. You gonna tell me about the leg?"

"God, no. Let him. Please let him."

Phelan laughed. "Will do, Miles, owe you a drink. Or a bottle. What'll it be?"

"Milk. The wife's pregnant."

"Well, hey, congratulations."

"Thanks. We're pretty excited, first grandkid for both families. Gotta go. If Mr. Fortram loses his Jag to Mrs. Fortram, he's gonna drive one of his Ford 250's through my office. But I guess in your line, you know about divorces."

"Apparently not enough." Phelan thanked him and hung up. Daughtry seemed to lose but won. Enroco won. That was happy. Who lost? Phelan could think of a few possibilities.

The chemist. Think about watching something you invented pull in millions for your boss and squat for you. But he was dead. Maybe the assistant chemist, who was not? He lost. Margaret, long-time secretary, Our Lady of the Keys? But she hadn't lost her job. She was moving to the new office. Neither of them was likely to be blackmailing the company lawyer.

He'd check out that angle though, yes he would. Not right this minute but some minute very soon and without telling Delpha Wade. Now he would clock in on the Leg Case. One that Thomas Phelan, Private Investigator, would like to conclude satisfactorily in order to make the world less crummy for Miles Blankenship, Esquire, Attorney-at-Law.

James T. Miller, Jr., a.k.a. Private First Class J.T. Miller, retired, a.k.a. Nutbox, had two hostile siblings and an artificial leg. Thoroughbred of a leg, courtesy of a deluxe insurance policy owned by the trucker who had T-boned him after burning through a cherry red light. Mr. Miller was cut out of his '61 pickup and ferried away to Baptist Hospital, bleeding from most of his natural orifices and several newly opened ones. To hear him tell it—and Phelan had been required to hear Mr. Miller narrate it twice—James Miller had died on the table that midnight and floated up beyond his own body on a net of gold light.

"Wasn't white light?" Phelan had asked, just to interrupt the flow of the second telling.

"No, gold as 24-carat. With sparkles," Mrs. Miller put in, her tone solemn.

James, stump and rolled pant leg propped up on a coffee table, elbowed her and went on. There he lingered, hammocked on gold light beneath the ceiling tiles while surgeons cut away the leg the 18-wheeler had turned into strips and mush. Then he was sucked through a reddish channel wide as a good-size drainage pipe. Standing at the other end was his granddaddy who shooed him on back into the operating room.

"He didn't wanna come back. Not even to me." Mrs. Miller was ten years younger than her husband, a row of barrettes shaped like some kind of birds perched in her blondish hair.

"I'm telling this, Linda. You just go on." James hiked a crutch toward the kitchen and his wife went. He was a naturally wiry guy around thirty-five whose forehead sported creases already. Hadn't pumped-up his pecs and biceps, he might have weighed one forty and looked something like James Dean would have looked if he'd limped away from the Porche Spyder. A weight set and bench sat in the living room blocking a tall entertainment center.

James was proud of the leg. It fit the stump comfortably, bent smoothly at the knee, and had the right size foot so he could buy a regular pair of shoes just like anybody else. Or so Phelan understood from his wistful description because Mr. Miller was no longer in possession of his leg.

"You sure the police handed it over?" Phelan asked. Since he had an in with E.E., if the police were still holding it, he'd just have had to go down to the station and negotiate.

"Yeah. They showed me the paper. My brother Byron signed for it. Byron." Hurt and injustice compacted James Miller's forehead creases. "My big brother. I'd a walked hot coals for him, he asked me. Byron told them he was taking it to me. Cops got what they wanted and washed their hands of it. Said it's a family matter now." James Miller laughed sourly.

"Why would your brother and sister want your artificial leg?"

James turned to gaze out the window where there was nothing to see but an alley of grass and the side of the next house. His face was fixed hard. A muscle in his cheek twitched. "Jealous, maybe. I got this settlement." He waved his hand at the room as though toward stacks of gold newly spun from straw. "But I paid the price for it. They ain't."

OK. Phelan would leave that alone for now. He flipped open his small notebook. "Now tell me again why the police came to have it." He had some notes from a newspaper article Delpha had dug up. And he'd read it in the paper in the first place. But he wanted to hear his client's version. That part of the story had been rushed by for the sake of the celestial light, which an astounded James Miller still favored above little details like his getting shot.

"OK, I was at Barney's having a few beers and got into it with this know-it-all motorcycle rider. Beard, long hair—kid looked like a haystack with tattoos. He claimed Cassius Clay that calls himself Muhammad Ali was better than Joe Frazier. I said, "No way, no how." Now I didn't mean Ali can't fight, 'cause he can. What I meant was character. Ali dodged the draft. Joe Frazier didn't call him down for that. Hell, he testified to Congress *for* Ali, said they should let him back in the ring. Then come the Fight of the Century, Ali danced around calling Frazier Uncle Tom, callin' him a ugly gorilla."

Phelan murmured, "Fighting words. James, could we—"

"You said it. Fighting words. Ali promised if Frazier won, he'd crawl across the ring and admit Joe was the greatest. Well, Frazier won. Fifteen damn rounds. Unanimous. And Ali didn't admit shit! Listen here, in '64 Frazier won a Olympic gold medal with a busted left thumb. Didn't tell nobody he had it, just kept fighting for the U.S. of A. That's heart. That's balls. You understand that? Some people don't." James Miller's unshaven chin stuck out and his eyes burned.

"I'm not arguing with that. Appreciate your viewpoint. But cut to it, OK?"

Miller shot Phelan a sullen glance. "First tell me who you'd vote for."

Phelan had complicated feelings in the matter, but he knew the right answer here. "Smokin' Joe, straight down the line."

His client grinned and raised a crutch. "A'ight. Me and this hairy kid's arguing, and it got out of hand. Got hot. Bartender told us to shut up. Kid rared around and cussed at him, and bartender jerked his thumb and told us both to get out. Longhair growled, 'Make me.' Bartender snapped a wet rag in his face, stung him good."

"That was..." Phelan consulted his notebook for newspaper details. "Mr. Roy Breedlove, the bartender."

"Guess so, I don't know. Man, did I laugh. That's when he did it."

"Did what?"

"Asshole pulled out a little special and shot my leg. Knew it was a prosthetic and shot me anyway!" James Miller made a face that Phelan judged a pretty fair reproduction of his original shock and aggrievement.

"Cops claimed they had to take my leg for the bullet. Kept it for six weeks. That's ridicalous—six weeks I been crutching around. Then they say I can have it. My brother Byron says he'll pick it up and goddamn him, I wouldn't never of believed it, he pulls this stunt. You gotta get my leg back. I can pay you. Got a little settlement money left."

James Miller cracked his knuckles and looked away, all around the small living room, past an old short-back rocker with a box seat upholstered in faded brocade, possibly his wife's heirloom since the rest of the furniture looked to have just had the price tags yanked. Oak, high-varnish gleam: glass and veneer coffee table with three *Redbook* magazines Mrs. Miller had artfully fanned, oak-veneer entertainment center that held the 21" TV, stereo and turntable housed in smoky gray plastic, Harvest Gold wall-to wall shag. He looked anywhere but at Phelan. He had the money, all right.

"But your brother signed for it. Asking him to give it back to you didn't work?"

"Said he gave it to my sister Sherry. That bitch. All my life she called me Nutbox, not James. That's shaming to somebody. That's hurtful. Kids at school took it up too."

"I'll need names and addresses."

"Linda! Bring that paper you wrote!"

Mrs. Miller hurried in from the kitchen with a sheet of tablet paper and a can of Schlitz, which her husband promptly drank from.

"You want one too, Mr. Phelan? I'd a brought it, but I figured maybe because you were working—"

"Should of brought one anyway, darlin'. That's just plain manners." James Miller looked at Phelan, one etiquette expert to another, shaking his head like *What you gonna do?*

"No, thank you. You're right. Just need the list."

"Good. Go get 'em." Miller levied himself up from the couch and hopped over to the weight bench, lay down. "Turn on the TV, sugar."

Phelan took his list and his leave. Mrs. Miller followed him to his car. Maybe, Phelan thought, her way of making up for not offering him a beer right away. But that turned out not to be it.

"Can I ask you a question, Mr. Phelan?"

Phelan managed not to say, Shoot. "Sure."

Her smooth young face, two streaks of blusher up high on cheekbones she didn't have, looked daunted. "You like this lipstick shade? It's V.I.P. pink."

"Real nice."

She frowned a little. "That's not really what I wanted to ask. It's this. James' daddy passed last year. His mama's off her head with hardening of the arteries, and they just put her in Restful Ways. You know, the nursing home? They don't believe she's got long. Now I think, because Mr. Miller's already there, he'll be waiting to pull Mama Nettie on across. But James is young. What I wanna know is, if you were on an operating table dying and had a chance to come back to your wife, wouldn't you want to? Would you go off and leave her?"

James hadn't mentioned his mother's decline. Phelan nudged this bit of information aside to try to answer the wife's question. He opened his car door, rummaging around for something to say. The moment dragged on.

Her eyes were flat. "No bullshit," she said. "This is serious to me."

Phelan's grandfather had liked calling *Bullshit!* on politicians, the federal government, and neighbors. Shorter-tempered all the time, he was years older than his wife. The evening after he died, Phelan, fourteen or so, had entered his grandmother Lila's house unburdened by the weight of sorrow. If he'd thought about it at all, he'd have thought she would feel the same—only reasonable, the man was *old* and when you get *old*, you *die*. But he'd found Lila bowed like a storm-crushed primrose on their bed. Phelan felt ashamed when he saw how deeply wrong he was: she told him in a yearning voice that if Grandpa were to come through the door again and hold out his arms to her, she'd go back with him tonight.

He cleared his throat. "Couldn't say what I'd do, Mrs. Miller. Think you got to be there yourself to gauge that choice."

She nodded thoughtfully, her pink lips pursed. The bird barrettes in Linda Miller's hair, he saw, were ducks.

XVIII

DELPHA JUMPED OUT of the Ford Falcon to watch the bridge
swing round on its pivot. She wanted a clear view and a closer
one of the red tugboat, flying the star of Texas and towing a
loaded barge. Isaac got out too, shoving against the breeze to
open his cranky door. They stood off the side of the road in the
gravel and weeds and primroses. The car—Isaac's dad's, carrying
a rusted wound in a fender—was third in line, and they weren't
the only ones to spill out. This was the beach road on a Sunday,
and everybody in a hurry to get there. Delpha had Joe Ford's
permission to travel that sixty miles and back. Sunny day topping
ninety-three, their hair blowing in the steady wind.

"Look at that!" She had to holler it, delighted, over the
wind.

The white-haired man steering the tugboat was smoking.
The barge's deck was painted brick red, and it carried stacked
yellow shipping crates, one blue. The wind was pulling waves
in the canal and bending the tall green grasses by the girders
of the bridge.

With the windows rolled down, it was too noisy to talk.
Neither of them minded. Isaac played a tape of Credence
Clearwater Revival and kept hooking her by the neck. She'd
stretch over and kiss the hollow beneath his jaw. He knew
she'd been to the Gulf once before—or her mother had
told her she had when she was a kid. Not since. They were

eagled-eyed on the last rises until Delpha flung out her finger, screaming, "I see it! There it is! There it is!"

It was what children did, competed for who could see the water first. When she twisted to Isaac, he was watching her, long hair crazy around his head, grinning.

The land was unclutching them, falling away to a blue seam that reached left to right as far as she could turn her head and past. It wasn't possible to fit it all into her eyes at once, to inhale deep enough. Stunned, Delpha expanded, immense, uncontainable, taking in this horizon and its wide salt breath. Not long ago, she had wanted *to be* Room 221 in the New Rosemont Hotel. Now she beheld the live, immeasurable ocean, heard it, smelled it, knew she would not fit in that room in the same way again.

Isaac stopped the Falcon right on the beach. They pulled off their shirts and jeans, joking. Shy of the bikini rack, Delpha had bought a black one-piece bathing suit she had to tug down on her butt. Isaac stripped off to some long, flowered shorts he called jams, too big for him. He made her submit to being wiped with Coppertone, and she rubbed it on his back and chest, smoothed it onto his face with his eyes closed. He kissed her. Then he wanted to charge straight into the Gulf that was turning over and over out there.

Delpha shook her head and walked barefoot across the powdery dunes, feet sinking in, sand sifting between her toes, sticking to her. Hair whipping back, she walked across the hard-packed sand scattered with shells and bottle caps, tar and dead jellyfish and a kid's red shovel. Onto the water-washed sand and into the clear, lacy, cool nipping tide that chased ankles. Water chill as she let it climb her legs, Isaac squeezing her waist. Delpha nudged him away and lifted her arms. The waves came on.

She bobbed, jumped and was propelled higher, broke through the wave. Or she let the brownish whitecap crush her down into the sucking, swirling water, rush her to the shore till she foundered, stomach in the sand. Then she plowed back out to the breakers, shoving against the heavy, warm water with her thighs. Such a pleasure to lose form and weight, become motion and sensation. Delpha squinted against the sun and the salt in her eyes. Her toes didn't touch the bottom except to push off again. The sunbeams she couldn't look at headon flashed down in intersecting rays, bent into diamond shapes. She lost time out there.

Finally she let Isaac, chopping out, drag her through the churning waves back to two towels, a white one from the New Rosemont and another sizable one patterned with green seahorses. The wind chilled the water on her skin, but the sun heated shivers away. They lay facedown a while on the hard sand, cheeks mashed, hair dripping, breathless, hearing kids' windblown shouts and jeeps blasting rock and roll. Isaac's hand crept over to hers and held it.

He hauled out the cooler and Delpha a grocery sack, more towels, and Calinda Blanchard's straw hat. Towel for her shoulders, fresh towel for a tablecloth. She laid out the picnic: containers of tuna fish with egg and dill pickle and chicken salad with sweet. Some of Oscar's puffy dinner rolls. He'd rolled her out some extra dough to bake early that morning. Sliced tomatoes and cucumbers, salted and peppered, little jar of Spanish olives. Jar of watermelon chunks and peach crescents, juices running together. Half a dewberry cobbler, also courtesy of Oscar, a rich man with shortening. His golden crust crunched in their teeth and buttered their tongues. They were sun lotion-greasy, salt-sticky, hungry, ate sand with every course. The Gulf roared and crested and broke, ran toward them and crept away.

They took the ferry to Galveston, Isaac insisted. Driving a car onto a boat was something, they had to get in line, watch the man with the pocket flag beckoning them to a stop. People slammed out of their cars, kids shrieked and ran up the stairs. Isaac fetched the sack with the leftover rolls, and he and Delpha planted themselves in the back of the ferry, feet spread against the sway. White bubbling wake piled up on itself.

The gulls! Dark wings hooked into the air, the white-breasted gulls hung crying. Layer upon layer of them. Hold up a piece of bread and a gull swooped. Another slid into its place before the first had snapped the tidbit from Isaac's or Delpha's fingers. Laughter bubbled out of them continuously like the wake behind the ferry. They couldn't stop until all the rolls were fed, the wall of gulls treading the air still demanding. Long-beaked pelicans were strung out across the water, floating with decorum like cats settled with paws beneath them.

They took a promenade through Galveston where Isaac pointed out the tall, stately houses—turrets and white filigree balconies, palms and pink oleander. The Sunday traffic suffocated Delpha, and soon they were back in the long line for the ferry. On the return trip, Delpha caught Isaac's arm, her own speared out. "Sharks! Look!"

"No way, no way! Dolphins!" Isaac yelled over the ferry's engine, and they leaned on the prow's rail watching the two dolphins make their curved leaps until they faded into the glitter of the water.

They stopped at Swede's store's outside shower to wash some of the sand out of their hair, off their sunburned faces and shoulders and necks, and bought hotdogs and Cokes to eat while they dried.

Parked down on the beach again, they leaned against

one another and tracked the low yellow sun as it marked its lighted road on the waves and then reddened the clouds as the water rose over it. Delpha loosened Isaac's jeans and put him in her mouth.

It was midnight when they arrived at the swing bridge again, and no commerce was waiting. The canal was dark and empty, busy about its own, subject to no human business. They drove through the rickrack metal framework and out the other side to unlit two-lane.

Isaac wanted to stay, but he didn't fight about it. He dropped her off at the New Rosemont's door, kissed her, gripping his hands over her ears so he could bring her face to his. Delpha walked through the dim lobby, two lamps on, and into the kitchen to drink a glass of water. She wiped her mouth with the back of her sunburnt hand and rinsed out the glass.

Such a day.

The harelip chaplain spoke up from the stool nearest the stove, out of the path of the yellow, backdoor light. He repeated his farewell line. Always the same line, standing to leave because he could leave because for him the gates would swing open. Telling Miss Wade he'd see her next time. Gentle, jagged smile. Before his two hands closed on hers, he held them apart as if the world fit between them.

This is a day of good tidings.
This is a day of good tidings and we hold our peace.

Reciting those lines to a prisoner—the pinch she'd felt at his presumption was tempered because he'd seemed aware of it. Eventually she'd asked, *So what angel said that?*

No angel, the chaplain answered contentedly. *Lepers.*

XIX

BYRON MILLER LIVED in a close-plotted neighborhood on
the eastside of town, little bitty wood-shingled house with
two runners for a driveway and weeds growing up the middle.
He'd been fishing over the 4th of July holiday, away from
home. Now Phelan came upon him in the driveway after
supper, working on his pickup. He was taller than his brother
James, sturdier-boned, and had more forehead creases, deeper
set. Probably not a lot of hair under the ball cap. The brother
put down a timing light and wiped his hands with a red rag,
finger by finger, as Phelan introduced himself.

The friendly blinked out of Byron Miller's cinnamon-
brown eyes. "My brother sent a private eye to come get his leg.
Damn if that ain't the end."

"End of what, Mr. Miller?"

Byron Miller squatted down, replaced the tool in a slot
in a green metal toolbox. He talked to the box. "You know,
my wife's brothers, she got four of them and any one of
them'd walk through fire for the other. Work on each other's
plumbing, paint their houses and stuff. Kinda like a crew. I
like being around them. But they's pretty close in age."

He latched the toolbox and stood up. "James, he was a
change-of-life baby. I 'member Mama and Daddy not getting
along all that good and Daddy, he had a fit when he found out.
Me and Sherry, we were at that age to be embarrassed having

all our friends seeing our mother pregnant. Kids. But when they brought him home, it was like we had a brand new toy, and he had two sets of parents, with me and Sherry. Now he wouldn't piss on either one of us if we's on fire."

"That's a shame."

"Sure is. I'm the oldest. You get older, your folks pass or lose their minds, you think about that." The wiping hands paused, and Byron looked at Phelan, a straight-on, steady look. "You have brothers?"

"I do."

"I bet y'all hang together, help each other out, all that shit, don't you?"

Phelan pretended to consider. "Can't say that we do, sorry to say."

Given the pained cut of Byron's mouth, he thought it best to run with some small talk a while. "So he's the youngest. Tells me y'all call him Nutbox. How'd he come to get that nickname?"

Miller's featherweight smile hardly dented his dour expression. "Aw, isn't nothing to do with being crazy or nothing. You know those cans say Peanuts on them, and you give it to somebody they open it and a spotted snake on a spring jumps out. He's about five and Daddy, he played that trick on him. James thought it was a real snake. He run a mile. Just hollering. Got night, Mama had to hunt him and drag him back home. Daddy and Sherry called him Nutbox after that. Just family stuff."

"He didn't like it, though?"

"Used to sull up. Always thought it was cause he's so little. Not just when he was a kid. Hell, Sherry's tall as me and I'm six foot. She got a boy on Forest Park's team led them to State. Plays center. James, Nutbox, that is, he took after Mama. Fine-boned as a finch."

"So he didn't play any sports?"

"They let him on the football team his senior year. Should have seen him. Pads were wearing him. They put him in the last game of the season when they were down 45-7 and he couldn't hurt anything. Playing Charlton Pollard. Damn if he didn't get hold of a kickoff and run it to the ten." Byron Miller's smile was a little more genuine now. "Then those black boys just piled on and sunk him into the ground. You know, they don't have birth certificates. Some of 'em probably thirty-five years old."

Phelan remembered hearing that rumor every time a game with Charlton Pollard, the all-black school, came around. And only at that time. He also remembered James Miller's eyes burning as he described Joe Frazier slugging it out with a broken thumb.

"But James kept playing."

Byron Miller looked at him surprised. "Yeah, quarterback threw him a pass. Set it right in his hands. And James dropped it. Daddy ragged him all the way home. Didn't shut up till he saw his hand next day, took him over to Hotel Dieu for a x-ray. Wrist broke."

"Must have been a little hard on your brother."

"Daddy could be hard. You messed up, he sat you down in Mama's rocker and wailed the back of your neck with his belt. That was the judgment seat. You jumped up, he pushed you back down in it. Hurt like hell, but you had to take it. I took it. Nutbox liked to've squalled down the house."

Byron Miller's eyebrows lifted. "Daddy was just kiddin' James about that pass. Kidded everbody, not just my little brother. With the heart congestion, more'n ever, seemed like. Not 'sposed to smoke or eat any salt, drove him crazy. Only thing sweetened him up was to play cards with the couple buddies he had left. Hell of a poker player. Passed last year, and Mama's mind wandered off after him."

"Sorry to hear it."

Byron Miller gazed down on the weeds between the driveway's two concrete runners. Then he made fists to clean his knuckle creases.

"Thorough man with a rag." Phelan smiled.

Miller looked up at him, hooked his chin toward his front door. "Old habit. Try to leave the dirt outside my house." His gaze was steady.

"Admire your policy. You got the leg, Byron?"

The man stuck the rag in his back pocket. "Couldn't tell you if I did."

Phelan put his foot up on the bumper, leaned in. "What's the beef? Your brother didn't tell me anything, but there must be one. You don't strike me as a man'd be mean for meanness sake."

Byron squinted toward Phelan, then folded his arms. "Don't have a beef. Sherry does, and I'm standing by her. Didn't even tell you, did he?"

Phelan shook his head. "Said you and his sister were jealous because of the money he got after the accident. How about, he owed you money, then got this big chunk and didn't pay you, and you're holding the leg hostage."

The brother hawked and spit by Phelan's toe. "Accident was three years ago. Money. 'Salways bout money, isn't it? That's what ninety-nine percent of folks're after. You just ran into the one percent, buddy." Byron Miller latched the truck's hood, picked up the toolbox, and went into his house.

XX

PHELAN LICKED THE chocolate off a donut and scanned the newspaper. The chocolate went down sweeter than the news that President Nixon had refused to testify or to turn over so much as a weather report to the Senate committee, claiming "executive privilege." Which meant, as far as Phelan could interpret, *Nyah nyah nyah, I'm President and you're not.*

Focused on that political message, he tripped over this line in the *Beaumont Enterprise* Divorce column. "Neva McCracken Elliott vs. Lloyd T. Elliot." Phelan hustled it over and showed it to Delpha, who read it, raised her eyes to his without moving her head, shrugged.

He felt compelled to say, "You have less curiosity than me."

"You can learn to lose curiosity."

"I still wanna know the skinny." Belatedly, he shut his mouth and thought about what she'd said.

"We already got paid. That's the skinny, Mr. Phelan."

He scooted up a wooden chair to her desk. Her light brown hair was alternately blowing in the fake breeze from the fan and framing her face. A face a little marked, a little stormy.

"It's just," he said, "somebody in that marriage'll be a couple hundred grand poorer, but neither of them will ever be short a sandwich."

"Judging by your pictures, looked like he's gonna be happy."

"So Lloyd's wife paid us to do him a secret favor?"

"Maybe she was really the girlfriend."

"No, that wasn't it."

Delpha clicked her ballpoint. In. Out. "Know that for sure?"

"I saw the girlfriend, remember? Took her picture a dozen times." Phelan rose and stood in front of the fan, hands behind himself, catching the air. "And checked out her plates at the DMV. Got a friend there."

"Gotta lot of friends. And?"

"Annie McNeill, second grade teacher, Eugene Field Elementary. Watched her walk out of school three o'clock, saw who she's with. Managed to shoot the breeze with some mothers. Said I was a daddy, 'magine that, inquiring among all the mamas about the best teacher for my baby girl. The picture they gave me of Annie McNeill, uh uh, not your blackmailing type."

"She's your cheating type. I'm thinking you didn't do all that in one afternoon, did you?"

Phelan slid his hands in his pockets, ducked his head. "Annie McNeill in a wig is not our girl." He moved out of the way of the fan, releasing the office wind, and her hair riffled again. Her eyes were narrowed.

"I know, I get it. The business has to eat, like I do. But to get back to the point, our client wasn't Annie O'Neill. They don't look alike. Our girl wanted to sock it to Lloyd Elliott. In a bad way."

"'Sock it to him' meaning do him dirt."

"In this case, yeah. That'd cover several meanings, I guess."

They listened to the fan.

After a while, not looking at him, Delpha said, "This woman come in for killing her brother. Diddler and a beater and a lot of other things, hear her tell it. Name was Sue Jones, we called her Plain Sue. She didn't like men. Wasn't there a week fore she fell for this woman named Forever. I swear that was her name. Colored woman with green eyes." Delpha smiled a little.

Not even looking his way, and his stomach tightened.

"Sue, she was this scrub-bucket white girl in love. You could tell it was like she'd been in a tomb for twenty-odd years. Now the stone had rolled away, and she was standing in clear spring twilight. Do anything to be next to Forever, let their fingers touch. This guard name of J. W. got wind of it and headed off any pitty-pat. Switched Plain Sue's work detail to toilet-scrubbing. Threatened Forever with losing the radio in her cell. Just did it 'cause he could."

Plain Sue had got the guard alone in a storage room, shed pants and underwear, raised up on her tippy toes, and braced the wall. Delpha wore a Mona Lisa smile while she related this part.

"What's the punchline?"

"Touch of syphilis to start with. Later on Sue took a bad fall, went to the infirmary with two black eyes and a grin. Got some crushed ice, penicillin."

Phelan kicked this around for a minute. "Well, but so? That's kinda winning the shit sweepstakes."

"Yeah, that was Sue. She was always winning those."

"Don't get it. What's the connection to Elliott's case?"

"May not be one. But story we heard was, J.W. was engaged to be married and when the blood test come back positive, the bride-to-be jilted him. But she had syphilis too, now didn't she, despite the lace dress in her closet, and that was news she wanted to carry to the grave. J.W. told his people she give him a social disease, so hell yeah he called off the wedding. His people blabbed to everbody and their dog. He come out on top."

"So...you're saying—"

"Saying you can plan. Don't mean your plan works out. Plain Sue spited that guard, but in the end, son of a gun squeezed a truckload of poor-me out of the deal."

"So your moral here is revenge might head north or it might head south."

"These stories don't have morals, Mr. Phelan. They're just things that happened."

"J.W. mess with Sue's love life again?"

"Naw. He didn't."

Delpha copied James T. Miller, Sr.'s obit word for word, drew a line. She flipped through successive years of Yellow Pages, running down James T. Miller, Sr. and his painting business, recording her notes on a long yellow tablet.

She got her stuff together and made a call at the pay phone, speaking sincerely into its dirty receiver while the sun beat on her head. She walked over to State National, blouse sweated through, humidity dampening her hairline, forming wandering wisps that tickled her cheek. She took last place in Debbie's line, noticed her earrings: cute red triangles that swung around as she talked to customers and thumped her ten-key. When Delpha got up front, Debbie said, "Hi there. How's my old boyfriend Tom?"

"Fine. Mr. Phelan's out on a case."

"He make you call him that?"

"No," Delpha said evenly, "that's my choice. It's businesslike."

"Well, good for you. What can I help you with today?"

Delpha told her. Debbie directed her to a woman off to the side of the bank, a loan officer behind a nice desk with a stack of files. She gave Delpha a bright look that said she'd like to ask some questions but she wasn't going to.

Delpha did question the woman at the desk, who was late fifties, minimally made-up so as not to scare any bank presidents. After saying she was a business customer and offering a short, adjusted version of the case Phelan Investigations was pursuing, Delpha produced a modest, friendly smile. Broadened it when it didn't turn the lock. Became more conversational. The loan officer warmed just enough to give her some details, a few anecdotes, and Delpha, satisfied, thanked her and stood up.

She made way for a black man in a double-breasted suit carrying a handsome briefcase. Determination on his face, high polish on his shoes. Behind him was a young couple, clients or relatives, clenching hands. They all three settled in to speak with the woman, who cocked her head to listen. Some pre-decided flatness in her gaze, her artificially-raised brows told Delpha they might not close on the loan they came for.

XXI

AFTER CONSULTING THE tablet page supplied by James Miller's wife, Phelan headed to Sherry Boatwright's, the sister's, house. He pulled up to the curb in a brick neighborhood near Stephen F. Austin Junior High. Nice houses, full-grown trees, two-car garages, smooth concrete sloping driveways. The garage front featured a basketball hoop that looked to be regulation height. Backyard was chain-linked, with two collies patrolling, nosing into the links. Near the back door, a cement patio and a barbecue grill, lawn chairs and a chaise lounge. Clearly, the Boatwrights were more well-off than Byron. Possibly better off than James too, depending on the amount of his settlement.

Sherry was waiting for him. Knew he'd be coming because her brother would have hit the horn as soon he got into his house yesterday evening. Though it was ten o'clock in the morning, Phelan had expected her to be flanked by a husband. That was not the case. Another thing. The pony-tailed woman in shorts, situated in a throne-like posture, open legs planted, arms bent and large hands dangling, appeared to be sitting on air. She let him cross the yard, inspecting him as he came. When he was a few feet away, Sherry Boatwright stood up, allowing him a view of a tortured lawn chair. One hand on her hip, James and Byron Miller's sister was Phelan's height and had at least thirty pounds on his one-eighty, not much of it flab. Thighs like telephone poles, calves like cantaloupes. The double D's just served as advertising for the range of her shoulders. If he hadn't known whose sister she was, he'd have guessed the giant boxer, Primo Carnera's. The Ambling Alp, seventy-two knockouts, counting the one that didn't wake up.

"I know who you are," she said, cutting off his introduction. She'd already looked him up and down. Phelan was on *her* walk by *her* front door, but this was a woman would've owned any space she chose. And liked owning it. He had trouble seeing her tenderly mulching the flowers in her backyard, less trouble imagining her hosing down a California redwood.

"Won't take up more of your time than I have to," Phelan said, which did not necessarily mean he intended to be quick about this interview, only to make it sound that way. "Your brother James hired me to retrieve his prosthetic leg, and I was hoping we could come to some agreement about that."

"Maybe," she said. She did not invite him inside her house, nor did she punish the lawn chair again. She stood eye to eye. "I want my rocker back."

Lost her rocker was the first thought that came to mind. The second was an upward appraisal of Nutbox's nerve, holding out on such a sister. "Mean a rocking chair?"

"I sure do. Don't act like you didn't know."

Yeah, like I'd do that, Phelan thought indignantly.

His gaze level, exactly level, he asked, "And your brother has this chair?" Mentally he re-inventoried James Miller's living room, recalling, among the new furniture, that low-slung old thing with the brocade seat cover. Short-backed, pine probably and painted by Sears during the dustbowl.

"James," she said, upping her chin, "took it outa our

daddy's house during the visitation, when Byron and us were up at the funeral home. He knew I wanted it special. I got a son in high school and three daughters. Two're engaged. One's married and due in October. I promised her her grandmama's rocking chair for the baby. James doesn't even have kids."

"Yet." Phelan slipped his hands in his pockets. "Has a fond wife."

Sherry Boatwright's prison-guard stance gave a little. "We got nothing against Linda. This is between us and Nutbox. They can buy themselves a brand new chair they get a baby coming. Heck, I'll even loan it back to 'em. But I want the keepsake for my daughter's baby."

"Well, doesn't seem unreasonable. How come James won't give it to you?"

The big woman's lower lip pushed into the upper one. She turned away toward the street where a late-model Chrysler with a Student Driver sign was creeping by, a boy completing his stop five yards from the stop sign. "Not a reason in the world. Rocked him myself when he was little."

"Maybe that's why he took it."

She laughed rustily. "Fat chance. Seem like he turned against me with Daddy's passing. "

Phelan shook his head, studying an oleander hedge bordering her front yard from her neighbor's. White and pink. Pretty scent, pretty leaves, waxy green. Mouthful'd poison a horse.

"Sorry to hear it. I got two brothers. We hardly give each other the time a day. I wish it was different, Mrs. Boatwright." Didn't hurt his acting, the little sluice of deadness through his chest. "Think your brother Byron wishes that, too."

The tight ponytail of brown hair, streaked with gray at

the temples, might be pulling her eyes, but they managed to widen themselves a tad anyway.

"Then you know. James was the baby, and I guess we spoiled him."

She told the story of James's nickname that Phelan had already heard. Added new ones. How she and Byron didn't leave him out of stuff just because they were so much older. They played with him. Keepaway, tossing Nannit—that was his old rag of a baby blanket. Let him be the batter when Byron practiced fast-pitch. Laughed at him when he couldn't hit; they had fun. How she stayed outside the door to the dark room where James, two or three years old, was huddled sobbing in the very same rocking chair he refused her now. Their daddy had sworn he wasn't growing up any titty-boy ascared of the dark and locked James in there. James wailing. Few hours later, after their father went to sleep, Mama had got the key out of his pocket and rescued her little boy out into the light of the kitchen.

"James wrapped himself around Mama like a baby monkey, I swear. And she always let him." There was a hitch in her smile.

Phelan nodded, glanced toward the Boatwright driveway. "Heard you got a boy plays basketball."

The wistful smile gained in wattage. "Six foot four and three quarters and still growing. Farley's just a sophomore, but he can get his elbows in the rim. Nine rebounds his last game."

Phelan whistled. Then he grinned at her. She grinned back, swelling into her full height, a mountain shining proprietarily over a brood of thrusting foothills. He could see her inching onto the fulcrum of friendliness, so he went for it. "I talk James into parting with that rocking chair, you give his leg back?"

Slowly she nodded. Estimating that the usual cutting-some-slack man's handshake with a woman wouldn't work for Sherry Boatwright, he shook with her, forcefully. Drove back downtown to the office, right hand pulsing on the wheel. Glad you didn't shake with your left because she'd have crushed his stump. But mostly he was thinking about what Byron Miller had said, about his brothers-in-law. About the one percent money couldn't buy.

He recapped his interview for Delpha, what Sherry looked and acted like, where she lived. He added one detail. The tell that had lightly curled one side of Sherry's maternal smile.

Delpha folded her arms. "This a plain old slat rocker?"

He shook his head. "Nope. It's short in the back and upholstered, got a seat cushion. Faded cloth, sorta thick, with a figure to it."

Her voice was sharp. "Then I think why'd you come back here instead of speaking to the chair. Well-to-do woman jacks her little brother's pegleg to get a rocking chair—and she smiles crooked when you act like you gonna help her."

Since when was it a capital offense to seek consultation with a colleague? Phelan registered a certain irked calculation in her attitude, as if she were determining whether he was testing her smarts. Why'd he stop back here? Well, he'd wanted the information he'd sent her to the library for: details of Mr. James Miller, Sr.'s obituary. She ought to know that.

Delpha did know that. With the eraser end of a pencil, she'd tapped the notes on the legal pad. Sherry Boatwright had other reasons for wanting that chair than rock-a-bye-ing her grandbabies, and his secretary understood that same as he did, once he'd described the tell.

He strolled the little room and sat down on the second-hand couch underneath the secretary window, lit a cigarette, stretched out his legs. Slow-poking into his mind, a glimmer: he'd just wanted to talk to Delpha a while. That's why he'd described his visit to Sherry. He liked hearing what she thought.

"I'm just asking you for your opinion."

She was squinting at him, charcoal glints in her eyes. "Or wanting me to tell you some cute prison story?"

He sat up. "Jesus, Delpha, you couldn't get much wronger than that. Couldn't you let down the ramparts for five minutes?"

At the sound of her name, the graceful neck lengthened and her chin curved down and inward, like a swan's. All Phelan knew about swans came from a day in his childhood by a slaggy Houston pond. Pretty white things, floating, but they could cruise like steamers, they liked bread, and they bit.

Phelan flicked ashes in his palm. "You got some concentrated experience of female human nature, and you said I could ask about it long as I didn't act like your slip was showing. I'm asking straight out. So what law did I break now?"

The squint stayed in place while Delpha processed this. Then she pulled out a drawer, took out a black plastic ashtray, walked over and gave it to Phelan, walked back, tucked herself into the desk, pushed back a strand of brown hair, and looked up.

"Fair enough. Just this ain't a case needs Sam Spade, and both of us know it."

Phelan studied a hardy hangnail on his thumb. "Not saying it is."

The slight inclination of her head indicated acceptance and the reestablishment of cordial relations.

"Awright." She steepled her hands like a banker with phony bad news.

Phelan sat still.

"Girl by the name of Sandra Ann, in for lonely heart scams. But they hadn't run her outside Texas, and she still got a couple of out-of-state husbands sending her money ever month. Cartons of Lucky Strikes under her bunk, shoebox clinkin' with bottles of fingernail polish. Way over the number allowed. Had a bargain-size Oil of Olay, Pond's Cold Cream, nylon panties. One supper, for grins, the cook didn't give her any pie. I'm not talking fancy pastry, this was a convicted arsonist using canned apples. Sandra threw a fit so wild it took two guards to wrestle her down."

"You're saying Sherry Boatwright's like this Sandra Ann."

"I'm sayin' them that has craves more."

Phelan considered that.

Delpha tilted the yellow pad. "You ready for this stuff now?"

"Yeah."

"James T. Miller, Sr. passed bout a year ago from emphysema. Seventy-four years old. Survived by wife Nettie, former employee of State National Bank, and three children. Whose names you know. Veteran of the U.S. Army. Self-employed at H&M Painting as a house painter. And…" She looked up from the legal pad, trace of a smile.

Finally. *That's all I wanted anyway*, Phelan thought. *Little gab and a smile, be on my way. Christamighty, I'm a simple son of a bitch*. "And what?"

"And I looked up H&M Painting in the old phonebooks at the library. H&M stopped listing in 1958. If Miller, Sr. ever did another lick of work in his life, they didn't write it down in his obituary."

Delpha flipped a page over. "I called up Restful Ways Home

where you said she was and asked about Nettie Miller. Said I was a niece from out of town and what should I bring when I came to see her because I'd heard her mind was plumb gone. Asked a few questions in a concerned voice. Asked what she could still do, compared to what she used to do, and all such."

Mrs. Nettie Miller tended to wear her brassiere on the outside of her clothes. Spit okra on the floor. Her kids had written down that she was a member of Rosebud Baptist, but the receptionist couldn't swear about that because that pastor had not yet paid a visit. A friend from the bank had stopped by though.

"From the bank."

"Where she worked. Our bank, where your friend Debbie works."

Phelan laced his hands. Out of sympathy with the stump, the left pinky refused to bend. "You go see Debbie?"

"I did. Nettie Miller was before Miss Debbie's time. But not the loan officer's, she's an older lady. Nettie worked at State National for twenty-nine years. One of her duties was managing safety deposit boxes, keeping records of the contents and all. Know what she was specially good at?"

"Leaving off a few of the contents."

"I 'magine so. And—handling grieving family members who came to close out boxes of the deceased. They all liked Nettie. Some even opened up their own accounts at the bank afterwards. She was good for business. Until she started forgetting to do stuff and doing other stuff twice. Then one day she went to the bathroom at her desk."

Phelan winced. He put his hands on his hips and considered her. "That's first class work, you know. Thank you."

He received another smile from Miss Wade, and this one was full.

XXII

LINDA MILLER MET Phelan at the door with a petroleum smell and a stained towel around her shoulders, see-through plastic gloves, and porcupine-head: strands of white goo-coated hair pulled through a frosting cap. Didn't seem to faze her meeting the public like that, even though it was about fifteen hundred miles farther down the ugly road than those women who wore curlers to the store. She brought Phelan into the living room where James, leg propped on the coffee table, watched *The Edge of Night.* Then she disappeared into the bathroom. James stared at Phelan's empty hands.

"Sherry wouldn't give it to you."

"No. She said she would if she got that rocking chair." Phelan pointed to the Judgment Chair. Low-backed so that the sitter's head would clear its last rail, painted black with plenty of chipped spots, especially on that last rail. "Said you knew she wanted it. Means for her daughter to have it when her baby comes. I'll run it over there, pick up the leg, and bring it back to you."

A flush had stained James Miller's neck and was rising to his jaw. "Sherry can get Missy a load of rocking chairs with her credit card. This is the only one I want." He had his crutch under his arm and hoisted himself up. "Linda!"

Linda Miller flip-flopped out of the bathroom missing a plastic glove, blowing on one hand of fingernails painted orange-pearl.

"Go hold the back door open. I was waiting till I got my leg back but shit, you do what you got to," James Miller said, planting his crutch. He grabbed the rocking chair by its top rail and stumped toward the kitchen, dragging the chair.

"James," Phelan said, following, "what's the deal here? I can be back with your leg in twenty minutes."

"You can take her the chair, all right. Just hold your horses." The red climbing his face flooded high tide into his hairline. "Promised myself I'd do this if it was the last thing I ever did. Goddamn it!" The rocker had skidded through the kitchen over the slick linoleum, but now it locked legs with a tall stool that sat at the bar dividing kitchen and dining room. James yanked. The bar stool crashed into the one next to it, which crashed into the last one, which hit the wall and remained there.

"Don't mess up my furniture," Linda's voice complained around the back door. "It's gonna get scuffs on it. "

Phelan righted the three bar stools, then took the black rocking chair from James Miller's hand and set it down outside a few yards from the door, at the head of a small yard planted in Bermuda grass. The Millers had a wood fence and a barbecue cooker that looked new, a redwood picnic table, benches attached, and a couple of old metal lawn chairs with the scalloped backs. A spindly tree had not resigned itself to a cramped spot between the house and a metal storage cabin. It twisted away, branches thrust out toward the yard like a man with feet caught in cement.

James crutched over to the storage hut and came back out with a chain saw. "Stay where you are, baby."

"Sweetie. That won't change a thing."

James Miller just clamped his jaw. His wife walked over to him and set her hand on his shoulder. "Just so you know."

She leaned over to kiss his cheek, and her husband turned his face so that they kissed on the mouth. A red-faced gimp muscling a chain saw and a woman with her head spiked like a medieval weapon—and it was a tender kiss, like a permission or a leave-taking.

Linda Miller shook her head at Phelan as she passed him.

"Fifteen minutes," Phelan said. "Lemme trade her the chair. I'm guessing your sister won't go for splinters, James."

But Phelan's client squinted defiantly into the distance, like a squad of rifle barrels topped his fence, and he was about to feed them some dirty last words.

Phelan tried again. "Leg's worth more to you than spiting Sherry, isn't it."

"Not Sherry he's spiting," said Linda, back in the door.

James wedged the crutch into his armpit.

Phelan got it. OK, nothing complicated here. This wasn't any Democratic Headquarters with secret files to B&E for — just a guy's last gesture to a daddy who regularly humiliated him. James Miller was destroying a crime scene.

The chain saw sputtered and caught. James revved it a few times. Not many human beings Phelan would have charged a chain saw for. He was tempted to sit down in the blue metal lawn chair to watch the show, but knew he should stay on his feet.

James Miller, Jr.'s chainsaw split the rocker's top rails down the middle and bit through the lower rail. About twenty seconds later, James leaning, his crutch punching into turf, the saw chewed into the upholstered seat bottom. James's chin jutted trembling—maybe from the saw's vibration, maybe on its own, his eyes were wet. The guy was soul-deep in this mission.

The saw was biting through the seat cushion when Phelan

charged forward semaphoring for James to cut the motor. A greenish edge had emerged beneath the old batting. But there was no halting James. The chainsaw hacked and spit through brocade and cotton batting and two slim stacks of green money. Some of the half-bills spurted up as in a shuffle gone wrong. The saw didn't stop till the front lower rails parted and the sudden lack of purchase lurched James forward.

The chair's two halves, yawning apart, lay themselves down. When neither a staggering James nor Linda—plastic-clad hands over her mouth—moved toward the corpse, Phelan squatted and autopsied its innards. He extracted three stacks that had book-ended the severed Franklins splayed on the Bermuda grass.

"Keepsake, my flat white ass." James used his crutch to sit on the ground. He was shaking his head, but he couldn't seem to shake his sister's name out of it.

Linda stood there a minute longer, her eyes white-rimmed. Then she whirled and ran into the house.

"Baby!" James called.

"I'mon get some scotch tape," his wife called back. "And this frosting has ate through my scalp."

Phelan and James sat at the shiny oak veneer dining table over beers while Linda taped. Her wet, platinum-striped hair lay down on her head now, but her right-hand nails still lacked the orange-pearl polish. $47,800. She chattered about the four-bedroom house they could buy outright over on the west side. The kind of house that had a kitchen with an island in the middle of it and swag curtains in the living room and no check to write to the Savings & Loan.

Ever so often she'd peek at James, who had some kind of convention going on inside his head. A spectator, he registered

a frown here, a twitch there, as various speakers elbowed to
the mike. He inhaled his first beer and plucked eight hundred
off the pile of unsliced bills. James scooted these over to
Phelan, who thanked him and reminded him there would be
expenses on top of this generous fee, and his secretary would
figure out the bill. Didn't faze James.

Linda rhapsodized over a page she'd seen in *Southern
Living*, and Phelan asked one question. A girl who knew too
good to be true when she saw it, Linda let *Southern Living*
drop and got herself a Tab from the refrigerator, pulled the
lever on an ice tray and knocked out some cubes. She reached
down a pint of Jim Beam from a cabinet shelf, topped her Tab
with just enough to get a roach drunk.

She brought two beers to the table and tossed Phelan the
can opener. They waited on her husband. The delegates at
James's convention grew so rowdy he pushed on his temples.
But finally they must have gathered their satchels and lit
out. James answered the question, and they drank their beers
while they worked it all out.

"You shittin' me, right," the cabinetmaker said. He pushed
safety glasses up on his forehead. "Or you're crazy as a betsy
bug. Glue ain't gonna hold a chair been sawed in half. First
person to sit on it busts their rump."

Phelan assured the aproned man that consequence was not
his problem. The rocker's repair was for legal purposes only.

"I never...what?"

"Glue it, including the cloth, and clamp it. Here's twenty
dollars." The guy's craftsman-brain was roiling, but his hand
closed on the twenty.

Phelan picked up the Millers' rocking chair several days
later. Glued, restained, retouched. "Way too good a job."

"What in the world...listen, you—"

"No. Really. Buddy, you're an ace." He hefted the chair, angled it gingerly into his trunk and tied down the trunk so it did not touch the rocker. He drove to Sherry Boatwright's, constantly checking the no-view in his rearview.

The question he'd asked James was *You want to keep on fighting about your leg?*

No.

Phelan and James had waited, silent and respectful though occasionally making eye contact, while Linda mentally downsized her dream-mansion blueprints. Down, down, down to one third of $47,000—$15,666.00—and the super-deluxe family room she could add on with that amount. Pool table, wet bar, fireplace. Maybe a swimming pool out back.

Sherry Boatwright, her acreage upholstered in plaid Bermuda shorts, held wide her door so that Phelan could carry the rocker into her tiled foyer. She approached the chair, but he shook his head. The big woman frowned, left and returned to the foyer with her brother's tan leg. Phelan lifted the chair farther from the door, setting its runners down on the pale carpet of a formal living room. Sherry's broad face pinked, as though the rocker was now safe across her state line. She laid the leg into Phelan's waiting arms.

"Thanks for talking some sense into my brother. Now my daughter can rock her baby here, keep up a family tradition."

Side of her mouth curled. Sherry walked over to the chair, bound on claiming her prize, and turned her fifty-inch hips around.

"And there's this from James, too," Phelan added hastily, bending to slap onto the entryway tile a manila envelope containing her share of the cash. "Thank you, Mrs. Boatwright." He shut her front door, sprinted, dove into the driver's seat and had the car started and rolling before he reached his door shut. Imagining the winsome crack of glue releasing its hold and her plaid ass hitting the floor, he screeched out of Forestgate with the leg.

Twelve minutes later, James Miller strode on two legs over to Linda Miller, bent her backward, and stuck his tongue inside her V.I.P.-pink lips.

That was heart-fluttering to witness, but Phelan Investigations was now officially between jobs again.

XXIII

THE TELEVISION FRAMED a stricken white man with gray eye-bags, licking his dry lips. A former aide to President Nixon had just admitted to the Watergate Committee that the Oval Office was equipped with a secret taping system. At the New Rosemont, Mrs. Bibbo scooted down the TV couch to make room for Mr. Finn and Mr. Nystrom. Oscar from the kitchen, waiting on Calinda to figure his paycheck, pulled up a chair. He had the evening off and the next day, and he'd done a job on himself in the employee bathroom, brown three-piece suit, lavender shirt, and kiss-me cologne.

"See! See!" Mrs. Bibbo was shoving her hand at the replay on Channel 4 News. "It'll all be on the tape recorder machine. You saw how nervous that assistant was. They know they did wrong."

Mr. Nystrom scoffed. "You believe everyone has a conscience, just because you do. No Italian woman your age should be that naive, Roberta."

Delpha looked toward Mrs. Bibbo and the television. The room receded like a tide, hazed, and then abruptly splashed into its former placement. She verified that she was indeed perched on the worn arm of a velour couch, in the middle of a conversation with four people who were not in prison. Later in a room upstairs, a boy would make love to her. She tuned in again to Mrs. Bibbo's polka-dot shirtwaist, her sandals with the thick straps.

"That John Erlichman has eyebrows like Satan," Mr. Nystrom was saying.

Mr. Finn said, "I suppose you'd know."

"I would. In restaurant supply, I met Satan at least twenty times. I sold him a fryolator. Who I'd really like to meet is that chickadee, that John Dean's wife. Her blonde hair and her little button nose."

"That's what all the women look like where your people come from, huh, Mr. Nystrom? White as cake flour."

"That's what people say, Oscar, but lots of Swedish women are as ugly as anywhere else."

Mr. Finn nodded toward the television. "The system's working."

"What they want you to think," Oscar countered. "They get off camera where you can't see 'em, they're slapping each other's backs."

"Not this time," Mrs. Bibbo said. "They're in trouble. They're on the tape recorder—and there's no way they can fix that."

Mr. Finn nodded in agreement with Mrs. Bibbo. Mr. Nystrom began to side with Oscar, but the young man hopped up and jogged to the lobby door where a girl could be seen peeking through the glass. They all watched his easy run.

"How you doin', Shayla? Lookin' like a stone fox this evening." He leaned into the girl in the doorway.

Mr. Nystrom sighed heavily.

"Don't be sad, Harry," said Mr. Finn.

"Little Simon Sunshine. This system"—Mr. Nystrom pointed at himself—"it isn't working."

Oscar came back in, bent to Delpha's ear, and told her Miss Doris wanted a word. The Rosemont commentators were off again.

Calinda was in the little office room at the end of the kitchen, bifocals on, writing in her big two-ring checkbook. Delpha poured a cup of coffee, left a dime on the kitchen counter, and took it out.

Miss Doris, stationed in one of the New Rosemont's sidewalk-viewing chairs, welcomed the cup. "Hot coffee cools you off on a hot evening, folks don't b'lieve that. Looky here now, what a artist-man give me." She lifted up her speckled arm to show a bracelet made from all sorts of stuff—washers, buttons, toothy watch gears, brass keys.

"Clever. That a bullet casing?"

"Don't it make a jingle?" Miss Doris shook her little wrist and clinking and tinkling broke out. The women smiled at each other. Delpha had to catch a bus, but she didn't feel like hurrying. Still hot as Arabia out here. She slouched in the chair and stretched out her legs.

"How you getting along?" Miss Doris turned her wrist one way and another, admiring every angle.

"Way ahead of where I was day we met. Got work. Got a place to live."

"Got a friend too, huh?"

Delpha turned her head.

"Somebody watching you one night. Pants, hat, middle-size-tall, skinny, stay back in the alley cross the street. Coulda been a man, coulda been a woman. That business, you know"— she cast a shrewd sidelong glance—"it ain't so cut and dried. You and your friend come out the side door and whoever it was picked up and studied you. Left when you went back in."

Delpha absorbed this information uneasily.

"Listen at it again." Miss Doris set the little metal pieces dancing. "I cain't get over how sweet it sounds."

"Miss Doris, how come you stay out so late?"

"Oh, honey. The moon. She make me feel like a queen nobody knows about." She laid the hand with the bracelet on her trousered knee and spread out its charms, regarding them with wonder, one by one. "You feel like you're back yet?"

"Sometimes it slips."

Miss Doris smiled at a tiny key. "Good to be out here, open air, see all over, go all over. Don't like being inside much."

"Got that. You have somewhere you sleep?"

"Well, I sleep me some odd hours. I got a little Social Security—don't you go thinkin I'm no-count." Miss Doris regarded her fiercely, lower lip pushed out.

"Oh, now." Delpha smiled. "Never thought that. Thank you for what you told me. Got to get my purse and go to work now. That bracelet is precious."

She passed by the television-watchers. Oscar was standing, slipping his paycheck envelope into his brown jacket's inside pocket. His cursory glance at Delpha lingered a tick longer than usual. It said he was clued into her legal history in a general way, but not curious enough to press for an explanation that would cut into the evening spreading out starrily ahead of him.

"Look at you, young man," Mr. Nystrom sneered, from his spot on the couch. "Aren't you just clean and neat and smelling sweet."

Oscar floated above the old man's nasty tone. "Accurately observed," he agreed. "I shall hit the street. Good night, one and all."

"Night, Oscar." Mr. Finn smiled him out.

Delpha ran up and retrieved her purse. She was running late. Mrs. Speir might be marinating even now, poor old body. No sign of Oscar when she got out to the bus stop. Shayla either.

It ruffled her, what Miss Doris had said, but then Miss Doris also saw haints. In particular, a striped-shirt gent from the pool hall who'd sometimes light-foot it down the alley. He didn't open the back door to get out there.

XXIV

PHELAN HAD ALREADY been told to get lost.

Nevertheless, holding a manila envelope containing a road map of Louisiana, he rang the bell of Lloyd Elliott's red brick, two-storied, porticoed and white-columned former home. The curved drive was bordered by azalea bushes. Must have been snazzy back in April, blossoms lit on the bushes like a thousand dark-pink butterflies. No cars in sight.

A young woman with flawless, melty-brown skin, a modest Afro and green wrap-around dress answered the door. Phelan told her he had a package to deliver to Mrs. Elliott. The woman held out her hand.

"Not to...the housekeeper. Which would be you, right? I have to deliver it personally."

"I'm filling in for my mother today." She pulled in her chin. "You're not a messenger from the firm."

"No."

"Not from the drug store."

Phelan shook his head.

She crossed her arms. "We don't let in salesmen."

Phelan explained that he was just a businessman who needed to deliver an order. He was the one who had just called, remember? Five minutes, that was all. "Three," he said when she didn't budge. He wagged the envelope. "She wants this today."

The young woman frowned, but turned. With stern back, she led Phelan past a palatial living room through a stadium-sized kitchen to a closed door. She knocked, called, "Mrs. Elliott? A man here says he's got an important order for you," retreated in the direction of the kitchen, where she fixed her suspicious self with her back to a kitchen island, spotless copper pots hung over her head.

He grimaced on entering the huge sunroom, bank of windows on one side, blue curtains framing a wall of pulsing summer light, masterful AC to defeat any trace of natural warmth. Phelan had seen photos of people on skis. This is how he imagined the air on a mountain: bone-gnawing but dazzling.

Built-in white filing cabinets and bookcases formed the opposite wall. Flowing out from them, a maybe 18' by 24' patterned rug, jewel-green with minty leaves and little pink and cream shapes like flower petals scattered on a spring lawn. Nothing he wanted to put a shoe on. The furniture in the room was white, an icy glass-top desk piled with newspapers and three phones on it, a white princess phone in reach of the daybed the woman was propped up in. The rich rug contrasted with the disarrayed newspapers, the twist of dark hair pinned to her head, the wide, pallid face—and the plain brown of her eyes.

Regular brown eyes, a little on the small side. Not reddened, not weeping. And they didn't know Phelan from the man in the moon.

Mrs. Lloyd Elliott set a tinkling glass next to the lamp. "You can't be the one who just called me. Because I hung up on him and that meant he was not welcome to occupy my telephone line, much less my residence." The voice was an imperious child's, the accent pure Texas.

Well, yes, ma'am you did hang up, but let's see what you say next. Phelan retracted his head and raised his shoulders in a way that might have conveyed either yes or no but certainly conveyed humble.

"Merrill Lynch or one of those cut-rate huts sent you, didn't they? Incorrigible. I've been managing my own portfolio since...you really don't have an inklin' who I am, do you?"

Well, actually, now I do.

"How dare you intrude on me. I have no intention of transferring my account out of my own hands. Surely not to one of you little Fuller Brush brokers. Leave. One more word and I'll call the police."

All right, not one more word and none about some pictures that must have been a riveting topic in your house. Phelan'd been prepared to feign a mistake over the delivery, wrong Elliott, wrong address, whatever, but this was his easy day. He arranged chagrin and puppy-dog-tails on his face and exited the brilliant room.

The young woman escorted him toward the door, her lion-colored eyes half-mast. "You're running some kind of hustle, huh? You'd never have got past my mom."

He believed her. "Bet you're a college girl. Go out at Lamar?"

She shot him a superior glance. "Business major."

"Just barely got past you," Phelan said. "But your bouncing days are numbered. Once you graduate, I see you, wait a minute, hmm"—he touched his middle fingers dead center of his forehead, squinted. They were almost at the door. "I'm seeing brick and carpet, leather chairs..."

"Law school." Superiority fell off her smooth face. Suspicion returned.

Phelan was pleased. His hand dropped to his side. "Well, damn. I'm not always that good."

She shut the door on him. He'd got a flicker of a smile out of her, but he'd lost his own.

XXV

BUS RIDERS PERKY this evening. Conversations flew over people's heads to land on people farther away. There was greeting, a story here and there, little acting-out to go with the story, chin-thrown-back laughing. Delpha nodded to familiar faces, even broke out a smile.

She washed up, heated Chicken Noodle, and carried the tray upstairs. Mrs. Speir's head hardly moved, but the blanched face on the pillow fastened onto her. The vertical wrinkles stretched to accommodate her open mouth. She was panting.

Delpha abandoned the tray on the vanity table, shoving the atomizer back into the mirror's base. She sat on the edge of the mattress, sinking it down, felt Mrs. Speir's forehead, took her hand. Cool. Her eyes were not fixed. They seemed to be seeing, though who could say for sure. Delpha had to call Calinda. She stood, and the hand closed on hers.

"Mrs. Speir, I'll call your niece, then I'll be back. Not leaving you, understand? Understand?" She squeezed her hand.

She had seen a woman, not an old one, keep up that panting for five hours, her eyes wild and black with knowledge then still and slitted, but panting. Heard of others slipped away with a gasp. Delpha ran to the stairs, then whirled and ran down the hall. "Miss Pittman, you here? Miss Pittman? Ida! Ida Rae! You here?"

The brass bed was unmade, empty. White boots, pantyhose, a black brassiere on the floor.

Delpha bypassed Mrs. Speir's bedroom with its black phone on the table by the leather armchair, hurried down the stairs to the telephone in the kitchen. Got Calinda in the Rosemont's kitchen on the fourth ring.

"Miss Blanchard, Mrs. Speir is going and most probably tonight. You want to see her, best come on over. Less you want me to call a ambulance."

"No! Don't do that. They'd plug her in and keep her going. Hundred years is plenty. I'll be there soon. Wait! Wait a minute. Is Ida Rae there?"

"Called for her, no answer. She's not in her room either."

"Good." The phone hung up.

Delpha returned to Mrs. Speir. She straightened the twisted sheet and covered it with a light, clean blanket, plumped the pillow, tamped the salt-white corners of her lips with a moist rag. She dragged a chair next to the bed. On second thought, she pushed up the window for fresh air. Then she sat down. The beebee eyes rolled toward hers, flared darkly. Stale breath came rhythmic, regular out of her open mouth, and her flat chest heaved. Her fingers plucked.

Delpha captured her hand. "Calinda's coming, Mrs. Speir." The old woman did not blink.

The rough panting went on. Labor, surely was. The way might be short, but it was rocky to traverse and only the single path. No matter what Isaac said, only the one path here.

Delpha spoke Mrs. Speir's name softly. "Jessie." Mrs. Speir's head turned then, her gaze latched onto Delpha's, and she was seeing.

"Gonna be all right, Jessie." She said it with what she could remember of tenderness, holding the loose-skinned hand. Despite the AC's efforts, despite the chill hand she grasped, Delpha had sweat on her face and on her palm. Her mouth was dry.

It was at least eight o'clock before she heard the door downstairs. Calinda Blanchard walked into the bedroom in a pantsuit Delpha had never seen, dark blue with pockets, double-breasted, navy-looking, her short gray hair brushed. Rouge on her thin lips and pearl ear screws on her ears. A canvas tote bag she set down on the horsehair sofa while her gaze stayed on her aunt.

"Know I'm late," she said softly. "But I wasn't kissing Aunt Jessie goodbye smelling like hog and hog gravy."

Delpha surrendered the bedside chair. Looked back to see Miss Blanchard mash back the topknot of white hair and kiss her aunt's forehead.

Delpha went downstairs and gulped water straight from the faucet. She took out an ice tray and pulled its lever, popped out cubes to fix a big glass of ice water and delivered it to the bedside table, received Calinda's nod. Delpha removed herself to the wide leather armchair in the corner and waited in case anything was needed. What Calinda said, she said private. Nobody had turned on a light.

Wasn't quite dark out. Delpha closed her eyes. Relieved of duty, she stretched in the spacious armchair, that sturdy, well-made chair, resident in herself, ready to do what was called for. Yes, she was serving, but there was not the futility, the mockery, the cheerless halt there had been in prison where you did what you did because you had to. There, you were not working for yourself, there was no fruit of your labor. You were not working for others, not in the right sense of the word, the sense that meant your work left people better off, stronger or cleaner or more soothed. You were working to keep the prison walls standing, keep the guards clocking in and out, the warden's office vacuumed, and yourself and all the other women separate and punished.

She looked up when the whispering developed a rhythm. Miss Blanchard had her gray head bowed toward her aunt's, touching forehead to forehead. She was barely rocking, and she sang in a whisper-voice: "Amazing Grace," all those verses. "You Are My Sunshine," the heartbreak anthem. She'd sip on the water and repeat a song, sip and begin another. An hour passed, more. The panting slowed.

From this valley they say you are leaving
I will miss your bright eyes and sweet smile
They say you are taking the sunshine
That has brightened our pathways a while.

On the third or maybe fifth time through "Red River Valley," a skip of silence prodded Delpha to look up. Mrs. Speir breathed, then she held it. After a long while, another breath, then the wait. A minute, two. Three. Breathe, don't, like she was flat-foot at the top of the path, picking through stones to find the place to ground her staff or to take hold of rope or rail while gathering strength to hoist. Her eyelids lagged half-way down. She was not seeing now.

Delpha took herself out to the stairs and down to the bottom step to leave the two old women alone. Miss Blanchard washed and singing, Mrs. Speir laboring to leave the valley.

The order reversed once Calinda pressed shut Jessie's eyes. She had laid her gray head a while on the bone chest. Then she sat up and wiped her eyes. To Delpha's quiet question, Calinda replied *No*, she sure should not call Thibodeaux the mortician right now. The lights switched on, and a last-ditch hunt commenced. This room, had to be, unless Ida had already got it.

"Maybe Mrs. Speir left word with her lawyer that made the will."

Calinda snorted, glanced at her watch and rose. "My cousin fixed that. She winds old Dinwiddie's clock ever once in a while. Huh. I'd bet you a year's property tax she doesn't remember she told me that."

"Mrs. Speir didn't say one thing 'bout where it was?"

"Maybe she did, but have you heard her talk? She was looking straight at me, and I picked up 'Tiffany' and 'in here.' Ruffled Ida, I can tell you that. She thought she'd already got everything, and I thought she had too. Moselle though said, 'Calinda, hear that? Miss Jessie's wanting to give you something,' and Ida had to shut her trap."

Miss Blanchard rifled through the vanity's drawers, not bothering to shut a one of them. She dumped the four empty jewelry boxes onto the floor with an exasperated hiss at Ida. Delpha, silently glad she'd stolen the Three Blossoms powder, went downstairs, fetched a wide china bowl with warm water and the squeeze bottle of Dawn dishwashing liquid. Slid the last diaper from between Jessie's withered legs, bone and hanging flesh, wiped and washed her bottom region clean.

She pulled off the blanket and top sheet, loosened the fitted sheet from its corners. Lifted up Mrs. Speir's shoulders and tugged on the sheet. Did the same from the bottom, and wrenched it out from under her. She bundled the dirty sheets and the blanket together and set the pile by the door. Coming back to the bed, no eye contact with Miss Blanchard who was now pushing hangers in the closet, she said tersely, "Maybe you know the Tiffany company made a lot of stuff."

Delpha maneuvered off Mrs. Speir's nightgown. Poor naked thing lying on a plastic sheet.

Calinda clapped the dresses, parted the clothes hangers and craned into the back of the closet, squatted down and pawed through shoes that hadn't pressed pavement in years. Then walked over to the bed where Delpha was washing Mrs. Speir's feet.

"A lot of stuff. Like all kinds of jewelry, you mean."

"Yeah, but not just that."

Mrs. Speir's toenails were yellow pearlized horn. Delpha reached over, pulled out the night table drawer and felt around, knocking over pill bottles. She came out with heavy-duty clippers, positioned the pinchers on the overgrown big-toenail.

"Tiffany made dishes and pretty silver things and colored-glass lamps. Little glass statues and vases, perfume even."

The navy blue pantsuit was smeared with dust. "You went digging around. I told you not to."

"You want a confession, Miss Blanchard, I used to spray my neck with your aunt's perfume. But the Tiffany Company, I went and looked it up in the public library. It's a old company."

When Delpha finished with the toenails, she dumped the rinds in the wastebasket by the night table. Resumed her sponging. The feet, the withered legs—take this stale smell away, replace it with the fragrance of soap-flowers. *There you go, Jessie Speir.*

"I didn't fall off the turnip truck yesterday." Miss Blanchard sat down on the horsehair sofa and counted on her fingers. "Jessie used to have a Tiffany fixture hung over the dining room table. Prettiest blue you ever seen. Dishes downstairs are Wedgewood bone china. They're here, but the silver's gone. And a couple of landscape paintings from the living room by an artist last name Durand. Tall trees and little bitty people. They had a big old rug from the Orient. Chandelier in the entry. Those're gone. But there was something in here that wasn't gone, or she wouldn't't've promised it to me. She was real intent that day, and until those strokes, Jessie was feeble-bodied but sharp in the head. She still had something Ida hadn't scavenged."

She turned away, then back. "That's the only reason I'm bothering now. And I'm here, and Ida's not, and you know that rule."

"The one that says possession's nine tenths of the law?"

"I was thinking Finders, Keepers."

The hunt proceeded.

Delpha washed upward of the slack belly, over the empty bags tipped with surprisingly rosy thimble-nipples and the rutted bone-chest. Under the sweatless arms. She wiped the folds of Mrs. Speir's neck, the cheeks, the forehead, wrung out her cloth, wet down the sparse eyebrows. Strange, she felt cleaner herself. Stroked her wet hands through Mrs. Speir's matted white hair.

Calinda had banged around the entire room. Then held her head and abruptly gone downstairs, stayed down there. When she finally trudged back up the stairs, Delpha had long finished her washing. She was nodding off on the leather chair, and Jessie, laid out straight-limbed in a pale blue gown, was growing cold.

Miss Blanchard lowered herself onto the horsehair sofa with a groan, set her elbows on wide-spaced legs. Her face was creased in defeat. "I guess she was talking gibberish when she said she had that Tiffany for me. I shouldn't of taken her so serious," she said with a mix of resignation and hurt that was painful to hear in the voice of an old person.

"Uncle Hardin he was fond of me and me of him. I never doubted that. Which is kinda funny, cause he didn't care for how I was. Tried to marry me off to the son of a friend of his. Didn't we have ourselves a knockdown drag-out. I expected Aunt Jessie to take up for me. But she stayed on the sidelines." Miss Blanchard removed her glasses and flicked the corner of an eye, slid them back on. "OK, fifteen minutes, then call the mortuary."

Delpha climbed from the leather chair and peered at the mantel clock. "Miss Blanchard, it's not but four fifteen in the morning."

"Undertaker's not an eight-to-five man, girl. Thibodeaux's got some fifty-cent-a-hour boys sleeping in a back room'll take a call. Besides, we have to tidy some." She gestured toward the bureau drawers, standing open, then said, "And lean over there and get all the pills out of that night table drawer, will you, so Ida doesn't get hold of 'em. What I brought that sack for."

Delpha got the tote bag from the couch. Pulled open the narrow top drawer of the bedside mahogany table and crouched to see inside it. There were the Q-tips, the Vick's Vapor Rub. Army of plastic pill bottles might make some bucks on the street. She threw them, handful by handful, into the tote. Done. Uncovered was some paper on the drawer bottom, and she fished it up, a large envelope. Old, stained, brown with age. She squatted and reached her arm toward the back of the deep drawer, felt around. Instead of wood, her fingers hit cloth. She got on her knees and peered in sideways. Pawed it out. Let a yellowed handkerchief fall away from a pack of envelopes tied with string.

"Lookahere," she whispered to Miss Blanchard. "These too." She leaned over the bed holding out the envelopes.

Calinda pulled the big envelope's sleeves apart, said,

"Nothing in it," dropped it onto the plastic sheet. She shifted the pack of letters so she could take out the top one's contents. A page ripped as it unfolded, she cursed and scanned it, muttering "Business talk, business talk," flipped it over, and stood still.

Sound of an engine outside.

Did Calinda hear? Her mouth had drifted open and her eyebrows were reaching toward her hairline. Still reading, she made her way to the vanity and sat down on its gilt bench. She laid down the letters and took another from its envelope, carefully smoothing it flat. Calinda propped her forehead on her hand. And read.

Delpha stood fixed but no other sounds came. The night, a cricket somewhere in the room, the silent woman on the bed.

A car door creaked open.

Delpha's head whipped around to the window and back. She was wide awake now. The circus was about to hit town, and she didn't want a ticket—whether it was lions or clowns. Miss Blanchard acted like she didn't hear a thing.

Car door slammed.

Miss Blanchard spit out a laugh and said, "C'mere."

Delpha skirted the bed and went over to the vanity. Miss Blanchard's finger pecked, and Delpha read a paragraph of Palmer script informing Mrs. Speir what Mr. Speir wished to do with several cherished parts of her body as soon as the train rushed him home. He proposed they carry out his wishes in the automobile and asked that she wear her French-heeled shoes and white stockings and leave off her drawers. Delpha glanced back at the woman on the bed.

A grin flashed across Miss Blanchard's face.

Faint ratchety noise from downstairs.

A scratchy rattle. Miss Blanchard motioned for Delpha to get her the bag she'd brought.

A caw, then another, shrilled downstairs in the foyer, as if a melancholy crow had made its way through the front door.

Footsteps, a dragging sound.

Calinda carefully laid the bundle of letters into the tote bag Delpha held. "Call the undertaker now. And if it gets to be five-thirty and I'm busy, call Moselle. She'll be up."

Step, drag, thump. Step, scuffling drag. Low conversation going on, with plaintive question marks in it, then some crying *hoo hoo hoo*, then steps.

Standing by the small table next to the armchair, Delpha dialed the black phone as fast as she could force its rotary wheel around. Miss Blanchard was right. A man answered on the first ring, and all he wanted from her was the address. Delpha faded back as Ida took the doorway.

Short pink tent dress banded green at the hem, sandals, blond flaps frizzed from the humid night. She clutched the torn shoulder strap of a humiliated purse that trailed behind her on the floor.

"I had to think all the way home from the casino boat," she said. "I thought till it was all clear and right in front of me, like a kaleidoscope. All this time and I refused to see it." Ida abandoned her purse by the doorway and tripped over to the leather armchair, sat herself down into it and stretched her legs out straight on the ottoman, lining up her tiny ankles and her white sandals. The piney gin-perfume accompanied her like a theme song.

Delpha edged sideways toward the vanity table.

"Calinda. We've been at each other like cats and dogs, and it's time to stop. Just stop. Honestly, it is. We should comfort each other when we need comfort. Besides Grandma, we're all each other has in the world, and she could go any day. She holds us together, but when she's gone, who's going to care about us?"

Calinda Blanchard tipped her head and sent Delpha a meaningful glance. Delpha bent and gathered the empty jewelry cases, quietly stacked them back in the lower drawer.

"Know what I remembered? You holding me in your lap, do you remember that? You were more a mother to me than anybody. That's what I realized driving home. All those years of pining for my mother who left me, and you were my mother. I loved you. Did I...did I ever mention that?"

"No, Ida."

"Come here, hug my neck." Ida held bare arms wide.

Delpha could see only the back of Ida's head. The muscles of Calinda's weathered brow and jaw softened so that her face sighed downward and her hooded eyes began to glint. Hands behind herself, Delpha pushed shut the drawers that Miss Blanchard had heedlessly jerked out. Then—Calinda probably wouldn't want Ida to have the marijuana either, not that Ida had a snowball's chance of finding it—Delpha pulled the top one back out and dislodged the fake back. Reached in and drew out the pouch and the packet of rolling papers. She dropped both in the tote bag bulging with pill bottles and checked back over her shoulder.

The two women's heads side-by-side, one gray and tipped down, one yellow and tipped up.

"Calinda, do you believe it's too"—a hiccup of weeping—"late for me?"

Calinda, staggering in the shorter woman's grip, sat down heavily on the leather footrest. Her hand went automatically to the trailing bangs, brushed them back in a way she must have done many times before. "No, baby, I don't think it's too late for you."

"Really? Oh, God, please. You really think it's not too late?"

"You're only forty-two. But you have to keep company with a different kind of people."

"Oh, I will! I'll change people, I will!"

"And you have to stop drinking, Ida."

The sobbing ceased. Ida raised her head. "I will," she said. "I'll...I'll stop tomorrow."

Calinda peeled herself out of her cousin's clutch, but she retained one small hand and rubbed it tenderly. "Good deal, baby," she said. "Good deal."

Delpha sighed without sound, jerked up the pile of sheets, and ducked out of the room. She was stepping quietly down the worn carpet of the stairs when the front door's knocker tolled. Four heavy strokes.

Two men in wrinkled suits and water-combed hair bumped in a gurney.

A scream from upstairs made Delpha about jump out of her flats, but only the younger man reacted, raising his head glumly. The jowled man in the lead, eyeing the staircase, muttered, "Fold the legs up, Jake," and pulled some lever under the gurney.

"Oh, man," the young one said. "It a fat person up there?"

"Shut *up*. I 'pologize for Jake, ma'am," said the older.

She held the door as they wheeled Mrs. Speir out. Quarter to six, birds chittering in the bushes telling the news, quiet upstairs from Miss Blanchard and Ida. Delpha used the kitchen phone to call Moselle, who surprised her by breaking into sobs. Was growing light outside, the sun beaming out its spokes. Delpha was sweaty and wrung out.

Sniffling, Moselle told Delpha to tell Calinda she had the papers Mrs. Speir had wanted to give her. She'd bring them down to the hotel at nine.

"Papers."

"The papers that was in a old envelope in the drawer with

her pill bottles. I brought 'em home to my house, 'cause Mrs. Speir said whoever had the papers was who they belonged to. She wanted Calinda to have them, and I was fraid Ida'd find them."

"Miss Blanchard was looking for jewlery last night."

"That's what Mrs. Speir said she was looking for too, more'n sixty years ago. Jewlery for her first anniversary. But Mr. Speir, he gave her paper, according to the rule."

"What rule?"

"Lord, some made-up rule. Gold for married fifty years, silver for twenty-five, I don't know what all. But for the first year, it's paper. You tell Calinda."

XXVI

MONDAY MORNING PHELAN was raring to tell his secretary about Real-Mrs. Lloyd Elliott, but he was held up by the sight of Delpha's snap-button western shirt with history, tucked into blue jeans, and pink flip flops. Her brown hair was tousled. She looked younger. He smiled, and she stood up.

"Morning, Mr. Phelan. Rustled up some money for the kitty."

She told him Mrs. Speir had passed on Friday, and the burial was today. Miss Blanchard was putting on some food at the New Rosemont and had asked her to help with that, and probably with her cousin Ida. "Dressed for the kitchen," she said, glancing down.

"Looking good anyway."

She held out an antique-looking envelope. "Here's the job. I told her I'd see if you had time. Mrs. Speir left these papers for Miss Blanchard, and she wants to know if you can find somebody to tell her what they's worth. She doesn't trust the lawyer. The library's not open on Sunday, or I'd've seen what I could do. Oh, and I wrote up a note that says what you're doing, and Miss Blanchard signed it."

Phelan took the envelope. "Miss Wade, you are one excellent employee."

Her face lifted, bright. "Thank you for saying." She

handed over two hundreds from Miss Blanchard and broke her own rule about the business having dibs on all the money. "I won't write that in our income, you don't want." She descended the stairs quick and light.

Phelan folded the bills into his wallet. Old lady Speir: a score and ten past her given years, no surprise there. He went over and peered out his window—sure enough, broad black bow drooping on the Rosemont's door.

He opened the envelope. Heavy, yellowed papers, two of them. Once he'd studied the goddessy, Miss Liberty-type figures, read the different-sized numbers, the large and the spidery print, he knew exactly where to take them. How he'd get in to see her, he didn't know. He sat, put his feet up on the metal desk. See, if he had a classy, varnished oak one, he'd have to worry about scuffing the thing. Phelan watched the sky, clouds drifting, and thought and then picked up the phone and left a message for Miles. Two hours later, Miles called him back and answered his question: yes, his firm did hire college kids for summer, but all interns were already hired.

"Interns? Thought those were doctors."

Miles told him interns were gofers who worked for minimum wage, the experience and the contacts. Mostly partners' kids or their friends' kids.

"How about next summer?"

"We don't schedule that far ahead. You changing careers already?"

"No, what I'm wondering is if your law firm or one you know might extend itself and offer some experience to a college kid that isn't related to anybody with his name on your letterhead." Phelan floated the particular idea he had in mind.

The other end of the line was quiet.

"Being as America is the land of equal opportunity," Phelan added. He played his ace to the silent receiver. "We inherited a crummy world, Miles. How we gonna fix it 'cept one by one?"

Half a minute after he'd rung the bell, and probably ten seconds after the woman on the other side had inventoried him and his suit through the peephole, she opened the door with mathematical calculation, her stance such that she could slam the heavy oak with minimum effort. Phelan gazed onto a strip of unsmiling face.

"Morning, ma'am. I'm Thomas Phelan, and I'm here to see Mrs. Elliott, please."

"She has no appointments on Mondays. Goodbye."

"Wait, she'll want to see what I brought." Surely she would. Maybe she would. Maybe not. He hoped she would.

The door shut.

Phelan knocked on it. Knocked again. Spoke loudly to it. "Ma'am, your daughter's the business major, right. Right?"

The door cracked again, the black woman still unsmiling, but looking toward him. "Your daughter said I'd never get past you, so I didn't come empty-handed."

The woman glanced down at his hands and back up to his face.

"Job for your girl next summer. Law firm."

Her head lifted.

"Well, I can get her an interview anyway. A friend promised me he could do that, and he's a good guy."

"What do you have that Mrs. Elliott would care about, Mr. Phelan? I will not let you in if you're selling anything."

Phelan pulled out the yellowed papers. "Not selling, scout's honor." Hastily, he flipped her a peace sign. "I just want Mrs. Elliott to look at these because she's the only expert I know. Or know of. Not for me, ma'am. Tell Mrs. Elliott I'm a private investigator doing a job for friends. A lady died Friday night and left these to her niece. Niece is an old lady herself. She's not a rich woman and not the trusting kind."

A palm extended toward him. Phelan set the papers into it. The door closed.

Presently, Mrs. Lloyd Elliott's front door opened again, and he crossed her threshold.

XXVII

TWO FANS RUNNING full blast over the measley central air
and the straining stoves. Delpha liked deviled eggs but disliked
making them. It was so easy to tear the rubbery white boats
that the cooked yokes—mashed with mustard, mayonnaise,
cayenne, pickle, and salt—had to fit into. This was the task
that Oscar, presiding over a Calindaless kitchen like a hard-
eyed Santa over two backward elves, had assigned her—boil
four dozen eggs, peel them, cut them in half, devil them
without tearing them up. He had his friend Shayla, who'd
already pared three dozen apples, chopping celery for Waldorf
salad, sacks of Diamond walnuts beside her. Delpha noticed
that the shine Shayla once directed Oscar's way had dimmed
a mite. A ham was baking. Oscar, smelling of cinnamon and
nutmeg, was crimping dough on the piecrusts and whisper-
singing *Ain't Too Proud to Beg*. It'd be out with the ham and in
with the pies.

"Ain't nobody begging here," Shayla muttered to Delpha.
"Lotta ordering around going on. You know he be this bossy?"

"Been nice to me."

Delpha tore an egg white. Oscar wasn't looking. She ate
it, which made Shayla titter and elbow her. The mood in the
kitchen elevated. They labored on through the storing of the
deviled eggs and Waldorf salad, set the ham to cool, then the
baked pies Oscar favored with a Cheshire-cat grin. Now he

was lining up restaurant-sized jars of bread and butter pickles and pickled pearl onions, cans of cashews for them to arrange in dishes and set out before five p.m.

The manager of the pool hall across the street had sent over ten pounds of brisket and hot links. Mr. Dinwiddie the lawyer had sent the centerpiece, lilies. The bank had had three boxes of pecan pralines delivered, and the CPA's wife had tottered through the lobby with an iced sheet cake she'd baked herself.

The two extra leaves were already installed in the big table in the lobby. Delpha dressed it with a linen cloth she'd ironed—first-class pain in the butt, you had to sprinkle water and press hard on the iron to flatten wrinkles out of linen—and warned off the residents. No one was to sit there to drink their coffee and put coffee rings on the fine cloth.

The residents watched her work. Mrs. Bibbo evened out the corners of the linen tablecloth for Delpha, stood back and then adjusted again, received her thanks in sober silence. The lobby's air was not grim, not with such a holiday spread to anticipate, but it was determinedly solemn. No checker sets in evidence, no Bicycle playing cards. This was Calinda's family today being laid in the grave. Calinda's elder, which left her now the generation next to heaven, a member of their club.

At three, the funeral home's car arrived for Calinda. Delpha knocked on the door of the back apartment that adjoined the kitchen. "Car's here, Miss Blanchard."

"C'min."

Cautiously, Delpha opened the door. She hadn't seen inside this apartment before. A spacious room with busy old wallpaper—vines and leaves and berries—wide-plank floors, a sitting area with sofa and upholstered chairs, double bed with two night tables and a lamp with a white shade. Miss

Blanchard, smoking, rocked slowly in a high-backed chair, her legs crossed. She wore a black dress and hose *hose* that gave a sheen to her shins. There was a sheen to her face, too, and an acrid smell in the room.

The tobacco pouch lay on a round table by the rocking chair, its packet of rolling papers open like a tiny cabinet with orange doors. Delpha had smelled reefer before and this was it.

"Funeral home sent the car."

"I heard you. Where'd you find this stuff?" Calinda gestured toward the pouch.

"In the back of a drawer, kinda hid."

"Hid." She rocked for a while. "One of the rolling papers had handwriting on it."

Delpha nodded.

"Like getting a letter that was thirty years in the mail. That's Hettie's writing."

"Y'all keep the pouch back in that drawer?"

"No, we did not. Kept it in this room. It disappeared. Before she did. Ida would've been twelve or thirteen, and she was one nosy child. Always had her eye peeled for things could've been her mother's. Bless her drunk heart." Pinching the cigarette between finger and thumb, she took a pull, held it, closed her eyes, rocked. Miss Blanchard blew out the smoke slowly, then spit-tamped the fire from the tip.

"Hand me that jacket, will you please?"

Delpha gave her the black jacket lying on the bed. Miss Blanchard stood and put it on over the shapeless black dress. "Shoes're already killing me. Oscar and y'all got the food ready?"

"Ready to go."

"Good. Thank you. I am grateful to you."

Delpha understood she was not talking about the food.

She stepped back from the door. The old woman held herself loosely, like there was no hurry in the world today.

Don't smoke all this without me, sunshine
I wouldn't never, baby, you'd been here. Why'd you go?
Had to. No choice, sunshine, no choice at all.

The whole hotel, some eighteen retired citizens, was assembled in the lobby. Residents approached and offered condolences as Miss Blanchard passed, each coming forward to meet her where they were, as if they lined a boulevard. They were mourners today, significant, confident in their part, if not in other things. Near the door, which was held open to the seething summer heat by a moist-faced chauffer in a black suit, Mr. Rabey hoisted himself to his feet. He did not speak to Calinda, but he removed his cap, revealing a bristling head of iron-gray hair, and nodded to her.

The polished black car drove Miss Blanchard away from the Rosemont.

"Didn't she look peaceful?" Mr. Finn said.

"That's what you say about the deceased," Mr. Nystrom chided.

"I can say it about whoever looks peaceful, Harry."

XXVIII

PHELAN WAS NOT invited to sit. He stood near the door
to the white room like a private without an army while
the woman scoured his face and mode of dress. He wasn't
any hippie or hobo, had his suit on, and he'd had the Magic
Weavers mend the rip in his pants. Maybe the suit had
accumulated some wear he hadn't noticed, maybe his tie had
a butter drip. She was hardly dolled up for a gala—not a lick
of makeup, half-glasses balanced on her nose, uncombed dark
hair clipped up in a rooster-tail. As she leaned forward, her
cherry-blossom kimono gapped, revealing packed cleavage.

"My housekeeper tells me you are asking about these"—
she raised the papers in her left hand—"for the legal heir. You
want information about their value, I assume. Do you know
the first thing about stock certificates?"

Phelan Investigations might not know a lot while Phelan
Investigations learned on the job, but lack of knowledge ran
counter to the image Phelan Investigations cared to project.
"Just that you own a little bit of the company," he said. "That
paper tells you how much. I'm guessing it's the number up in
the right-hand corner."

"Who is the owner of these certificates? Let me see some
authorization."

Phelan unfolded Miss Blanchard's note from his inner
jacket pocket and handed it over to Mrs. Elliott. "Not a formal

contract, but you can see it says she's asking me to find out for her. They're burying her aunt today."

Neva Elliott pushed the glasses up to read the note. "Today. Your heir certainly is wasting no time."

"As Miss Blanchard's aunt was a hundred years old, her death didn't surprise anybody. And Miss Blanchard's sole living is a downtown hotel. I'm betting its value shrinks every year about the same amount its maintenance costs rise."

"Well. What was the aunt's name?"

"Jessie Speir."

"Speir." Mrs. Elliott let the glasses drop on their chain. The furrows between her eyebrows drew tighter. "Speir, Speir. Hardin Speir. Haven't heard that name in many a day, and he had a partner in his brokerage. Wexler, something like that. Saul. Why aren't these certificates with the attorney?"

"This is a...special bequest to her niece. Made orally, in front of witnesses. Her granddaughter inherited the rest of the estate and has disposed of a lot of it, I understand, uh... premortem."

"I see."

Neva Elliot tucked her little feet into low-heeled slippers, rose and toddled over to her white file cabinets. If only she'd been standing the first time, he'd have known in an instant that his client was not in front of him—this woman was five feet tall. She pulled out a slim folder and turned pages in it. Her fingernail speared a line. She laid down the stock certificates and leaned over to get a pen on the desk, jotted a while on a pad.

"All right," she said, turning. "Your Tiffany is a hundred shares purchased in 1910. It's worth around twenty thousand dollars, plus sixty years of dividends, which will be considerable. The niece should take it to her broker who'll tell her its precise value."

She put down the Tiffany and picked up the second paper. "This one, I don't need to look up. Even you, as long as you brush your teeth and wash your hands"—one eyebrow lofted—"will know Colgate-Palmolive."

"Even me."

"You may tell the niece it's worth a nice little bit. But it's ten shares. Ten. Her uncle would have done far better to have purchased a hundred of Colgate-Palmolive, and ten of Tiffany. It never ceases to amaze me, the foolish choices intelligent people make. Hardin Speir had his own firm. Presumably he knew markets and values. He's handling business in the time of the titans—*my god*, J.P. Morgan, Astor, Carnegie. Off he goes to New York City and ignores Standard Oil and U.S. Steel, gives short shrift to Colgate-Palmolive, and instead invests his money in arty French trinkets."

"I understand the stock was an anniversary present for his wife."

"A hundred shares of soap and toothpaste, now *that* would have had true love printed all over it."

Mrs. Lloyd Elliott laughed without smiling.

There must have been thirty people in the lobby, whose thumping heart was a table laden with platters, cut glass dishes, bowls, and coffee urns. The strong scent of lilies mingled with coffee and ham. The middle-aged were on their feet chatting to other middle-aged, with the exception of a blond woman who appeared dazed, planted in a blue chair knees apart, both hands clinging to a glass. The elderly fetched food or ate from plates balanced dangerously on their laps.

Phelan passed an old guy in a cap who was working on half a plateful of cocktail onions and big square piece of cake. Delpha's slender back disappeared into the kitchen. Feeling some intensity directed his way, he surveyed the room until he caught sight of the gray proprietor, honed in on him like a searchlight.

She shook his hand and guided him to armchairs on the lobby's periphery, set down her coffee on a table in between, and listened with a pleasant expression. Phelan offered condolences and reported on his initial consultation. For a more accurate accounting of the Tiffany and the Colgate-Palmolive stock, she would need to choose a financial expert—he handed her a block-printed list of legitimate stockbrokers in town he'd interviewed (called on the phone), who were prepared (drooling) to examine and discuss Miss Blanchard's certificates at her convenience.

"Twenty thousand for the Tiffany?"

"Yes, ma'am, plus dividends. Sixty-three years' worth."

"At *my* convenience, you said."

"Any of these gentlemen would be glad to get your call."

Miss Blanchard rose with the ease of a young woman and nudged a cabbage-rose footrest closer to her cabbage-rose armchair, sat back down, and put her feet up. Her searchlight aspect was extinguished. She settled herself into the chair, crossed her ankles, reached for her coffee and sipped it.

"Fast work, Tom Phelan. Get the girls to cut you some ham and fix you a plate. There's plenty."

Phelan accepted a cup of coffee from Delpha, dressed in her white blouse and navy blue skirt. Her hair was swept up and folded around somehow, the scar on the back of her neck covered by trailing tendrils. He reached out to trace a light brown strand, but caught himself as Delpha turned. She'd poured herself a cup, and they clinked.

XXIX

TWO FULL WEEKS. The phone was suffering a siege of drought, except for several parties who inquired about Mr. Phelan's rates and lied that they'd call back. The bank account was withering.

Delpha's Gatesville business course had included a chapter on marketing. She set herself the job of writing a letter advertising their services and, in the library, compiled a long list of likely companies. Whir of activity in the secretary part of the office. Sometimes she hummed. She'd call to identify the head of Personnel or some other manager figure at each company on her list, type up a letter, add Phelan's business card, lick an envelope and a stamp.

Phelan signed letters. He worried. He stepped out for lunch, leaving his secretary to her campaign. Noon, faint church bells tolling mass, sun like a full steam iron on the top of his head. Bought a shrimp sandwich to go and a Coke from a lunch wagon and parked down by the port. Jacket in the car, sleeves rolled, baseball cap pulled down, he seated himself on a new bench, conveniently situated for river-watchers like himself.

Black-hulled tankers were anchored in the port, white topsides, striped flags riffling against the drift of summer clouds. The big ships rose like courthouses from the river, not a sailor in sight. Only things moving were the flags and the sunlit currents of the Neches, its water infinite sparkles. There would never be diamonds the like.

He ate his sandwich. *Mmm*, they'd buttered and fried the roll before they packed the saucy shrimp in. Chefs. He smacked, mopped off the mayonnaisey sauce and sucked his fingers. Privy to the food/bird network, a pigeon appeared expectantly. Phelan sacrificed the last of his bun, tossed out a handful of crumbs to the guest. Soon the rest of its party arrived, a second pigeon with a raveling nether region, and something small and nondescript, maybe a sparrow, with a startling, jack-hammer-like hop that propelled it to Phelan's toes.

OK, one more go-round and he'd file this case away. Phelan leaned back, one foot on the other knee, and filled in columns of a score-sheet written on the air. Daughtry. The formula developed in his R&D belonged to him. That Enroco ended up with it was industrial sabotage. John Daughtry must have been ready to rain fiery toads on the stealers. Instead, in keeping with these progressive times, he'd sic'd Lloyd Elliott on them.

Phelan moved to the Enroco column. This particular formula was stellar. Someone tiptoed it over. Big E hooked it and cooked it. So Daughtry and Enroco squared off over the formula. Which Daughtry legitimately owned. Suppose some people would say a decent employer might ante up some compensation, a bonus for a formula like this one. Especially since, according to Margaret in the proper black suit, the lead chemist Roberts or Robertson...no, Robbins had been in the process of dying.

Phelan pictured those bosses from company headquarters, the ones who'd tour the rig every so often, starched white shirts rolled to the elbows, borrowed hard hats sitting up high. Those execs, they'd have said that sentence in a different tone of voice: Hey, the chemist is *dying*. S.O.L. shrug, crinkle at their eye corners. They were the kings who'd paid marine geologists to locate the site, have the rig towed there, hired the workers on it, financed its dollar-devouring operations to the tune of six zeros and ticking. Righteous, straightforward gaze out at their own—nobody else's—laden ships, sailing into safe harbor.

The spruce pigeon beat out the raggedy one for the biggest piece of bun. Phelan found a lettuce shred in the sack and lobbed it toward the loser.

OK. Back to the Daughtry column. Say Daughtry leaked the formula himself. Why didn't he just sell it? Phelan didn't get that part. Then he did. He did. Margaret—Margaret had said John Daughtry missed his business more than his wife. Man like that wouldn't sell off a product that stood to make his company talked about, envied. He'd keep it and himself in the bosom of the petrochemical world. But he would have had to scramble for such an expansion while Enroco could easily handle nationwide production, distribution, exports.

Lloyd Elliott column. Like Miles had said, the lawyer would have known the whole deal.

Last column: Wallace Daughtry. A sick John Daughtry retires suddenly, conveniently for Wallace. Wallace and his brand new office/nouveau antique house designed for him to sit behind a tennis-court-sized desk and accept calls from his investment counselor. No oil drips on his cuff, no mud on his boots.

These kinds of things happened all the time. Case was done. Didn't matter anymore.

The pigeons and the sparrow, having cleaned Phelan out, took to the sky. Breeze off the sunlit water played on his sweating face. Finally he wadded sandwich wrapper into the paper bag, tossed in the Coke can. Had to get back to the office so he could sit around.

Funny. Used to think it was the ships, but all along it had been the river that drew him. It stretched him until his blood streamed with it. The river remained itself, its wholeness a power beyond any of the puny daily forces in Tom Phelan's little life. He could drive down here and study it, gray in the days, black at night, white gleams of moon, port light carried on the rippling skin of its wide back. After a while he wouldn't bother with understanding anything.

"Phelan Investigations. How may we help you?" A couple beats of quiet then "Colored man," Delpha whispered, covering the mouthpiece. "Nervous-sounding." She transferred the call to Phelan.

The voice told Phelan Dennis Deeterman was around again.

He'd never heard the clear voice before, but it had to be him. Phelan said, "How do you know, Marvin? You see him?"

Silence. Then "Yeah."

"OK. When and where?"

"Las Saturday. Comin' out of a 7-11 on Pine Street. I 'as bout to get outa the car, and once I seen him I didn't."

"Sure it's him?"

"Yeah, he so tall. And he got this funny walk, butt scoot around sideways. Iss him. Got a mustache now."

"You didn't see what he was driving, did you?"

"Old maroon pickup."

"License number?"

"Mud on it."

"You tell the police this?"

"You can tell em. Bye."

"Wait a sec. You and your mom stay at the same place you used to?"

"Naw, we at another place."

"Good. You talk to Ricky Toups?"

"That fool. Hell no."

"Fool. Wait, why's he a fool?"

Clunk. Dial tone.

Phelan called E.E. and reported this information. "I've been driving by Deeterman's house ever so often, you know, just checking. Hadn't seen any sign. Y'all heard anything about him?"

E.E. dodged the question. Muttered that awhile back they'd got a call on a teenage boy. Fifteen years old. Mother on the line insisting he was a missing person, stepfather on the extension butting in with the theory that the boy took off. "Call us you see anything make you think Deeterman's haunting that house on Concord. Don't be traipsing in there after him, you." Click.

Phelan put down the phone, ambled into Delpha's office, and repeated the news about the boy.

"Missing. Mmh, mmh." The envelope at Delpha's lips lowered. Her shoulders pulled forward as her forehead creased. "Hate to hear that. I hate it."

"Guys like Deeterman are born with their wires crossed. Or else somebody crossed 'em when they were too little to know the difference."

She laid the envelope on the desk, sealed the seam with her fist. "And they wanna do what they do."

"Pretty simple view, Miss Librarian."

"Yeah. It is."

She placed the envelope into a cardboard box holding its sisters and brothers, rolled more letterhead into the Selectric.

Four hours later, Phelan cruised by the Toups', marking the solitary living room light.

He drove by the white ranch. The house was a pile of night. Just enough moon to see the yard standing in weeds, strip of cement driveway, no pickup parked on it. Couldn't make out the track to the backside of the house.

In the next minute, Phelan's heart beat fifty-nine times instead of sixty.

The street light nearest the old white ranch was dark. Streetlights burned out. But they could also be smashed.

XXX

THE MARKETING LETTER had taken major figuring. What would Phelan Investigations help these companies with? Stealing. Cheating. Lying. Double-crossing. That would be your embezzlers, pilferers, fake-identity employees, crooked partners, sabotagers, etc. You couldn't use those words though, they weren't businesslike. Not classy. People didn't want to broadcast they'd been taken in by crooks like that. Make people throw the letter away.

In the course she'd completed at Gatesville, Mr. Wally had taught how to use larger words that weren't plain from the get-go, that hinted, let you read the page and sit back and think about it, apply it to yourself gradually, not all at once like a sharp stick in the eye. Accordingly, Delpha had written bland and broad, picking a few of what Mr. Wally called *utility words*. Phelan Investigations could help you straighten out *difficulties* in business *dealings* or *personnel activities*. Those problems that distracted a *successful* business from its *goals*.

She'd written a catchy enough first sentence. Then a little about their services and their standards: they aimed to assist your business in returning to profitable operations. They were quick and discreet. *Discreet*, she looked up because there was "discreet" and then there was "discrete." Mr. Wally had a droning lecture about bad spelling or using the wrong word of a pair that sounded alike but meant different things.

Like *their* and *there*. Didn't matter if you were smart. Those mistakes made you look like you were sporting a dunce cap. Delpha's last paragraph was dedicated to their contact information. Please do not hesitate to call or to stop by, should your business…etc., etc., address and phone number.

Her back hurt between the shoulder blades from tensing up about the letter, from intent typing. She'd felt relieved when Mr. Phelan thought it looked fine. She had a bunch of letters to go.

A Thursday evening and Delpha was drinking coffee in the Rosemont lobby after dinner, not much attending to conversations unless they insisted on being attended to.

The special prosecutor had called for President Nixon to turn over the secret tapes, Nixon had stonewalled, and the Senate had hurled a subpoena into the Oval Office. The discussion of these dramatic events had carried over into a contentious debate about whether Henry Louis Aaron would chase down George Herman Ruth's 714 career homeruns.

Mr. Nystrom finally scissored his arms like a ref calling "Safe," then pronounced that he could not. Hank Aaron was thirty-nine years old, and youthful as that was, it was old for a professional athlete. Okay, so he'd squeaked out 700, but he'd never reach 714. He didn't have another season in him.

"Squeaked out!" huffed Mr. Finn. "Gimme some of that squeak. You just don't want him to beat The Babe."

Mr. Nystrom fired back, "So what if I don't?"

"Newspaper says Hank Aaron's been getting death threats. For hitting homeruns. Harry. What kind of person wants to kill a baseball player for hitting homeruns?"

Mr. Nystrom's face swelled. "The record should hold."

"Wish it could. 1935. My wife was in the pink and a looker

still. Kids were running in the back door and through the kitchen. I miss those days. We all do."

"Oh, quit bumping your gums," said Mr. Nystrom.

Mrs. Bibbo, regent of the television, rolled her eyes and beckoned for Delpha to come watch. With no night job anymore, Delpha usually walked or read a book upstairs. Isaac wanted to see her earlier, but she couldn't feature him sauntering through the lobby past all the residents like he was picking up his aunt for a date, or them climbing the stairs side by side, turning all heads in the lobby. She didn't want judgments, stares, or confidential advice to unburnish her time with Isaac. Their time was good where it was.

A commercial interrupted Mrs. Bibbo's program: "Socialites, the choosy woman's choice"—a beanpole in a short beige dress murmuring *Yes, yes* to a pair of black patent leather shoes with stocky heels. Delpha looked away to see Calinda steering through the lobby toward the TV couch.

"You got a letter."

Her chest seized. She let Calinda reach her before she accepted the envelope, which lacked a return address and so had not been issued by the Texas Department of Corrections. Therefore, she was not, today, being ordered back to prison. She breathed again. Delpha abandoned the television and ran up to her room, locked the door.

Linen paper, cream-color like the envelope. Typewritten.

Dear Delpha Wade,

I am writing to you as Isaac's mother to ask that you stop seeing him. Perhaps you will not believe this, but it is not your criminal record that concerns me. Neither is it the large gap in your ages. I want you to stop seeing my son so that he will agree to finish his education on the East Coast. That is where he belongs. He has a future in science. He has friends from families who can help him make a first-rate start in life, though he is not presently in contact with them. Isaac has completed his junior year. There is only the final year left. Now all he talks about is staying here in Beaumont.

You may judge me prurient when I say I am not sorry he met you, but I believe young men need first affairs like the one he has had with you. Isaac is changed. I would go so far as to say he is able to be kinder. I can persuade him not to worry about his mother any longer, and I can persuade him to return to Princeton, as long as you will break off with him.

A woman with your past undoubtedly understands how a situation can call forth necessary if regrettable actions.

I wish you well. Truly.

The letter had no signature, but the writer had stated who she was in the first line. Delpha read it again. What a difference that third paragraph made.

Undoubtedly understand.

Necessary if regrettable actions.

Right. She did know about those.

Delpha put the dry fountain pen, nib-up, in one skirt pocket and five dollars in the other. Passed head-down through the lobby and went out walking on the openness of Main Street and Liberty Avenue, past the Jefferson Theatre where the marquee hawked "The Day of the Jackal," starring no names she knew. She took long strides, hands in pockets, feeling the pen, the folded bill, and her own hipbones swinging along. She stayed away from Crockett and walked

Forsythe Street, Bowie and Fannin, Neches, and Archie. This old downtown was not really a wide acreage until it met and opened up to the port and the ship basin's oily water. She stopped in front of St. Anthony's, looking up at its brick towers with the white columns, the white crosses on top.

"You lost something, ma'am," a voice called. An old man, sitting on a bus bench the other side of Jefferson Street.

Delpha waited for a car to go by and then crossed over to him, slowing up as she saw he wasn't so old as she'd thought he was, late forties or fifty. Broad, mixed-race man wearing a thin-lapel suit new maybe the year she went away. A cane leaned against his knee.

"Why you think I lost something?"

He flipped a finger toward the red-brick church. "St. Anthony. The saint of lost things. I'm a deacon there, so I'm qualified to tell you"—he smiled, gap-toothed—"if you pray to St. Anthony, he'll help you find whatever you lost. Or I could pray for you, if you like. Would you like me to?"

The chaplain at Gatesville used to ask that. Used to say, You don't tell me no, Miss Wade, I'll pray for you anyway. That chaplain visited Huntsville too, even the men on Death Row, and he loved and prayed for them, he said. That impressed Delpha, made her think. One of her thoughts was the chaplain was loving humbled men, not free ones bent on harm. Could he do that too?

"Like to ask you a deacon question."

The man straightened and looked at her hospitably, as if she'd stepped into his office.

"A chaplain once told me if you harbor hate in your heart, if you don't let forgiveness in, it'll poison you. You believe that?"

"Yes, ma'am. I do believe that."

"Chaplain said if you harbored hate, you had hate. If you

found love in your heart, that's what you'd get. Love. You believe that too?"

"Oh, yes."

"So how is it you get from the hate to the love?"

A car approached, lighting them both up. It was slowing to the curb. At the wheel, a black woman with a white scarf on her head and a cigarette in her mouth. The man held up his hand, and she doused the lights.

"You don't get there once, Miss. You get there over and over. You have it, you lose it, you find it. That's why St. Anthony is powerful. We have to keep finding." The man stood, jacket in hand, leaning his weight on the cane. "I know a long prayer to him and a short one. Which would you like?"

"Short."

"St. Anthony, St. Anthony, please come round. Something is lost that needs to be found."

Delpha smiled at the rhyme.

So did the deacon. He said, "Hey, baby" and maneuvered heavily into the passenger seat, drew in the cane after himself. He spoke up at her. "You're gonna find it now."

He was right. She had it already. Delpha had just wanted more opinions on the matter, more time for her decision to form. Decisions took time, took scrutinizing and sifting and measuring and weighing. A decision wasn't sure till it settled in the body.

And then she liked finding out things—had known that before. Knew it more now.

The matter at hand tonight—a knowledge, an understanding—hadn't been lost. Just postponed. She herself was holding off looking at it.

Delpha walked on, toward the New Rosemont. Her blouse was sweated-through under the arms. She'd have to rinse it out in the sink with a smidgen of Ivory, drape it over the back of her chair.

She'd had to walk to overcome the old push-pull feelings of receiving a letter. Happy when she got a birthday card from her friend Barbara Jean. Happy when her great-uncle Lafayette sent a letter every month, though he mostly wrote the same talk about the weather. Letters were just measures of distance between her and the free world, but it was better to get them. It was empty to receive no Christmas card in '71, even when she'd been notified that Lafayette passed. Nothing after.

She climbed the stairs, unlocked her door, locked it and kicked off her flats. Sitting on her bed, she reread Isaac's mother's letter aloud in a low voice. *Perhaps*, a common word anybody could use except everybody around here would say "maybe." Didn't prove anything. But *prurient*, that was the word Delpha'd had to look up in the dictionary. That word their second client, who was not Mrs. Lloyd Elliott, had used on the telephone—explaining herself when she didn't have to. "Prurient, perhaps, to have my husband and his lover photographed at a motel room. But I must. Some things cannot be let pass."

"They can't, and that's the truth," Delpha had replied and given her the amount that was owed on her account. The woman had not offered to send a check but named the steakhouse museum for the payoff.

The red pocket dictionary had informed Delpha that *prurient* meant "having an excessive interest in sexual matters."

Perhaps. Prurient. Both words on the same page of stationery.

Coincidence? Perhaps.

✳

Sandwich in her purse, Delpha stepped through the library on Friday at twelve. Sun-flooded stained glass jewels, creaky old wooden floor. She stationed herself in the periodicals, searching through the year's newspapers backwards by date until a square-inch, handsome, middle-aged Isaac startled her, staring out at her from the obituary page. A strong-boned face, confident, casual, the smile in the eyes rather than the mouth.

Dr. Charles Robbins, 47, lost his valiant battle with cancer on June 2, 1973. Survived by wife of twenty-two years, Lucinda, and one son, Isaac. Dr. Robbins employed since 1961 by Daughtry Petrochemical of Beaumont in the department of Research and Development. In lieu of flowers, the family requested that donations be sent to the Dr. Charles Robbins' Memorial Scholarship fund established at Lamar College.

Isaac's dad, Charles Robbins, the chemist at Daughtry.

He'd devised the formula that attorney Lloyd Elliott had been engaged to defend against Enroco Oil Co. Was married to a woman with an educated vocabulary and a mind on the bedroom part of marriage. Maybe because she'd never ever make love to her husband again. Forty-seven wasn't old. Maybe the last time, they hadn't known it was the last time. Or maybe they had.

The real telephone number, not Walgreen's payphone, would be listed in the book. Now Mr. Phelan would have at least part of his outsize curiosity satisfied. Delpha would pass on this information to her boss, if she was right. If she and Mrs. Robbins got straight about her request to let Isaac go.

That had to come first.

Angela rounded the stacks and paused by the remote table

for a whisper-chat. An assistant librarian, sweet girl who overdid her makeup, she'd caught Delpha stealthily biting a sandwich and shown her a more secluded lunch spot, out of the head librarian's route.

They talked from time to time, which pleased Delpha. It was like she had a friend she wasn't assigned to. Angela wanted to know if Delpha was going to the festival on Crockett Street this weekend. Her uncle's band was playing. "I'm hustling up an audience, you oughta go. They're pretty good, really. They can play everything on the radio. Sometimes they let my cousin sing a song. He's just twelve but he can really give you the creeps."

"I don't know. I might."

"You finding everything you need?" Angela had individual, black lash-strokes painted on the skin beneath her eyes, and above a panorama of mermaid green. Her solicitous smile was framed in a thick shade of nude.

"Yeah, thanks, I'm 'bout finished here."

Procrastinating, Delpha walked for a while. A cloud above the downtown was trying to shed the rest of its water but clumsily. A few drops fell and slacked off. St. Anthony's bells were sleeping. She brushed rain from her hair and scanned for the deacon but didn't see him. She walked on. A man with roses sprouting from his arms hurried into the florist shop managed by a lady with a black mask. Delpha liked flowers. Drawn into the shop once, she'd spoken to the woman, asked how she learned to place flowers in vases so they looked pretty. The mask covering the spot where the woman's nose had been ruffled at the edge when she spoke about horizontal and vertical, oval, S-shaped floral arrangements.

Delpha nodded through the window to her now, as the manager brought a rose up to her mask.

In a few more minutes, she stopped at the payphone by the library. The smile fell from her face, she took a breath, and dropped in a dime. A female voice said hello.

"Mrs. Robbins?"

"Yes. Who is this?"

This was it. This was the voice she'd heard before. "My name is Delpha Wade."

Satin quiet the background at Mrs. Robbins' house, no music, no television. On Delpha's side not much noise, car every now and then. Twelve forty-five on a sweltering day, air steaming, streets wet.

A tight, coiled silence persisted. Delpha wiped her neck.

Finally the woman said, "If Isaac had answered, what would you have done?"

"Hung up."

"Well, that's something. You received my letter."

"I did."

"Will you do it—let my son...get on with his life?"

"There's a bench in front of the City Hall and Auditorium. Pearl Street. Across from the library. Can you meet me there tomorrow evening? Won't be that much traffic on a Saturday."

"Why not tonight?"

"Cause I'm still thinking."

"You want money."

"I want a little of your time."

"But will you do what I asked?"

"First tell me what 'necessary but regrettable' means."

Sound of an indrawn breath, then one breathed out into the receiver. "What time?"

"Eight, eight thirty. That work?"

"I'll be there."

Delpha hung up and walked toward the office. Their phone might be ringing with fresh business and her not there to answer it, "Good afternoon, Phelan Investigations. How may we help you?"

XXXI

PHELAN POPPED A Tums, pulled into a Texaco. He threw
his jacket on the seat and filled up the tank. Sixteen gallons,
Jesus Christ, almost seven dollars. He accepted his measly
change and fed it to the pay phone.

Half a ring and a gasp.

"This Ricky?"

Nothing.

"Mrs. Toups, that you?"

Sobbing.

Phelan touched the ear part of the receiver to his throat
and paced as far as the phone cord would let him. Swiveled up
the earpiece.

"Mrs. Toups, this is Tom Phelan."

"I know who it is." Snuffling. "I need you to help us, Mr.
Phelan, but I was fraid to call you. Ricky's at it again."

"Deeterman?"

"Yes. Ricky used to take up for him, say that man fixes sick
animals, that he cured a hurt raccoon. Said he just got mad
that last time. But now Ricky doesn't like him. Goes because
that man gives him money. Ricky's not the same boy. Not my
boy—," Mrs. Toups broke down again.

"Call the police and tell them just what you told me.
They're looking for Deeterman. Seriously looking. You want
Ricky safe, you have to call the cops. He's not at home now?"

"No."

"Where's Georgia Watson live?" Phelan jotted down the address. "I'm gonna be out of my office. But I'll call you back. Need to talk to Ricky."

"Will you scare him, please?"

Mrs. Toups. Caroleen.

Way, way too late for that.

Maybe scaring would be a workable plan for Georgia Watson.

A van in her driveway advertised P&C Karpet Kleaning. Jacket on again, he rang the bell at the small house, got a paunchy man in a tan T-shirt didn't open the screen door. Said nothing.

Phelan showed his card. "Could I talk to Georgia, sir?"

The man studied the card through the screen. "No. My wife's about to cook supper." He said it with just a little reluctance.

"I'm sorry to interrupt, Mr. Watson, but I got reason to believe your daughter—"

"Name's Prewitt. She's my stepdaughter."

"All right, Mr. Prewitt. I believe you should know that your stepdaughter and her friend Ricky Toups are hanging around with dangerous company—"

"Hold on now. Where you getting something like that?"

"Ricky Toups' mother."

Mr. Prewitt's brows drew down. He cracked the screen door and took the card. "Georgia!" he yelled. "Get your butt out here!" He lowered his voice. "Investigator. You stake guys out, catch 'em catting around. That what you do?"

"That's one type of case. There's others."

"Yeah? What other kinds?"

Phelan was half-choking on his impatience. He coughed, calmed down. "Industrial sabotage case."

The stepfather's resistance wavered. He motioned toward Phelan's tie. "Wouldn't like dressing up ever day. You mind it?"

"Helps. Some people"—he glanced around like those people crowded Mr. Prewitt's porch—"suit makes 'em feel at home, you know. They need this kind of apparel."

"Apparel." The man was with him now. "Bosses, you dealin with them."

"They got the money. You know how that is. Listen, Mr.—"

"Oh yeah. Man, I got this one office manager—"

"What d'you waaant, Glen, I'm hungry." Georgia Watson flounced to the door, a fist already stuck to her hip. Her eyes flicked wider as she recognized Phelan. The brass attitude retracted like a pair of balls from chilly water.

"I see you remember me. Came over here to warn you to drop whatever you still got going with Dennis Deeterman."

"Whatever you say, sir."

"Not working, Georgia."

"Aw, he's just an old weird guy that likes animals, and I don't hang out. I leave pretty much right away. He doesn't like having girls around."

"Old and weird. Right. You leave right away after what?"

Her dish-face fell into a careful nonchalance. Phelan continued to stare her down.

"After we get there, me and some boy, I leave, OK?"

"He hurt Ricky once before. You remember that."

Her eyebrows quirked upward, and her lips parted.

Well, look at that, maybe she didn't. Maybe Ricky hadn't confided that part of his very tough day. "You got a new address for Deeterman, a number or way to reach him, tell me."

Dark brown knowing lowered into her eyes. Now she had something Phelan wanted.

Prewitt tugged on her plump, freckled arm. "Who the hell's he talking 'bout?"

"Shut up, Glen." Georgia wrenched away from him and shot Phelan the bird. The door slammed.

Cussing this clueless little bitch he'd failed to terrify, Phelan drove back to the office, called Mrs. Toups. No Ricky yet.

Friday night, close to eight o'clock, his professional deck was cleared, but his brain was still zipping around. Tried to leave the phone alone. Night's second failure. He called E.E. at home and reported that "Once bitten, twice shy" did not apply to his former client. The teenagers were back in business. The office was hollow without Delpha there, his footsteps loud. Heedlessly, he asked that E.E. call him if he heard anything about Deeterman.

"Call you. Like you was a cop. Mr. Hawaii-Five-O. Mr. Mannix." E.E. read him the sorry-nephew code for a minute, finishing with, "You're family but don't mess in police business, you hear?"

"All right. But you have cases you can't let go of?"

"One or two."

"Me too."

E.E.'s shout of a laugh tripped over itself making more laughing. Bounced like a trampoline for ten seconds. "Thank you, Tom, bless your heart, I needed that. Oh, my. Get over yourself, boy. How long you been in business? All we know, this your summer job."

Phelan sat down, face heated. He hung up before E.E. could bust out laughing again.

Dug the bottle of whiskey from his bottom drawer and was about to pour a glass, but then—*hold up, have a Technicolor life here, Tom*—he tucked it back. Switched off the fan and the straining AC units. Tugged his tie loose, tossed it onto his desk, locked the door and walked down the stairs.

Twenty minutes and two shots later, he was bossing some emotional leeway. Owning some perspective. He'd bypassed Crockett's outdoor street fair and chosen the relative quiet of a bar, heels hooked over the rung of a bar stool. He was letting his vision blur out on neon, savoring the wide sweep of breeze from a big ass ceiling fan. The bartender had just rescued his loyal constituents from Top Forty and delivered them into the deft hands of a KJET jockey spinning this week's Jet Set of Soul Sounds. Phelan was ready to sip properly from a Jack on the rocks with a twist.

"You Tom Phelan?"

He angled his stool around to see a twentyish blonde in a yellow tank top. "My friend," she pointed her cigarette over her shoulder, "she told me your helicopter crashed in Viet Nam. What was that like?"

Phelan looked past her to a table where two other young women sat with fresh drinks, empty glasses, and a full ashtray, one of them...yes, indeed, Debbie from State National. She scrunched up her face in contrition, mouthed "Sor-ry." He angled back to the vision of yellow. A snub-nosed girl riding into the night on her mother's opinion that she was pretty, who hadn't learned yet that she was just bright-acting.

The silence between them paid out until she began to question her mother's opinion and her face turned a color he liked: rose. All rose over the cheeks and the neck. He didn't like that she was uncomfortable, even if she didn't know her nose from a drill bit. Maybe he was supposed to come up with a fun anecdote for her when a hazy glimpse had shimmed itself in, hills and mist, tumble of faces and soaked uniforms, oven-heat, the blowback of a chopper, stumbling stooped over at the head of a bloody stretcher. Roar and churn of blades above his ducked head, grit blown in his teeth, embedding in his skin, writhing of the man on the stretcher, the weight, the shifting twisting living weight. Lift-off, up, up, noise, smoke, door gunner's face as he pitched back, clawed at the metal insides of the lurching chopper. The glimpse flared into a black, breathless fear-wall that was himself body and mind, and the wall rammed forward, crushing.

Then something clicked in, and the fear cleared.

Snap, packed away.

In its place, beige calm.

The wide breeze brushed his sweating cheek. Music sluiced by. *If you want me to stay I'll be around today...* Someone screamed in a modified fashion. Horsing around, not meaning it.

Oh whoahh.

Good

Wish I could

Get this message over to you now. A better scream this time.

"Fast," he said to the girl, about the plunging chopper, and swung the stool away from her. Chugged his gleaming Jack on ice cubes from his clean glass. Time to go. He was over himself.

XXXII

A BLACK LINCOLN ruffled the skirt of a woman crossing the street. She abruptly sat down on the bench.

"You're her, aren't you," the woman said.

"Yeah. I'm her."

Mrs. Robbins angled toward Delpha, taking her in.

Looking into the woman's eyes, Delpha thought, *I'm dead wrong. Those words*, prurient, perhaps, *anybody can write them.*

No makeup, light lines at the eyes, one tracing up from the chin without reaching the corner of her lip. Nose like Isaac's now that it was healed straight again, not much of a dip at the brow. She wore a baby blue oxford shirt with the sleeves rolled and a khaki skirt. Loafers. With spatter-spots.

Paper-bag brown hair in an untended pixie cut.

Didn't rule out Isaac's mother as their client, a wig would fit over the short hair. But unlike their client, who Mr. Phelan had described as having dirty-brown teary eyes, Mrs. Robbins sported clear lamps there behind her metal-frame bifocals—outsize, blue, almost purple. And turned on Delpha.

"You have a delicate face," Isaac's mother said, with surprise. "After fourteen years in prison. My god. I thought *up-close* you'd be…blowsy. Harsh." Mrs. Robbins sat straight again, turning her head left away from City Hall.

Up-close. Did that mean Isaac's mother had seen her from far off? Must have. She too looked away, fixing her eyes on the greened copper trim of the library, the stained glass images of wheat and scythe, of bound sheaves.

"You thought blowsy is what Isaac would like."

"Not at all. But he's always been shy and...I thought you'd have brought yourself to his attention in some obvious way."

"The regular obvious way. I didn't do time for prostitution."

"I know what you served time for. It's not difficult information to find. The law serves man, not justice, and frankly, I'm not unsympathetic to you."

"Unsympathetic enough to threaten me."

A braless girl in a gauzy white sundress halted by the bench. She twirled an unlit cigarette backward into her palm. "Wow, hi! Dr. Robbins. I thought that was you. Y'all fixin' to go down to the Crockett Street fair?" She smiled expectantly.

"No, how are you—" Isaac's mother said.

"It's Susan." The smile dimmed a notch then brightened again. She raised on her toes and signaled toward the street, breasts bobbing. A motorcycle showoff-skidded to the curb.

"I mean to take Bio-Chem again. Hope I can get a better grade in your class this time." The girl's hopeful gaze overflowed onto Delpha, drenching her in good intentions. "Nice to see you, Dr. Robbins." She ran on tiptoe to the motorcycle.

Though light was leaching from the sky, Mrs. Robbins produced clip-ons from her purse and was about to fix them over her glasses, disappearing the wild-indigo eyes. "So. My language. It offended you?"

A beat in Delpha's throat, then she realized the woman meant the language in her threat, not the language that had led Delpha to call her. Not *prurient*, not *perhaps*.

"That's the sticking point, isn't it?" Mrs. Robbins expelled a breath. "It wasn't personal. I'd have written the same to anyone in Isaac's way. That's all you want, the threat removed? Not money?" The dark lenses left off scanning Orleans Street, amber-gold in sunset light, and focused on Delpha.

You brought what you had to the fight. Delpha decided to ruin that scrutiny. "Sorry about your husband. Isaac loved his dad a lot."

The straight nose flooded red at the tip, her lips clenched. Trembled and opened. "Oh, yes. Yes, he did, yes. Yes." Mrs. Robbins' wrist touched her forehead, the pose of a silent-movie actress, but effortful, as though she were propping herself up.

"Just break it off like I asked. Please. Allow Isaac to resume his education."

Delpha intended to do just that. She had never intended otherwise. But she had to know. "If I didn't agree to break it off...what is it you have in mind to do?"

Mrs. Robbins glanced at Delpha and rapidly away. "This is a problem. I know what happened to you. I understand precisely why you did what you did." Her voice dropped. Her head was shaking in stern disagreement. "I've no wish to hurt you."

"Really. How would you?" This was it, the information Delpha wanted, did she have her plan ready?

"Miss Wade, Miss Wade. Hypothetically, any number of ways. Other than with my son, you're not a powerful person. I could interfere with your parole officer, bring some sort of complaint. Or perhaps your employment. The latter. Interfering with your employment would violate the terms of your parole. You have to hold a job. You're a convict. Whereas I supervise a hospital laboratory and teach a class at Lamar College. Hardly Harvard, but respectable. You appreciate the leverage."

"Oh, I do." Delpha shifted away from her. "Isaac tell you what my job is?"

"It's hard to get much out of him. Except your name, he seems to like to say it. I gathered you're some kind of nurse aid."

"I did have two jobs, just one now. When you checked up on me, you didn't find out who I work for?"

"My research took another direction. Quite another. Direction. I discovered...well, let's wait a minute for that." Isaac's mother's mouth stayed open, she hesitated, as though about to reverse herself and spill whatever she'd discovered. But when she went on, she said only, "That minor point, where you work, that wouldn't be difficult, either."

"I work for Tom Phelan. The private investigator. Funny, you and me talked on the phone before I ever met Isaac."

Mrs. Robbins's head jerked around to Delpha, her gaze alarmed. Isaac's mother knew instantly what she stood to lose.

"I am not an extortionist. Sending those photographs, without any message, isn't a crime. I refer you to Black's Law Dictionary. I had no expectation of any gain but harm. Harm, like they had harmed us."

Delpha watched her steadily. "Why'd you want to hurt Elliott?"

"Monstrous. They were monstrous." Her fists beat against her knees. "My husband's work should have earned him international recognition and made us comfortable for life. They cheated him. His logbook disappeared, the notes he kept in the files disappeared, and Charlie...Charlie was undone. So angry and already ill. His strength just—they stole it from him. They took his character. Oh, he'd have regained it if he'd had time. Charlie would have gotten hold of himself, I know that. But I...we only had two months left. And they ruined our precious time together. Lloyd and Wallace saw Charlie would die before... It was an unbearably cruel betrayal. But not illegal. Not against the *law*. Miss Wade, please don't—"

"The police ain't in this."

Mrs. Robbins sat back. "My god." Doubt flickered across her face. "Are...are you sure?"

"Sure. The police are not in this."

"Thank you. But...don't tell Isaac. Don't make my son lose regard for me." Below the dark glasses, the bottom half of her face sagged, adrift.

"Oh, come *on*." Delpha herself was unlucky but not the kind of blind fool who would try to tie a twenty-year-old. The deal was this: she didn't want to go back to prison. How hard was that to understand?

Isaac, he was separate. He was a whole other matter, and hell if she was gonna discuss that with his mother. What she'd wanted from Isaac, she'd had. An ironed handkerchief and genuine respect. Some traded sweetness, some fun and companionship and cunt-jarring, brain-jarring, heart-nudging sex. She'd had a time—a time while he was still in her and a bright voice spread outward, filled her to the skin announcing *This, this is everything*—she'd had that. Being a woman who could choose a man, say yes, not the kind of woman who broke her fingernails clenching a desk-edge while her cheekbone scraped against the wood. Could go with a woman free-choice too, if she wanted. If she chose.

Same for Isaac, in Delpha's estimation. What he'd needed of her, it had been a fair and willing and joyful trade. He would know that a week or two after he went back to Princeton, went out with his buddies to bars, to city parks, sat in classrooms alongside long-haired girls, and that life sealed around him like he'd never left it. Just like, she knew to the soles of her black flats, if she went back, prison would seal around her like she'd never left it. And she never would.

"Only reason I told you about working for Tom Phelan is because in prison it's not smart to play like you didn't hear a threat. Need to keep your ducks where you can see 'em."

She didn't expect Mrs. Robbins to seize her upper arm, painfully, to press in close, but it seemed Mrs. Robbins had expected to do this all along. The woman talked fast directly into her ear. When she'd said it all, she released Delpha's arm and stood.

"You have my phone number. There are arrangements to be made, so talk to Isaac before August 15. Call me at noon— August 15, have you got that, noon?—and inform me how you want me to proceed. Are we agreed? I know you understand what I mean."

Delpha understood, but it was too powerful to think about all at once. She said, "Wait."

The woman's eyebrows raised hopefully.

"Tell me how you make those eyes of yours brown."

The brows fell. She reached into her purse, brought out a round plastic container, pried it open, and displayed the contact lenses floating inside. Mrs. Robbins squatted, tipped it so the lenses dropped onto the sidewalk, stood and ground them under the ball of her foot.

"I tinted them, but the tint aggravated my eyes. One last thing. It should go without saying, but…I feel I must say it. If by August 15, Isaac still refuses to go back east on your account, you'll hear from me thereafter. Indirectly, of course."

Her black lenses held Delpha's gaze.

"A paradox. I so deeply abhor cruelty, Miss Wade. I'm afraid it's made me cruel." She swiveled and headed into the street. A rocket-looking red Pontiac punched its horn and swerved around her without her missing a single stride. Isaac's mother stepped into long shadows. After a while, her straight back was gone.

Delpha pushed herself up from the bench, crossed her arms, and walked slowly toward Crockett's lights.

Paradox   you'll hear from me   indirectly of course

That she would cut Isaac loose, that there was ever a question about that, was insultingly obvious. But Isaac's mother hadn't got that at all. Cast in her own turmoil, she had communicated what she'd discovered. Quickly, as though she was unburdening herself. Roughly, getting rid of that knowledge. That other research Mrs. Robbins had done, in case it became necessary.

She'd located the man Delpha had stabbed.

Still alive, did Delpha know he was? She'd thought Delpha would know because if she had been in Delpha's position, *she*, Mrs. Robbins, Dr. Robbins, she would have known. *Oh yes*, she would have *made a point of it*. Furthermore, that man's *pitiful* adult daughter had two children. Two *deaf* daughters. Very possibly not a biological coincidence, in Mrs. Robbins's scientific opinion. One of them perhaps but not two. Recipients of *an autosomal recessive* gene, a *mutated* gene carried by *both parents*, Mrs. Robbins had *inferred. Perhaps Miss Wade was aware* of these children? Had she inquired? Did she *comprehend* the most likely agent of those two children's deafness? *They were fathered by that old man*—possibly some other close male relative. But Mrs. Robbins thought the old man the most likely, given what he was capable of. Didn't Miss Wade? A waitress at a café near the store they ran had refused to speak frankly. However, she was quite comfortable *insinuating* that this *intolerable situation* was suspected locally. There was disgust *in her innuendos*. And here was Mrs. Robbins'—Dr. Robbins', Isaac's mother's—very last offer, the one in reserve.

That man could be gone. A distinct benefit for several parties. Mrs. Robbins wouldn't even have to risk her person, it would not be a difficult thing. And it would be just.

Just.

Just four more years, *just* three hours till lights out, *just* let him pass me by, *just* don't get into it with her, *just* keep your mouth shut. *Just* go to sleep. That's the kind of *just* Delpha knew best. Meant "do this little thing and ward off bigger trouble"—that's what "just" meant.

But to Mrs. Dr. Robbins, *just* meant *right*. She had rights. She was used to having rights. She had always lived in a land of rights, they had worked for her. Until suddenly they hadn't.

A crescent moon rested in the blue layers over the red simmer of sunset. The end of the block pulsed a lively reach. The Crockett Street merchants had rolled out rows of multi-color flags to attract anybody driving by. They had Christmas lights strung. A band tuned as people drifted through a gate. It was a parole-breaker to patronize any of the establishments where alcohol was served, but she could stand back and watch their party. Tables, waitresses, pitchers, paper plates. Smoke and beer and laughter.

On the stage up ahead, faint call from the drummer *Uh-une deux trois quatre...*and like a party barge cutting loose from a dock, the band sailed into "Diggy Liggy Lo." Guitars rang, the loose-elbowed fiddle player thrust, accordion player squeezed, the spoon player rubbed knuckles to vest—hollers, whistles, and applause, two bobbing couples took to the portable dance floor.

Delpha lingered beyond the lights and flags, slapping

mosquitoes, dread ticking inside her, taut shoulders not quite touching a creosote light pole that would smudge her shirt. After the band blew through the Big Bopper's "Chantilly Lace" and some jumpy number about when you're hot, you're hot that she'd never heard, they hailed up a boy singer. Crowd noises died as the husky towhead delivered "Belle Lousiane" in the voice of a stone angel come awake at midnight to sing to the souls in the graveyard.

Ouvre tes bras et serre ton cher enfant.

Open your arms and hold tight your dear child.

XXXIII

HE'D GOT E.E.'S point about being...over-involved, he
thought, selecting that word instead of *fool*. He did not go
into business to freelance or to pro bono, in Miles' lingo.
But Mrs. Toups commanded his sympathy, and Daughtry
Petrochemical irritated the shit out of him. Besides, Phelan
Investigations was twiddling its thumbs, and Miss Wade was
not talkative these days.

Phelan scoured the Willises in the phone book and told
Delpha he was going out. Cruised down I-10 West and took
the Gladys exit, found the address. Let's see. Did an assistant
chemist live in the sandstone palace with the green slate roof—
or did he rent the garage apartment Phelan could spy the
corner of, '58 Rambler wagon parked by the wooden stairs?

Meeny, miney.

Phelan admired the fins and the chrome of the Rambler,
dusty as they were. Noted that, in contrast, the driver-side
door handle and a six-inch diameter around it gleamed.
Boxes were stacked solid in the back of the wagon. He
climbed the garage apartment's stairs. Bamboo curtain rolled
down behind the door's dirty glass. Phelan knocked, waited,
knocked again. He thought maybe he heard a cough, so he put
his ear against the door. He banged. Nothing. He took out a
little snake rake pick. Presto, knob turned.

Door barricaded.

Phelan shoved. The barricade scrambled away with a whimper, and the door hit the chain, opening its allotted amount.

By the window that faced the big house stood a folding table with a stack of colorful magazines, a phone, two large plastic bottles of something clear, wadded tissues. Pizza boxes, soda cans on the olive-green carpet. Against the far wall was a couch Phelan could see part of. It featured about half of Plato Willis's ass as he dove onto it, then spun around armed with a golf club.

Phelan produced his license, reached his hand into the room. "Tom Phelan, Mr. Willis. Private Investigation, check it out." He waved the license. "Mr. Willis?"

"It's *Dr.* Willis, I hold the Ph.D. Keep away from me. You've entered illegally."

"Almost," Phelan said and kicked the chain loose.

Way too much force, the door whanged back and dealt his elbow a crack. *Ow.* He strode into the apartment rubbing it. Place smelled like a hospital. He stepped over to scrutinize the two plastic bottles. Rubbing alcohol. Willis' chin was stubbled and his fair hair dank and stringy.

"You drinking this stuff?"

"Of course not."

"Good. Just have a question or two. Won't take—"

Plato Willis glowered at Phelan through his round glasses while wobbling the club in front of himself, like a peeved insect working its feelers. "You. You were the one at the lab during the week we moved, pretending to be a salesman. Sure you are. You have hands like a catcher's mitt."

Insulted, Phelan was inspecting his hands when the phone on the folding table rang.

Willis tossed the golf club and dived to snatch up the

receiver, listened, then with a quavering smile, exclaimed, "Thank god, thank god! Where've you been?" instead of hello. He shook his head vigorously. "No, no, I *didn't* know. No one told me. I thought that you...excuse me, I'm sorry. Oh no please, you go on." He turned his back on Phelan, hiding the receiver. He kept nodding, murmuring "Yes, yes" and "I would, so much" and "Thank you." He cagily informed the person he'd be at their house in the usual amount of time it took him to drive there plus four hours. "Absolutely self-sufficient. Not like last time. Yes, it is. A solemn vow."

He set down the receiver and squeezed his hands together beneath his chin in a kind of congratulatory self-hug. Then he dashed into the bedroom, commanding Phelan to get out.

Phelan followed. "Did Wallace Daughtry offer your head chemist's formula to Enroco—or did you?"

A cocoa-brown suitcase lay open on the bed, one side packed. Willis clapped the case closed, but not before Phelan had seen baggies filled with powder and capsules nestled among the clothes.

"Sure you wanna take all that relaxation? Starting a new life and all."

"It's only methaqualone. Like generic Nyquil." Willis snapped the suitcase's locks and hauled it out to his gracious living area through a slalom of beer and soda cans. He swiped a set of keys off the folding table and looked up at Phelan. "Who are you working for?"

"Employer's name is confidential, and I've been paid. Job's over. So I guess I'm working for me. I wanna know what happened at Daughtry."

"You want to *know*? Oh my god, a neophyte."

Phelan sighed and took a step toward the man. "I'm tired of you, Plato. Just talk."

Plato skittered away to the couch. "You're a big guy. If you're forbearing, if you let me be on my way, I'll mail you all that information."

"And I've got two dicks."

"No, I mean it. In case the police pursue whoever damaged John Daughtry, I want them on the right trail. And that is not my trail."

"Nobody damaged Daughtry, pill-head. He's in Arizona."

"Exactly."

"What does that mean?"

"Nobody wants to be in Arizona. Not John Daughtry either."

"But he's sick."

"Correct. And how did he contract said illness."

"I don't know. Ate a bad can of spinach?"

Plato blotted his upper lip. "Or someone gave him tainted food or drink. Or mixed some noxious, noxious bacteria into a solvent that would readily penetrate his skin. DMSO, something similar. Even you ought to see how simple that would have been in a lab."

"And that's why you're hiding."

"I'm not hiding, I'm relocating. At long, long last." The chemist's voice grew tight, high. "Wondering which toxic substance you might have come in contact with—thinking about that can be unnerving, all right? It can...absorb one's entire attention. Especially at three a.m."

"Well, come on, what's your nightmare? Nobody cares but me, so spill it. It'll be a relief."

Willis began to breathe faster. "I found a box in the lab. It had "BACTERIA" scrawled on it in red pencil. Inside were vials with dropper caps—amber, not our usual lab glassware. John was already sick. I freaked. Just let it crash to the floor. One vial bounced out and broke. I'm not"—he scooted over to the card table, soaked a tissue with alcohol, swabbed his hands—"a biologist. I took the other three vials to a med lab to be tested. One contained a ruffian strain of e-coli. John Daughtry might have had contact with that one. Or with the second one. Listeria."

"What's—"

"It's worse, that's what. The third—"

Phelan raised his eyebrows.

Plato swallowed. It clicked. "Mycobacterium tuberculosis. The immune system can contain it. Or not. You civilians think TB's been eradicated. It hasn't. There are hyper-virulent strains, and mutations can render them drug-resistant. Speak to a certain hospital in Boston, and they will assure you that is not science fiction."

Palpating the skin beneath his jaw, Willis lowered himself onto the couch. "But the incubation period is two to twelve weeks, and I'm not ill. There's nothing wrong with me, and as far as I've heard, there's nothing's wrong with Wallace. Or Elliott."

"It was you took the logbook."

"I never said that. I'm a mere gopher." His voice turned bitter, and he tipped his head like a seesaw. "Beaker here, beaker there."

"Yeah, right. Still have it?"

Willis's forehead ruffled. "Let's just say it is not currently in its designated location."

"OK. Let's just say that. And let's say Elliott may be healthy, but his marriage is terminal. Somebody sent a set of incriminating pictures to his house, and he's headed to court. With his own lawyer."

Plato hung his head between his knees. His back began to heave.

"You didn't know about the divorce."

Plato's head rolled back and forth. The gasps kept coming. Phelan slammed drawers in the kitchenette and found a paper bag, handed it to Willis. He breathed into it a while, then lifted his head. His flushed face began immediately to jettison its color.

"Lloyd's wife is...not the kind of wife I'd ever care to lose. She could buy Portugal."

"So? Lloyd's a lawyer. He makes a good living."

"Small, small change, Blue-Collar-Man."

"Why would you care whether Elliott's married or not?"

"I don't," Plato shrilled. "Weren't you aptitude-tested for this job?"

"If I knew what was going on, I wouldn't've broken in here. You say somebody poisoned John Daughtry. If the poisoner sent pictures to Lloyd's wife, you're in for a nifty surprise. You're the only chemist left in this picture, big man. Maybe *you* poisoned your boss."

Plato sat up, his mouth squeezed into a slit devoid of lips.

"Your lead guy Roberts—"

"Robbins."

"Robbins. He had cancer. My blue-collar guess is that you took advantage of that. Snuck his formula over to Enroco and collected. Took the logbook. Took the notes. Let them read or copy them, whatever R&D thieves do. This was a Plato Willis operation, start to finish."

Phelan didn't believe this. He wanted to see what would happen.

Plato's mouth still clamped shut.

Phelan feigned patience. "Look. Robbins developed this great product for Daughtry, but it escaped, didn't it, right into Enroco's lab. Daughtry sued. But the lawsuit ended up with him settling. So why didn't Daughtry settle with Enroco when he first caught wind of the theft? Why not take the money and give them the rights then? I may not know much, but I know that. Because Daughtry wanted it for his company. Loved his company. Your girl Margaret told me that."

"God, Margaret." Plato tittered hysterically. "Wallace fired her after the reception at his gaudy new office. Loaded her up with party leftovers. Her severance was chicken salad."

Phelan stared at him. "That's some shit after thirty-odd years. Maybe Wallace poisoned his old man."

"Oh, make no mistake. Wallace is the Real Thing, if you grok what I mean. He'd like to buy the world some coke. Except he wouldn't share."

"OK, and since Dad's disabled, everything's Wallace's. Right?"

"Why should I tell some freshman private investigator?"

Phelan stalked over to the wall, gave it a prodigious slap. Plato's gaze jumped toward him. He strode back. "Fucking talk."

"It wasn't all Wallace's. Charles had a cut written into the contract. He'd been fiddling with these compounds for years. Charles Robbins was extremely bright."

"And Lloyd wrote the contract."

"All of them."

"So what would happen if Robbins died? Like he did."

"His percentage was to be paid to his heirs."

"There it is. How'd they get around that, how'd they screw him out of it? Has to be Elliott. He wrote in a loophole."

The corners of Plato's dry lips curved, indenting sets of parentheses at the sides of his mouth. "Actually, he didn't. It was already there, and all Lloyd did was to push the magic paragraph under Wallace's runny nose. Charles's percentage was good for anything he developed *and Daughtry produced.*

That was just how Lloyd wrote it, no ESP involved. John Daughtry controlled his own products. Everyone in the industry knew that. Always had, always would. Charles believed his future was assured. But if Daughtry didn't produce, if Enroco became the producer, Charles was—"

"Out. So what looked like a settlement *was* a sale. Enroco'll manufacture Robbins' formula, package it, sell it, send Daughtry a check. Which the Daughtrys will not have to split with anyone. Wallace talked his father into it. How?"

"Don't ask me. Moondark's a soul-stealer."

"Lay off the kid stuff." Phelan stomped a Fresca can on the floor.

"Would you stop projecting hostility, my nerves are shredded. The nickname just fits Wallace. He doesn't even mind it." Plato coughed and deflated into the back of the couch, limp. "I don't have children and probably never will. But I was a child once, and believe it or not, my father loved me. I was his only son. Wallace is John's only son. Stretch your limited imagination."

Phelan paced the path by the table, enjoying kicking the cans and boxes out of his way. "Last question. Does Wallace have a wife, 5'7" or so, older than he is?"

"Please. Moondark dates strippers."

Phelan had the whole story now, except he didn't. No, he did. He really did. He mostly did. Give or take a few details, there was only one way this could have gone. He nodded to the man on the couch.

"OK, Plato, drive careful. Don't end up in Arizona." Phelan slipped out the door, hesitated, then stuck his head back inside. "Don't think about what kind of bacteria might have been in the vial that broke. Keep your mind off that one."

He closed the door.

XXXIV

DOOR LOCKED, BED pulled out from the wall. They could lie or kneel or sit on it and it might travel, but it would not hit the wall because once it had inched too close, they would lift the bed out into the room again and set its legs down easy.

After the very first times of muted, awkward amazements at what happened between them, there were one-word questions and adjustments, and plain simple doing so that their bodies learned each other's. She could come by sucking him off. Had to pause and shudder it out and then finish Isaac, then wipe her lips on the sheet and look at him and put her mouth on his. Isaac trailed his tongue down her belly, his hair tickling her skin, his palms spread on her thighs. They were as silent as they could manage to be. One might lay a hand over the other's mouth, then remove it to find a complicit smile. The window was pushed up far as it would go and the fan spinning and they were always slick with sweat.

The various lies she had thought of to end it would be more trouble than they were worth—*she was tired of this thing, she had met somebody else, she had a boyfriend somewhere who was coming home to Beaumont.* These would lead to false stories and arguments she didn't have the heart to make up, much less carry through.

"We got to quit now, Isaac."

"Let's don't. Let me stay a while longer."

"No. I mean you got to go back to your school and finish."

"What?" He lifted himself up on his elbows and stared down at her. "We talked about this. I can graduate here. At Lamar. I'll keep laying tile and go to classes. My credits will transfer. I can stay."

"No. You can't."

Delpha twisted so that he had to move. "It's not the same, and you know that and don't play-like you don't because that would mean you think I'm stupid—and that'd mean you been playing this whole time. And if you have, well, maybe that's OK for you because men do that to get laid."

"Yeah? Did men tell you that...or was it women again and who are *they*? They don't know me. They can't speak for me."

Isaac swung his legs around, snagged his jeans and jerked them on. He brought over the chair and sat in it, elbows on knees. "You're freaking me out. The only time I've ever pretended was when I brought back your handkerchief. I did that as an excuse to see you again. Is this about college, like you think college is exalted or something just because you didn't go?"

"It's about being where you're 'sposed to be. It's about being where I'm 'sposed to be. You're 'sposed to be there. Back there's your right place, Isaac. Not here."

"You've got it wrong."

"I really don't."

"If I was thirty, would you do this?"

"You're not."

"I will be."

She looked at him without arguing.

His head sank, and he tugged on his hair. "No. I had this. I had it. It's beyond great. Don't take it away from me. Please." He reached, blindly.

Delpha dug her heels in the mattress and pressed herself against the headboard. The sound of the fan spinning became more prominent, her awareness of the ends of Isaac's hair lifting and settling in its wind, the swell and sway of the curtains. Down the hall came shuffling footsteps—a door closing, clink of a toilet seat going up. After a while, a flush and another clink. Footsteps. Door shutting.

Isaac, folded over.

"Truth. Your dad was still alive, you wouldn't be talking any long-range tile-layin', would you? You'd be leaving this week, next week, something like that."

Isaac threw himself back in the chair and gradually the broad shoulders curved around his chest.

"I'd have made my case to him. Dad would have heard me out. He wouldn't have gone for it, probably, but he would've taken me seriously. God. He always did. Even when I was a little kid, you know like four or five, he treated me like I was... like I had some kind of dignity. Which meant I had dignity."

"Precious thing."

"That was my father."

"What about your mother?" she murmured.

"You know. She wants me back East yesterday. I worry about her. Mom's always been nervous, but now she's fanatic to the max, can't reason with her. Losing Dad crushed her. She wants to move because she can't stand the house without Dad. She watches for him to come through a door, I catch her at it. You're doing the distraction thing again. Stop it."

Delpha hooked the straps of her nylon slip around her wrist like a bracelet and slid from the bed. She walked behind him, naked, wrenched back his shoulders, ran the heel of her hand down his knobby backbone. "You want to be the man your dad was, don't you?"

He shrugged away from her hand, though not out of reach. "If it takes me all my life."

"Then listen to him. Be better if he was here, but he ain't, so listen hard."

She buried her lips in his thick, tangled hair.

They stayed there some time. Until finally he stood up, took the white slip out of her hands. He tossed it onto the bed and embraced her, his hands under her buttocks, then on them, then wrapped around her waist. She raised up on her toes and crossed her arms around his neck.

Delpha kissed him, released him. She pulled a dress off a hanger and over her head, fit her bare feet into flip flops. "Get your shoes on. Walk you down," she said. "You come say hello next summer and show me your diploma."

"*Don't* talk to me like that, like some casual friend. That's bogus and you know it." Isaac tried to lock her gaze, but she looked away. He skinned into his T-shirt, tied on his sneakers, jerking the laces, stuffed socks and underwear in his pockets. "Delpha."

"What?"

"Was I like this game to you?"

Delpha pulled his hand, towing him with her, and sat on the bed. "'Member those paths you explained to me." She curved the ends of her fingers into his, ran her thumbs over his knuckles. He let her.

"Whether your scientists are right about that or not, I thought a lot about what you told me. I listened to you, Isaac. My path, it ran a long, long time the same way, straight and low and rough. Took on some people like family and endured others I didn't want to know. Then it ran into your path and that way wasn't rough and it wasn't low. It was sweet. I wasn't playing for keeps, Isaac. But I wasn't playing. That's about the best way I can explain it."

She stood at the curb, tracked his red taillights into the

distance, thinking his name. *Isaac. Isaac.* Her body already was bereft and her room, her good safe room, would be wracked and haunted for some time. She had practice though. When a friend, a cellmate moved on to the outside or elsewhere, it was a wrench—often a relief, sometimes a loss, sometimes both, but always there was the refiguring, letting go, the empty space, the dealing. No choice, no exit. Deal.

It was around three in the morning. August 15. Delpha locked the side door, hung the key back on the nail, used the kitchen telephone in the dark. Streetlight angling in through the half-glass of the back door. The counters were sponged clean, deep gray in the shadow.

"Hello" was terse and immediate.

"I told Isaac we got to quit. He took me serious. He's headed home now. You treat him like a man 'cause he is one."

What must have been a held breath released into the receiver. "I...I'm in your debt. I won't jeopardize your freedom, you have my word. We also are quit, Miss Wade. Except for one matter—do you want justice for those fourteen years of your life?"

"Justice. I wish that old man would never ever cross my mind again—that'd be my very first choice. I'd pick that over anything. But there's a place in my brain where he is, he and his son, that son. Answer the phone at noon. I'll know by then."

Delpha sleepwalked downstairs. Mrs. Bibbo was sipping her breakfast coffee, as usual these mornings, watching Frank Blair read the news on *Today.* Delpha poured her own coffee and eased down beside her. This is what you finally learned to do after a hard-to-suffer change—all the things you did before. But you paid more attention to anything pleasing you could squeeze out of them. Anything. You didn't play like nothing was wrong, but you didn't cry in your beer either. Like she'd had beer to cry in. What she had now was a strong cup of black chicory coffee and a couch that was not property of the state of Texas and an acquaintance who was alert and friendly and had neglected to comb the back of her hair.

The camera swung onto somber Hugh Downs and Barbara Walters. Mrs. Bibbo rose and spryly turned down the volume. A fullblown editorial was about to roll. Delpha set down her coffee. She took a comb from her purse. Once Mrs. Bibbo had positioned herself to orate, she stood behind her and began working out the tangles. This small attention did not deter Mrs. Bibbo. She informed anyone not paying attention to Frank Blair that the President would be addressing the nation tonight in prime time.

"In *my* opinion, saying you take responsibility for what your employees did is the inside-out way of saying *you* didn't do it! The public has had it up to here"—she chopped her hand to her neck—"with lying and cursing. Nixon has to give up these tapes. He needs to lead our country now like he has some decency and respect for the office."

Mr. Nystrom, who preferred taking his breakfast at the little game table rather than the dining one, cackled over his toast until he choked. When he got through spraying crumbs, he said, "Roberta, if your body was as sweet as your mind, I'd marry you tomorrow."

Mrs. Bibbo stepped out of the range of Delpha's comb so that she could fluff her own hair. "If your Social Security check was as big as your mouth, I'd say yes."

XXXV

JOE FORD SAT on Phelan's couch, long legs stretched out
over the coffee table, big feet dangling. The orange glow had
faded from his cigar, and he hadn't bothered to relight it.
Chugging the beers, though. On his fifth or sixth out of the
case that guarded the petrified cheddar cheese in the fridge.

"How'm I gonna do it, Tom? I won't know what to do
with her. Counting on my wife making us another boy, and
she let me down."

Phelan was drinking vodka on ice, squirting it with
limes from a plate. His own feet were up on a cardboard-box
ottoman. He stuck to cigarettes, his ashtray a souvenir from the
Astrodome. Celebratory cigar poked out of his breast pocket.

"Tell me that again next year when that little girl is
running your life."

"You know she's gonna be six foot six."

"So what. Time she turns eighteen there'll be pro leagues
for women, and you'll have yourself a star. Listen at it. Give it
up for numberrr...what's today?"

Joe lugged his wristwatch up to his eyes. "August the 15th."

"Give it up for numberrr fifteen! Standing six foot six,
weighing in at 180 pounds, averaging 22 points a game and
leading the league in rebounds—All-American Jennnie Forrrrd!"

Joe sat up and smushed his face around. He was nodding.
"OK. OK, I can live with that."

"Yeah, but can you drive? 'Cause you better get a hour or two's sleep so you can bring the new mama home in the morning. And your daughter."

"I can always drive. I'm ticket-proof. Know every cop in town. No, don't get up there, Mr. P.I. Believe I can find my own way out through the box piles. Your décor is, I don't know, maybe *absent* would do it justice. Hey, Delpha Wade must be working out for you. She tells me she's still employed."

Phelan drained his fifth vodka including ice bitlets and let the heavy highball glass drop to his rug. "Seriously. Joe Ford, you whistledick. It was a good day you called me about her. Glad you talked me into the interview. I coulda hired somebody that wasn't, that just wasn't, you know...wasn't her."

Joe stared down at him, jingle of car keys, superior smile. "That's eloquent, Tom, it is. Well, thanks for the beers. And the company, poor as it was."

Phelan waved.

Snap, five fifteen a.m, had to pee. He opened his eyes in his bedroom, dark as Hades, read the shapes languidly arranging and rearranging themselves on the air. They finished their work and stopped and the dark was still.

Phelan got out of bed naked, pissed, and put on jeans and his watch. Tied his Adidas, palmed his car keys. He was at the gate to Golden Hills Memorial in nine minutes. Parked, snagged his flashlight and jumped the chain, hiked the oyster shell lane to his grandmother Lila.

Plato's hyperventilating crossed his mind. Guy'd been terrified of who might be knocking at his front door: whoever had decommissioned John Daughtry, dropped off a box of bacteria that might have wriggled onto Plato and nestled in to colonize. And that would be a weepy-eyed brunette in a charcoal suit. The chemist's widow. Plato should be worried. He'd probably started it all by whispering into Lloyd's ear. Or Wallace's. Yeah, Wallace's. By tiptoeing the logbook, with Wallace's blessing, to somebody in R&D Enroco. Phelan bet Plato still had it, on the bottom of his suitcase, riding in the back seat of his Rambler wagon.

Plato Willis had not woken Phelan up though. A glove did that. A glove sailed out of a dream and drew shapes on the air until the shapes settled in a particular formation that pointed to Lila. Which didn't make sense until it did.

He crunched along on the oyster shell until he found her.

Lila Pearl McNight. April 19, 1890—June 1, 1973. Rains had beaten down the raw dirt, grass blades scattered all across her. He told her why he was here. "But that's second, darlin'. First is, I sure miss seeing you."

He turned the direction he'd walked after the graveside ceremony and slowly walked that way. Played the flashlight along the headstones.

Johnson, Acuff, Radley. Smith, Mabel and William. Greco. Greco. Patterson. Reaud. Nance. Forrester, Rodney and Evangeline.

Robbins. Charles Francis Robbins. December 7, 1926— June 2, 1973. Single word chiseled in granite: *Beloved*. He aimed the beam rightward onto the other name.

Lucinda Scourie Robbins November 1, 1928—

Lucinda Robbins, the widow behind the veil, had slipped on a glove from her purse. Set her finger to the lips of a rueful old man who was trying to say something to her. One glove. With a spot of invisible, crawly stuff on it? Removed the glove by pinching its cuff and dropped it into a purse. He'd seen that. You could burn a glove. Or alcohol-dip it, donate the pair and the purse to the Salvation Army.

You could put invisible, crawly creatures in other places, too.

The old man trudging back to his car: had to have been John Daughtry, chiseled in shame. Simple to verify. Few days later, Mr. Daughtry feeling a worse internal disturbance than usual. Then worse.

Then Arizona.

Sky gray, few birds stirring, warm mist. Driving back to his apartment, Phelan pictured the executive meeting that deprived Charles Robbins of the rewards of his labor. The founding moment, as it were. Present, he figured: Wallace Daughtry and an ounce of stardust mounded on a dish carved from African ivory. Plato and Lloyd would have done their parts, but the final decision lay with Wallace.

Had he given the future widow ten seconds' thought? Phelan doubted it. If he had, that thought might have run along the lines of a Hallmark card, potted rhododendron for the funeral. Sufficient unto the day is the evil thereof.

Well, no.

Phelan found a parking spot, jogged up to his apartment. Six dead soldiers where Joe Ford had sat and a *Congratulations, It's a Girl* cigar butt. Place smelled like the club car of the Sunset Limited. He peed again and dove back into bed.

Gargled the vodka out of his sinuses and combed his hair. Getting long, maybe he would collide with fashion at some point. Fiddled with the knot in his tie and called it good. He was feeling pretty triumphant about his cemetery work, also sheepish. He veered into a 7-11, bought a packaged cinnamon bun with wax-sugar frosting and some weak coffee and called the office. Checked his watch—9:10 a.m.—as his secretary answered: "Good morning, Phelan Investigations. How may we help you?"

"Whoa, you sound like you're on your last legs, Miss Wade. You have a cold?"

"Just tired. Didn't sleep sound."

"Take the day off then. You sent all those sales letters out, right?"

"Marketing letters. Just about. I want to finish the last ones."

"Nobody'll die if you market tomorrow. Whyn't you go on home."

"I'm OK. I get a sense of satisfaction when I put another letter in the box."

He wasn't going to tell her about his visit to the assistant chemist, but suddenly he was telling her. "Know I was 'sposed to leave off, but I went and talked to Plato Willis. Ninety-nine point nine percent sure I know who blackmailed Lloyd Elliott."

Delpha said nothing.

"Thought that would interest you."

"How...how'd you find out?"

"Process of elimination." He was leaving out a glove dream and shapes in the dark. "Let's talk about it later. You know, I kinda count on you for that. Talking things over, I mean. Right now, can you see if there's a Margaret Hanski listed? Phone book's gone at this phone."

He heard a drawer slide out. Pages rustling. He leaned against a plate glass window, blocking a hand-scribbled advertisement for six-packs of Texas Pride. Mist had lifted, but a breath of dew hovered in the morning heat. Some lazy rooster crowed.

"There's a Howard and Margaret at 3630 El Paso Avenue. Here's the number—"

"Don't need it, thanks. Listen, if you start feeling worse, go home. Bye now."

He headed down El Paso Avenue, a neat, working-class neighborhood, calculating what he might say to Margaret Hanski to bridge his transformation from petrochemical company rep to investigator. Then again, she might not remember him.

But she did. Phelan cut his engine by a ditch that bounded a yard decked out with a Slip'N Slide and three shrieking little boys. No sign of the sober suit. Margaret wore a floppy sunhat, pedal-pushers, and a happy expression. Her feet were bare. "My goodness," she said, "what are you doing here, young man? I'm sorry, I don't recall your name, but I remember you. Salesman."

Phelan smiled. "Let me come clean, Mrs. Hanski. Margaret. Here's that card you wanted from me the day we met. Moving day, I believe."

She read the card, looked up quizzically. "Private investigator?"

"My apologies for misleading you. I was hired to check into a few things concerning the company, the lawsuit, you know, without stirring up a fuss. One of the people I interviewed indicated you weren't working there anymore, and since I enjoyed talking to you so much that day, I thought I'd stop by. I guess there have been a lot of changes at Daughtry."

The happy expression washed away. "Sure have. The company is Wallace's, and it's all about money now, not about making a product. Calls it Daughtry & Company. Could be selling tires or ladies' underwear, anything. Larry! Larry, you let Michael have his turn." Protests and general guff from skinny, wet Larry. "He's not too little. You let him slide."

Phelan cut in. "Wallace's no sweetheart, is he?"

"Oh, don't get me started. Wallace was the cutest little boy, used to ride him on my hip like one of my own. Grew up to be a weevil. He just flat fired me, after thirty-four years. I went to work for his father in 1939. My husband's up in arms, but I'm trying to put all that behind me, and you know what? Turning out to be easier than I thought it would be." She cast a look toward the boys, Larry taking giraffe-steps backward to get a running start on the Slip'N Slide, and her face softened.

"So you won't miss working at the new office."

"That house. Anybody with sense would've knocked it down and put up something modern. Not Wallace. Raved over it, called it authentic Queen Anne Revival style. He brought in an architect from New York City and carpenters and such, spent money like water. I give him this—it's a showy property, if you like old-fashioned. Fancy woodwork. Antiques everywhere, leaded glass, claw-foot tub. That scalloped siding looks like fish scales. Garish, if you ask me."

A wail pulled her from the lawn chair. She squatted down and opened her arms. "Those big boys not letting you play? Tum here, baby, tum'ere."

The smallest boy, mouth tragically downturned, staggered toward his grandmother. She swooped him up, streaming shorts and all, and sat back down with him on her lap.

"I see you're busy, Mrs. Hanski, so I won't keep you but a minute. Guess I was wondering what you could tell me about Charles Robbins."

Her head angled around to him. She contemplated Phelan with a blink or two, measuring. "Charles Robbins was the smartest man I ever ran into. He had a kind word for anybody needed it, and he seemed to know when you did. He was... well, it made you feel better to be around him. Mr. Daughtry respected Charles. I'll never understand how he came to let Wallace do what he did."

Phelan raised his eyebrows.

"Just because a contract allows you to cheat somebody doesn't mean you're obliged to do it." Margaret was swaying her knees sideways, rocking the toddler. "Who are you working for...Sam, was it?"

"Tom. Did Plato take the logbook or was it Wallace?"

This time the measuring look contained wariness. "I think you better answer me first."

He was aware that revealing what he believed could turn out to be a massively airhead move. But something told him to say it. "Mrs. Robbins."

Sympathy replaced suspicion. Still rocking the child, she whispered, "Well, why didn't you say so? You already know what they did to Charles."

"Professional ethics, Mrs. Hanski."

"Margaret. I believe Plato took it, but Wallace knew."

"Did it ever show back up?"

Her head jerked toward him, then she looked away, over to the older boys, who were flinging water out of their hair like wet puppies. "How *is* Cindy? My goodness, I haven't seen her since...well, the reception, I guess it was." Margaret suddenly developed a film of sunburn. "You know, I better get this baby inside. He's sound asleep."

The boy was judging Phelan from the corners of his eyes.

"The reception on Daughtry's moving day, you mean? I hadn't realized Mrs. Robbins attended that party."

"Oh good Lord, no. Wallace and Cindy in the same room? Cindy and me just...ran into each other afterward. Grocery store. Larry, you and Shawn turn off the hose. Let's go have us a snack."

Clearly his exit. Phelan thanked her, tendered his opinion that baby Michael favored his grandmother.

Cindy.

He drove thoughtfully over to the new office of Daughtry & Co. Sunny and talkative Margaret was, until the logbook was mentioned. And the reception. She'd run into Mrs. Robbins at the grocery store after that reception. How many people, after being fired from a lifetime job, went grocery shopping? Pick up some Hamburger Helper, Skippy peanut butter on sale. Phelan thought you'd more likely go to a friend you could talk to. Preferably one who knew the parties involved. You'd recount the terrible deed, get some outraged noises and a hug.

He drove right past Wallace's new place of business, a tremendous feat of non-detection. Banged a U-ey and drove a full four blocks back.

The sign was discreet, black with gold letters, small and rectangular, mounted on a pole like an old-time lawyer's. The house though more than lived up to Margaret's description of showy: peaks to the roof, wrap-around porch, goddamn turret on the side. Painted in a luscious jade-green, it looked almost animated, as if alligators in top hats might perform a song-and-dance number on its veranda. Phelan liked it at once. Maybe loved it. Wallace's Z was parked in the wide drive, along with several other late-model cars.

He admired the house for a while then cruised on to a Fertitta's grocery, bought some more coffee and four hangover nectarines. Ate them dripping over a fistful of napkins then washed his sticky hands in the restroom. Dialed Delpha from the phone outside.

"Be down there pretty soon. We get any calls?"

"Yeah, we did, good thing I stayed. We got a call for new

work, how about that? Some gentleman wanting us to find him."

"Find *him*. Like he's invisible?"

"More or less. It's the less he's concerned about. I'll explain better when you come in. Caroleen Toups called. Asked if you could go over there. Ricky's home, and something's wrong. She's just beside herself. Says you're the only one that can help. And then somebody left a package wrapped in brown paper at our door. Kinda tall like a business ledger you write your accounts in."

Phelan held the phone for a couple seconds.

Finally said, "The logbook. Plato must've put off his trip a while. Why'd he leave it with me? Him leaving it says it's still good for something." Phelan was trying to pace but the phone cord kept jerking him back.

"All I can tell you, there was somebody on the stairs. Ran up, ran down. I'll unwrap it and see, you want."

"No, hold onto it. There'll be prints on the paper, if that were to ever matter. Identify yours quick, any others belong to whoever left it, namely, one Plato Willis. What good's the damn thing now? The shouting's over. What...no, it's OK, I'm talking to myself here. I'm going over to the Toups, then I'll be in. We'll figure this out."

XXXVI

CAROLEEN TOUPS LOOKED like she'd smeared black shoe polish under her eyes and missed her last six meals. Right away, she pressed forty limp dollars on Phelan, who gritted his teeth and accepted. She hollered for Ricky. Then she fell into describing what was wrong with her son.

It was like gypsies had come and stolen the boy he was and left some kind of ghost that looked like Ricky. Used to do things for you without having to be told a hundred times. Now he was gone nights and slept days and when he was awake he acted deaf and scooped out empty.

"He's scared, Mr. Phelan. It scares me that he's so scared." She called her son again and when nothing happened, hurried down a hall.

Phelan invited himself to sit down in the Toups' pine-paneled living room that opened onto a pine-paneled kitchen. Deeterman had roped Ricky in again—had a hold on him, money or dirty hands or both. He slipped Ricky cash and dope, Ricky steered him boys. Too dumb to believe the son of a bitch would turn on him again, sure as the earth goes round. But he must know that now.

Wearing gray sweatpants and clutching an inhaler, Ricky Toups stumbled out into the living room, herded by his mother.

"I'd like to talk to your son alone, Mrs. Toups, you don't mind."

"You go right on," she said, and banished herself down the hall.

Skinnier, face hollower, bluish lips chapped and cracked. Weird—Phelan saw what Mrs. Toups meant. Ricky was kind of drifting and shifting in place, as though he was avoiding certain air currents.

"Sit down."

"Don't think I can," the boy said faintly. He wafted to different spots in the living room, a recliner, a side-table, but none worked for him. He couldn't stay anywhere. The kid was trying to run away, inside his body.

Whatever hopes Phelan had had, curdled. "How many you bring him, Ricky, and what'd he do to them?"

The flittering gaze landed on Phelan. The boy gagged. His shoulders raised up and did not go back down.

"How many boys did you bring Dennis Deeterman? Besides Marvin. Need names. Cops'll want to talk to them." Phelan got up and spoke right at the teenager, whose breathing was beginning to wheeze. That creaky sound, in and out.

"Look, you can be safe from him, never see the guy again. OK?"

Ricky put fists over his eyes, then his ears, nodding and wheezing.

"Use the inhaler."

"You know, maybe I, you know...won't."

"Use it. You're through with Dennis Deeterman, hear. Use the inhaler."

Ricky hit his inhaler, and his jaw jittered sideways like his head was trying to screw off. His next wheeze sounded like "Wait."

"Wait what?"

"We got his...diary."

"Diary," Phelan echoed.

The kid's eyes flicked like pinballs.

"Deeterman had a diary? Aw, shit, Georgia Fucking Watson, this'd be her play. And she's got it, too, doesn't she?"

Ricky's chapped lips parted. "She said we'd get money. But he found out where she lives."

Phelan pushed him toward the kitchen. "Call her."

The kid mumbled into a phone on the kitchen wall then hung his head listening. After a while, he slumped and the receiver fell to his side.

"Well, what? What's going on, Ricky?"

"Never mind, it's all OK now. Georgia's OK."

"She give him the diary back?"

"She'd already took it...to your office."

Phelan's stomach lurched.

The boy slid down the wall, sucked the inhaler. Let his head fall back onto the wall. Georgia'd told Deeterman he could go get the diary where she'd left it, by the outer door of this private eye's office. The guy wouldn't be there. He had to be out working. She'd talked fast, peeking through a latched screen door with Phelan's card taped to the outside of it.

XXXVII

11:49 A.M. CLOSE enough to noon. Delpha wanted this
call over with. She'd just picked up the phone when the
downstairs door opened. She set the receiver back in the
cradle and clicked her ballpoint. If it was Phelan, she could
step out in a minute, use the phone by the library. She had
Mrs. Robbins' number by heart.

Right decisions, she believed, were those when you knew,
brain and body. This one she'd sifted as though laboring
with handfuls of sand. To begin with, there was the sole,
heaped side: the old man dead with no risk on Delpha's part.
Blue sky.

But on the other side was Isaac. Anything his mother was
punished for would punish him as well and for all his life.
Isaac evened out the sides.

Whoever was downstairs was taking their time—last-
minute calculating, maybe: did they really need a private
investigator, could they pay for one?

Isaac was not solitary on his side. Add in common-sense
reasoning: Delpha knew where that old man was, she'd never
again set foot in his bait store. There were other spots to
rent a boat when she wanted to drift out on the quiet brown
channels under the green overhang of vine, willow, moss,
Spanish bayonet, past the downed logs populated by sunning
turtles, past cypresses towering from the water. Other bayous.

She never had to behold that one face, that scar again. Why pick the side with murder?

What he'd done to her. What he'd told his son, showed his son how to do, let him loose to do. Fourteen years that man had been living how he chose, and she not. His daughter. His two little granddaughters with their spelling hands.

But Isaac.

Delpha prepared to greet a client who'd decided on his need over his wallet. The ascending footsteps were not Phelan's light tread, not the running footfalls she'd heard earlier this morning. This was somebody heavy and in a hurry.

She had stood by her window at the New Rosemont, forehead propped in her hands, while the chaplain and the deacon had weighed in on her decision. *Harbor hate, you have hate. I visit the men on Death Row and I love and pray for them. You have to keep finding love.*

The decision set as she woke solitary in her bed. Bed that smelled like Isaac. She would not mar his future, would not take the chance. She knew that in her belly.

She would tell his mother to leave the old man alone. Let him be.

The office door opened forcefully and a bulky man barged in, cranking his head around. Politely, she asked how she could help him. His gaze passed through her to scan the room, lingered on the inner door to Phelan's office, partially open. Looking away from her, he said, "Girl left a book of mine here, and it's not layin' out by the door like she said."

He was a head taller than her. Faded red ball cap, long-sleeve work shirt. Mustache.

"I heard her and found it. I brought it in here, Mr.—"

"Gimme it. I got somewhere to go."

The man was still not looking toward her. Then he did. "Your boss not here, is he?"

Blood in her neck and chest thumped. Her head lightened. Her fingertips convulsed on the ballpoint pen and flicked it into her palm. They didn't have a letter opener, used their thumbs. Phelan had his gun with him. For a few seconds, the office remade itself into a flat picture, a poster of an office. She grasped hold by ordering herself: *you're here, you're the only one in this place.* The office fell back around her in its former depth. A flash of the brown-paper-wrapped book as she'd placed it in the bottom desk drawer, under the whiskey bottle—only a few steps away.

"You wait right there. I'll bring it right out to you, and you can go." Delpha crossed in front of the man to Phelan's office door.

"Your boss's out working." The voice, lower than before, was closer behind her.

She threw a glance back. His mouth hung open so that teeth were visible beneath the thick mustache. A smudge on the cheek or a bruise, one. White around the dull black pupils that blended into the shadow beneath the cap. He slid his hands into the pockets of soiled khakis. She dropped her glance down. The front of his pants was raised. Wasn't lust, she knew that like she knew her name, it was him knowing she was alone. Couldn't remember his name, though she'd heard it countless times. Could not call that name. Didn't matter. She recognized the face, and not because she'd seen him before. She recognized *it*. Blank as a clock looking at you. Until it changed. And it would change.

There sat the phone on Phelan's desk. If she went for it, it'd all start then, fast, few choices. She didn't try for the phone. She walked around the side of the desk to the drawer, said loud, clearly, "My boss, he's due any minute now." She did not trust that saying this would help or even postpone anything, but it was the only thing to say. Her fingers released the flimsy ballpoint, which rolled away on the desk. Straight-backed, she bent from the knees as she pulled open the bottom drawer. She gripped the whiskey bottle, was lifting it off the book when he rounded the desk from the opposite side, stretched out a long arm and lunged to snatch the book from her hand.

Done. He had what he came for.

Leave now.

Ripping. Brown paper was discarded onto the desk. A shove and Phelan's chair rolled away and banged into the wall.

Leave. Leave.

She tracked him through her peripherals so as not to stare directly into his face. Stuffing the book into the back of his belt, he stepped closer. Pulled his zipper down and cupped, breathing harshly through his nose. He'd like it if she tried to beat him out the door.

All she saw to do was slide one foot a couple inches behind the other, center her weight, shift a little forward. Slow, so slow. To suddenly stand full height might set him off and wasting one ounce of effort on persuasion, no, no, no. To this kind, she wasn't a human being, she was an animal that moved. A body in reach. A means to liberate the core need, she understood that, understood also that any humanity the man owned was already sloughed.

His left hand surfaced from the pocket with a black knife handle, he flipped the blade out. Four, maybe five inches, not clean. Now she looked at him. His face was in a stage of altering, recomposing. The thing behind his eyes breaking through. The knife separated from his trunk, moved as part of his arm, as his hand, weaved toward her and away, weaved closer toward her. Once he saw her following the blade, he began the threats. The voice that squeezed from him slammed the panic in her stomach up through her chest and into her throat, spread it over her skin. Over all her skin.

This, she hadn't foreseen, hadn't before even imagined—a hissing, rhythmic, falsetto whine. He rubbed himself, working up to it, savoring. A knife with a mouth whining.

I'm going to cuttttttt youuuuuu. I'm going to kiiiiillllll youuuuuuu.

He put the knife into his mouth and leisurely brought it out again.

A jab, and a spot on her ribs stung, prickled electrically, coldness entered and withdrew. She glanced down at the red leaf-shape on her blouse, up to see him lifting a red knife to his protruding tongue.

He had the face now. Not the clock one, the stretched one. The ecstatic eyes.

Phelan burned up I-10's fast lane, swerving around truckers balling for New Orleans. Took the off ramp at 50 per. But he climbed the stairs soft and worked the doorknob soundlessly, hoping Deeterman was somewhere ahead of the truckers on I-10, not sitting in Delpha's chair watching the knob turn. Phelan eased into the still office, .38 out.

Her chair was pushed back, not snugged to her desk like she usually left it. The box of letters was on the desk. The door to his office stood ajar. Quietly as he could, he crossed the floor. Once he was pressed against the jamb, Phelan pushed his door, swinging it open.

No one. The high-backed client chairs, his desk with some brown paper on it. Phelan's ribs constricted as he confronted the thought that Deeterman had been here and forced her off somewhere. No, surely she would have yelled as soon as they got to street level. Surely he couldn't wrestle her along a public sidewalk to his pickup truck, no, Delpha Wade would not have gone docilely. Phelan stepped over the threshold into a curtain of bourbon fume and iron and silence. Glass crunched under his shoe.

A client chair drifted around. "I put that package away in your bottom drawer," Delpha said. "Under the whiskey bottle."

Phelan got a good look at her. He slid the gun onto his desk next to the wad of grocery-sack paper, sank down to her.

She stared off to the left of him, her pupils dilated. Her left hand hung behind the chair arm but her right shivered on a worn ledger in the middle of a shiny darkness at her waistband. Different-size spots stained her white blouse, spray and spatter, one red channel.

"I'd a carried it out to him. Told him that. Coulda been long gone from here. But he had to do one of those things they do. Those extras."

Her gaze shifted to Phelan, and she shook her head. "They just can't resist."

He'd seen the blood, the legs on the floor by now, the rest of the body blocked from view by the big metal desk. He needed to get E.E. here, get an ambulance first, but he couldn't reach the phone, couldn't get that motion happening because he was listening to her, hearing her tell how she was still holding the whiskey bottle when the man licked the knife and cut her and when he went to lick it again she broke the bottle on the edge of the desk and drove it up two-handed through his throat then she wrenched the book out from under him and she sat down while he died.

The half of her face he could see wore a sheen of sweat. He passed his fingers through the brown hair, soothed it back. "Delpha."

A blood-smudged index finger riffled the ledger's pages. "God in heaven he's got a envelope of pictures in here, boys before and boys after, and the before's the most terrible thing there is."

He could barely hear her. Skin at her temple cold. Phelan grabbed hold of the curly cord and crashed the phone off the desk onto the floor. Dialed, urging it to ring fast.

XXXVIII

SHE SAUNTERED INTO the bait shop at nine o'clock in the morning, the boats that were going out already on the bayou. Just driving around, she said. Her husband traveled: he was in and out. Didn't take her with him, and she liked to see places. What could Mr....she peered up at the sign...Mr. Pettit tell her about this place?

Little nervous-acting but she had feathery red hair, the shade that'd always snapped his neck around. The shade he liked best in the magazines, whether the woman or the girl or the child was photographed or sketched comic book-style, red-orange hair falling over the chains or the rope. The man picked up a sack of Fritos from the display stand, strolled outside, fished her a Coke from the cold drink box and popped the cap off. "For free," he said. He set up a lawn chair that had been folded next to the door and offered it to her.

She smiled but sat down on the steps looking up to him and ate the Fritos right there, licking salt off her fingers. He sat in the chair, shook out a Pall Mall and lit it.

"Can you blow smoke rings?" she asked, her lips testing a little smile. She was holding on to some sunglasses, but she didn't put them on.

He manufactured a smoke ring, and the smile turned into a laugh. "Look at you! I admire that trick."

He lifted up his chin and described the type of fish they

had around here, the weather. She know about hurricanes? Where was she from originally? Didn't sound like here. No, she said, Oklahoma, and bit slow into a Frito. It interested her hearing about hurricanes, he could tell, and fact was, nobody'd been much interested in anything he said for some years now.

She took out some Juicy Fruit, offered him a stick, but he was liking the talking. This woman here, she probably thought she was smart. So many of them did. But one that looked like her, she could be smart for a while for all he cared. He gave her a history of hurricanes going back to Galveston in 1900. Course he wasn't there then—he paused for her to smile, and she did—but he'd heard the story enough. She just leaned back on her elbows on the steps, head cocked, listening. A damn boat was coming in, the choking Evinrude making him have to raise his voice as it brought the fool to the dock. He gave the man his deposit back hastily, out of his own pocket. He was afraid she'd get up and leave.

She didn't. He finished telling her about the Seawall, and then he asked her how a man might see her again.

"I'm a married woman," she said. "I'll always be a married woman."

"Don't mean you're dead."

"Near enough." She looked at her nail polish and looked at him over it. "My husband, he's an older gentleman."

He took that in, meaning she didn't think he was an older gentleman, though he clearly was, older anyway than her—at the same time he took in the ring, gold band, no rosette of sparklers on her finger. She didn't much sound like she was from Oklahoma. Clip to her speech. But the important part was that red hair, the bangs spilling across her forehead, the sweep of it onto her shoulders, red red red, and that she didn't walk off while he was talking.

"My husband is out of town until tomorrow. He's closed his office while he's gone." She said this like she was just holding up her part of the conversation. Wasn't even looking at him. Surprise drove back his shoulders. He'd heard liars report lines like this but none had ever been directed at him.

A cloud shifted, and the sun did its Bible pose, sending out separate, dazzling rays. That just made it all better.

She ruined it a little when she added that her husband sometimes changed his plans. That her husband carried a gun. He didn't like how that sounded. But the rays lit her up, and in the glint from under her long black lashes—she sure had the eyelashes on her and those eyes—he caught her drift. This was play-like. This was a bored woman's game. He heartened. "Don't make a hill of beans to me," he said.

She said she could see that. He was the kind of man who'd walk straight in the front door, not sneak in the back one. "You look like you can handle yourself."

It was the sentiment the man had waited all his life to hear. He wanted her phone number, but she took his, writing it down on the inside of the Juicy Fruit wrapper. She smiled at him. She had just the one night alone. Maybe she'd call this evening, maybe she wouldn't, she said. She couldn't tell yet.

His gut clenched. He felt like somebody was giving him a Santy Claus present, then snatching it back before he had good hold of it. He wanted to say something smart but couldn't think of the right thing, so he settled for holding his jaw tight. As she got up, she swept a hand behind her neck and flipped the red hair off her shoulders. Then she thanked him for the Coke. Sashayed to her car, a new white Chevrolet. Waved. He just watched her.

The man sat out on the porch as the day burned on, in a lawn chair surrounded by some zone repelling time and the store behind him, the bayou in front of him, the rotten old boats and their tinker-toy engines, always going haywire. He had a son who'd died and a wife who'd died, a daughter who didn't talk to him, and two grandkids that didn't talk at all.

A pretty woman had told him he was a man who could handle himself.

Wrote his telephone number on a gum wrapper.

Red hair. Eyes like bluebonnets.

XXXIX

THE AMBULANCE GUYS pounded the stairs, running up the
gurney. They left it parked in order to surround Delpha with
their medical attentions and careful voices. Not soon enough
for Phelan, they lifted her onto it, said they'd be taking her
to the closest hospital, Hotel Dieu, and he could ride along.
Knowing he couldn't, Phelan squeezed her hand, loathe to let
it slip from his. Her eyes shut.

He'd stood back for the swarming homicide squad,
handed over the book to some unfamiliar detectives and was
quarantined on the plaid sofa until he'd answered the same
questions five or six times. Once they said he could go for now,
he gladly put distance between himself and what was left of
Dennis Deeterman. He jogged past patrolmen holding off a
Channel 4 news crew, whose microphone he batted aside.

Phelan took up residence in Hotel Dieu's waiting room
and played the scene in the office over and over. How it must
have been for Delpha. How it could have gone. How it did go.

A kid popped a potato chip bag with a *smack-bam*, jerking
Phelan's head up. The kid's mother seized the hair top of
his head and yanked him, yelping, into the chair beside
her. People wandered out rattling change in their pockets,
wandered back in with candy and coffee.

Phelan got on the pay phone. Couldn't reach E.E. at
work, couldn't reach him at home. Talked with Maryann

until a banker-type behind him said, "Playing through, pal."
Phelan said goodbye, and the banker seized the receiver,
dialed, ripped off his tie, and crammed it into a pocket.
Snarled, "Get down here, you piece of shit, she's hanging
on just for you." Slammed down the receiver and marched
from the waiting room.

Families, singles, couples sitting there cast furrowed-
brow glances toward the exiting banker. People looked at each
other and then somewhere else.

Phelan sat back down again, but stood up any time a
white coat appeared in the doorway searching out next of kin.
He hunched forward, elbows on knees. Unwelcome pictures
flooded. He should have been there, *could* have been there in
the office instead of pigging out on goddamn nectarines. *Can
it*, he told himself, *you got cops down at your office wading in
Dennis Deeterman's venomous blood, which he will never ever use
again. Only thing that matters now is Delpha pulling through.*

Close to six o'clock, a slight, baby-faced doctor with Afro
sticking out from his white cap gave Delpha Wade's brother
the news that his sister was out of surgery and expected to
survive.

"Can I see her?"

"Not yet. She's gone back to sleep again. Take it easy on the
visiting for twenty-four hours."

Phelan's processing mechanism had a lag in it. "What?"

"Just a precautionary measure. Calm down, Mr...." The
surgeon consulted a clipboard. "Wade. Twenty-four hours of
solid rest. Come and visit tomorrow evening."

"But that sounds like there's some doubt that she'll—"

"No, no, she'll recover just fine."

"Swear."

The doctor's gaze tightened. His professional demeanor

gave way to the man behind it: he had a chest without heft, but he hefted it. "Your sister was stabbed, Clyde. All kinds of bad come with a wound like that, physical and otherwise. You're talking to the doctor that sewed her up, and I have assured you she will recover. You want another color doctor, I can send one out. And I'm a surgeon, not a sorcerer. Some winged monkeys fly through the window, carry her off, that'll be out of my league."

Phelan was waving both hands. "No offense, no offense, no offense, promise you. Just I'm kinda...I'm all...she's not my sister."

"Oh. Well, OK then, all you gotta do is believe me." The young doc bummed a cigarette to take back to doctorland.

Phelan called the station. Fontenot crowed, "She got that tahyo, I tell you, that girl—"

"Self-defense. I wanna hear E.E. say nobody's gonna arrest her or anything."

"*Alohrs pas, cooyon.* Nobody's touching that girl. Is the doctors fixing her up good?"

Phelan blew out his breath. "She'll make it. Don't you ever go home, Sergeant Fontenot?"

"*De temps en temps.* Feed the dog. You want the chief."

"Yeah."

The sergeant informed him that E.E., a Bobcat, twenty men with shovels, and a rig of lights had set up in the woods back of Deeterman's white ranch house. They were there along with County and some State, and what they expected to find left E.E. in no frame of mind to be interrupted.

Phelan thanked him and hung up the phone. Located a name in the phone book, jotted the address and number. He lit a cigarette and went to blow out the match when a man with a cigarette clenched savagely in his teeth loomed in front of him. Phelan held still, lit up the banker, too. Burnt his finger, *shit*, and the phantom finger set up a commiserating howl.

He swung out of Hotel Dieu's parking lot, wended his way through the downtown and back onto I-10 to HWY 69, leaving the freeway out by the LVNA canal. He passed the water-processing plant, paralleled the embankment that held back dark water. Found the street and turned. Big lots in this neighborhood, an acre, acre and a half each, brick ranch houses set back, nice lawns, oaks, dogwoods, shrubs. Chemists could afford these places. Plant managers could afford them. Lawyers, company owners, they could afford better.

He pulled into a driveway with two cars. '66 Ford Falcon with a primered fender. Last year's Impala 4-door, white. *For Sale* sign planted in the yard. Wind had risen, blowing his hair into what felt like peaks. He raked it down. This time, if it was needed, he had the right card. Several of them, as a matter of fact.

A tall guy, longish hair, answered the doorbell. Young man, he noted on closer inspection, it was the graven expression that conveyed age.

"Good evening, sir. I'm Steve Russell. Real estate." Phelan extended a card. "Would you be the owner?"

The young man automatically took the card, answered no, called, "Mom. Real estate guy." He handed over the card to the woman who approached his shoulder, but he didn't leave. Stood there, slightly in back of her.

The woman, dressed unseasonably in black slacks and a close-fitting black T-shirt pushed up at the elbows, glanced first at the card and then out at Phelan.

"Evening, ma'am. Like I was telling the young man, my name is Steven Russell. I see your house is for sale. You may be happy with your agent, but if you're not, I'd like to offer my services. Is there anything else I might do for you, Mrs. Robbins?"

She hadn't introduced herself, but any respectable real estate agent would have learned the owner's name. He wanted to use her name, the real one.

Wouldn't have known her in a million years.

A hundred, anyway. The dead, pale-brown hair she brushed back as she looked up was almost as short as a man's, chopped pieces on the crown, shaggy in front of her ears. Glasses rested low on her nose, and—a feather swiped his spine—he was not looking into the leaky dull-brown he'd looked into at Leon's. Nope, how'd she do that? Her face, thinner now, was dominated by her eyes, and they were blue as cobalt.

And alert—she knew him, all right. Soon as she spoke, it was a lock.

"We're satisfied with the company we've engaged, Mr.... Russell, but I wouldn't mind hearing what your firm offers. I'll show you the grove around back. My husband designed and planted it."

"I'd love to see it."

"Mom, the realtor we have's fine."

"I'm sure he is," Phelan said. "I only stopped by—"

"Excuse me," the young man said extra-softly. He turned from Phelan to his mother. "Thought you needed to go over to Margaret's, Mom."

"I've got time to talk to this man for five minutes. It's OK. Go on and finish packing."

Mrs. Robbins led Phelan around the side of the house to the back yard. There was no yard. He found himself gazing on a fairy forest that stretched far back to a wooden fence. Red brick pathways, lit by glow-lights in the grass, wound under the trees—must be fifty of them: fruit, pines, hardwoods, drooping willow yonder, nearest to him the broad waxy leaves of a magnolia, blooming its candlelight white. Fireflies darted and flickered among the trunks. The dampness here was cooler, breathing, murmuring, swaying, full of contrasting, leafy scents.

"Most every kind of tree that grows well here and some that don't. That one to the west side is a sequoia. Ten years old." Tension squelched the pride in her voice. "What do you want?"

"I'm a simple man. Had a little spare time and wanted to meet the woman I'd worked for."

"You met her."

"Lloyd's pictures worked out for you?"

"Yes, well enough, and I have no idea what you mean." The large eyes held him fixed until he broke off the contact and inclined his head, studying the pattern of the brick.

"Assumed that. Your husband's logbook—who ended up with it? "

"Margaret brought it to me as soon as it showed up again. Once the sale went through, the logbook couldn't incriminate anyone. She knew I'd want it. Because it was Charlie's work."

"Plato Willis is having bad dreams about bacteria. Who got which kind, Mrs. Robbins, and did Wallace get any?"

"Persistence *is* your strong suit, Mr. Phelan." She glanced at her watch. "You have more bacteria in your own mouth than there are people in the world."

He wasn't going to get any more. The breeze cut through his hair. Involuntarily he turned back for a last look at the grove. Found himself drawn to strolling into it, mosquitos be damned. Silly, given the circumstances, like he shouldn't be here in the first place and in the second place, this woman wanted to forget she knew him. Retroactively. But look at all this—he took in the waving branches, orchestra of murmurs, cut-lace shadows, the tiny auras of light. Out of the rise of insect din, he distinguished a tree frog's *ek ek*. Rain, maybe. Despite himself, he said, "Your husband, he was an amazing guy."

The woman collapsed from the middle. Phelan lunged, but she was suddenly sitting tucked, forehead on her knees and arms squeezing round, contracted into a tight package. Her head moved rhythmically, lifting and falling onto her knees, an odd, silent version of beating your head against a wall.

He held back till he couldn't, then he reached, and she allowed him to steady her upright. "I haven't found anything else yet that accommodates these ghastly...moments." She glanced back. "I have to go now. And so should you."

The son was walking toward them. He called, "Hey, Nixon's on TV swearing he never had a clue about Watergate." He seemed to be taking a wary inventory of his mother. When he drew even with them, he laid a loose arm around her shoulder. Said, softly again, to Phelan, "Full up on realtors" and accompanied his mother back into their house.

XXXX

PHELAN LEFT THE Robbins' and pulled up near the end of the traffic jam on Concord around the white ranch. If this was Pop the Whip, he'd have been the tail. He estimated they could have been working four, five hours already. Squad cars, unmarked, Highway Patrol, ambulance, a fire truck. News vans from all three local stations. The shabby house was illuminated to brilliance from the light rig set up behind it.

The rubberneckers, piled up craning behind the yellow tape, parted for a canine officer trotting by with a German shepherd. After introducing himself to a cop as E.E.'s nephew and as a private investigator on the case, Phelan persuaded the guy to ask E.E. if he could observe.

"Red Rover, Red Rover, you can't come over," said the cop when he came back. He took his place by the tape, stamping backward on the foot of a pushy onlooker.

"Hey," the onlooker protested. "My tax dollars and all that."

"Yeah and all that." The cop didn't turn around.

An hour. Two. Phelan milled around, picking up what he could. Mainly how many officers were there, little sniping between the cops and firemen. He passed the newswoman whose mic he'd batted away earlier. Her formerly sleek blonde hair had frizzed into a globe shape. She was positioning a compact mirror and dabbing the mascara smears beneath her eyes.

A middle-aged couple pushed up to the yellow tape and asked to be let through. The officers held them off. "But you don't understand," the woman said, her voice rising, "you don't get it. That could be my *kid* back there."

Everyone in hearing range oriented themselves toward the pair. The father was saying their son had been missing for two months, that he thought he'd run off, but—

The mother squeezed fists against her head. "He never ran away," she said. "He never, never, never."

The cop tried to convince them information would move through channels as quickly as possible. Home might be the best place to wait, he suggested. The woman ducked under the tape and squirmed past him. She ran.

"Shit," said one cop, and both of them jogged after her.

After maybe ten yards the woman slowed, plodded on another clumsy stride and then stopped, on her own. Stood still, her hair flagging out, her skirt blown against her legs. The palms of her hands met, flat, in front of her face, and then sank down to cover her mouth.

The breeze, with its scent tendrils from the dead, carried into the people gathered behind the crime tape. Jostling ceased, then talking broke out. A woman dragged her kids away.

The two cops bookended the mother and gently turned her around. The newswoman was already cornering the father when Phelan heard a loud *crack-k-k* that rumbled on for several seconds and then echoed away. A minute later, the fire truck pulled out. Phelan eyed his watch. 10:28.

"Where they going?" A boy jumped up and down to see as they hit the sirens and the flashing lights.

"Put the wet stuff on the hot stuff," his dad said.

He left Deeterman's ranch house, but knew he couldn't settle down in his own place, so he drove out to Leon's and landed on a bar stool.

Patty Peavey served him a freebie Pearl. "Your hair's standing up, Tom. You look like that white rabbit late for a date. Jesus, smell like him too."

Phelan lifted the longneck to his dry lips. Johnny Carson as Carnac the Magnificent was holding a piece of paper to his forehead when Channel 4 news broke in and went live to the scene of an explosion and fire.

"Would you look at them chop those windows. That fire's just rolling out now!" Patty's hands clutched Phelan's shoulder seam. "What's…what's that nut trying to do to the firemen?"

Phelan took a long look. Little hairs at the back of his neck levitated. Dug a dollar tip from his wallet, poured the beer into a go-cup and slid into his car.

He jogged to the outskirts of the blaze, cordoned off by squad cars parked crossways. Phelan mixed with the watchers. The neighbor that called it in kept retelling the story. Another pointed out the berserk homeowner restrained in the back seat of a cop car. Phelan hung around the flames, the shooting water, and the falling debris until there was just smoke rising from black. Then he left and bugged the graveyard crew at the police station. Returned in the light of day to the ruined house. Couple chimneys. Clawfoot tub. Backtracked to the station. He dragged home around noon, took off his shoes, and fell backwards on the bed.

Uncalibrated lighting in these hospital stairwells, combination of too bright and too dim that cast weird shadows. Phelan plowed up the industrial-gray stairs, emerged into a hall, and dodged a runner with a stethoscope bouncing on his chest. Paused to pump the nurse at the third floor station, and then counted his way to room number 303. He couldn't see her past a blue curtain drawn between the beds.

Fluorescents spilled over the bed nearest the door. It held a lump with a pointy, shelf-like shape near the top end. All covered up by the sheet. Maybe morgue was short tonight.

The sheet slid down past a new, black, squeezed-on Astros ball cap to inquiring eyes, then to a bandage over one cheek, then part of a chin. A moon-face.

"Hey there," Phelan said as he passed. He peeked around the blue curtain. Darker there, no light on, but the sheet wore the sweet undulation of a woman on her side. She seemed to be breathing steady. Phelan backtracked. He slung a plastic chair and set it down against the wall, equidistant to both beds, so he wouldn't be invading anyone's privacy.

"My mom *is* coming back," said the moon-face. "She promised."

Phelan nodded.

"You're not from Social Services, are you?"

Phelan shook his head. "Bet you're an Astros fan."

"Duh."

"Me, too."

"Coach Durocher, he don't take shit from nobody." The round face challenged him.

"Sure not any umpires."

"No way. Or batters. Hey, pitcher, stick it in his ear!" Lips that'd been compressed into a bud by heavy cheeks opened, and the kid looked pretty much like a chubby fifth-grader with an ear bandage.

"Durocher's the man. That your wife over there?"

"Secretary. And friend."

"She hadn't hardly woke up yet. What happened to her, car wreck?"

"Bad man hurt her."

"No shit?" The boy looked shocked for a few seconds, then cut his chin hard and resettled his ball cap to a low and serious angle. "If I had a wife, I wouldn't let anybody hurt her. Ever. Not till the end of the world."

"Then you're the man," Phelan said.

A middle-aged nurse with a wheelchair blocked the door. "Tommy?"

Phelan's and the kid's heads turned together.

"My mom back?"

"Oh, not yet. What say we go visit the babies. Got a new one. Need to tire you out, sport."

"Far out." The kid swung his legs to the side of the bed. Pinched the gown to cover a skinny ass and elbowed off the nurse as she tried to guide him into the chair.

"Now, come on," she said, "be nice."

Gurgley hooting from the kid. "Nice guys finish last."

The nurse said, "Men always say that. I don't get it. I like nice guys. Not that I know any." They rolled away.

Phelan rose and slid back the blue curtain. He felt a twinge, remembering her pushing the gold-stickered certificate from Gatesville across his desk without saying a word. The whitened scar on the back of her neck.

Delpha's hand fluttered. "Help me turn over."

He gingerly fit both hands beneath her side, lifted her body and, rounding his arms, let her slant back into them, stayed that way a while, holding her, then gently replaced her on her back in the bed, slid his hands back to himself.

She was grimacing, brow squeezed. "Thanks. How 'bout some real air?"

Phelan hoisted the blinds and pushed open one side of the window. Rain was falling through the smeary halos of the parking lot lights. It wafted in, little plinks of water along with the wall of heat and humidity. Tree frogs, crickets, katydids, cicadas sharpened their scissors, rubbed their wings, whirred, chirred *zzzt-zzzt-zzzt*, settled into the room.

"Better?"

Her head nodded.

"How you doing?"

"I hadn't slept like this since I was three years old."

"Doc said he fixed you up. Nurse said barring infection, in a week or two you'll be back to work. Mind if I turn on the lights?"

"Not the ceiling one."

"There's a little one on a pull-chain back of the bed. Mind that one?"

"OK."

Phelan leaned in to snap the chain, stepped back, looking down on her strained, ivory face.

"Police gonna charge me for Deeterman?"

"E.E.'s got a sergeant down at the precinct that'll call down a Cajun riot if that happens."

"Fontenot. I remember him."

"They got Deeterman's diary from the bottom of hell. And this is Texas."

"I 'as in Texas last time, too. Never been outta Texas."

The summer tune thrummed through the window, hospital hummed around them. The bag on the pole dripped without a sound.

"Close, wasn't it, Delpha?"

She laid an arm across her eyes.

Phelan went over and retrieved the plastic chair, set it between the bed and the window. He tucked her fingers in his, said softly, "Piss-poor timing, but I gotta ask you something. Yesterday night while you were sleeping, a house blew up and took somebody with it. The body, if you can call it that, belonged to the father of the man you went to Gatesville for killing. Or least, that's who the '62 Ford parked out front belongs to. Ronald Wayne Pettit. His daughter hadn't seen him since supper last night."

Her breath sucked in.

"House is a place of business belonging to one Wallace Daughtry, dba Daughtry & Co., Inc. You can see that…" A specter of ill flittered through him, and he shut up, mulling over how to put it. "It's just…there's kinda a collision of circumstances happening here. I know who blew the house. Fire marshal'll tell us how. But Ronald Pettit. Damned if I know why she'd do that for you. I can live without knowing, but it's gonna be awkward around the office."

She moved her arm down from her face, slipped her hand from Phelan's and laced her fingers tight together. Squeezed eyes, a crease between her brows made her exhaustion clear. A whisper, "You askin' me for a alibi?"

"'Course not. Etherized on a table. Ringed by medical personnel, A-1 alibi."

Her eyelids smoothed. The black lashes were glittering. "That old man dead?"

"He's carbon, honey."

The glitter bunched to water that pearled and the pearls flattened as they rolled down the sides of her face.

Damp from the rain sifted through the screen. Damp from the bayou. Phelan sat vigil until something began to leave from her. Her chest rose and fell as she drew in breath, let it go, open-mouthed letting it go, drawing breath and passing it out of her, passing it on somewhere and on and farther while he sat and felt it pass.

Gone to sleep, he thought after a while, *needs sleep and here I am keeping her from it*. He hovered his hand over hers, barely touching.

Delpha's head tilted on the pillow so that she was looking at him full-on. Not a cloud in the gray-blue eyes that met his. The horizon inside them was clear.

"I'll tell you why she did it but...first turn out this light."

Tom Phelan clicked off the pull chain.

Acknowledgments

A BILLION THANKS to David Baker for being my closest reader, cheerleader, and wise and tireless advisor. A million to Cindy Black for the secretary suggestion, to Kevin Flatowicz-Farmer for asking the genre question, to Deputy Sheriff (ret.) Gene Langston for the title, to eagle-eyed Eddie Elfers, sympathetic Ruth Elfers, and veteran librarian Laurie Macrae for great catches and comments, to my engineer brother for oil rig information, to my fabulous, generous writing groups: Lynda Madison, Shelly Clark Geiser, Suzanne Kehm, Jane Bailey; Barbara Schmitz, Karen Wingett, Neil Harrison, Lin Brummels. Thanks also to Barbara B. Brookner for getting me into her friend's office with the Neches River view and to her kind aunt Deanna Ford for the Cajun translation. I'm grateful to Bobby and John Byrd of Cinco Puntos Press for commissioning me to write the story "Phelan's First Case," from which this novel grew, to Johnny Temple's Akashic Press for anthologizing the story in their *USA Noir: Best of the Akashic Noir Series,* and—¿cómo no?—to the crafty Lee Byrd, whose skilled, guerilla editing made the book clearer, slimmer, and faster. Deep bow to you all.

In memory of NANCY RICE, 1950 – 2015.
Phenomenal Woman, that was you.